THE

CAUSE

THE CAUSE

C.M. MEERT

TATE PUBLISHING
AND ENTERPRISES, LLC

Published by Tate Publishing & Enterprises, LLC
127 E. Trade Center Terrace | Mustang, Oklahoma 73064 USA
1.888.361.9473 | www.tatepublishing.com

Tate Publishing is committed to excellence in the publishing industry. The company reflects the philosophy established by the founders, based on Psalm 68:11,
"The Lord gave the word and great was the company of those who published it."

Book design copyright © 2013 by Tate Publishing, LLC. All rights reserved.
Cover design by Errol Villamante
Interior design by Joana Quilantang

Published in the United States of America

ISBN: 978-1-62746-889-3
1. Fiction / Action & Adventure
2. Fiction / Crime
13.08.06

THE CAUSE

To Elaura Lilienthal (the Canadian) and Alex Krause, my first readers; to Mrs. Bills, who pushed me hardest to finish; and lastly, to Grace Pump, who cured my procrastination with terrible threats.

PART 1

Aleksei's Cause

CHAPTER 1

It's my first time in an airplane. Looking out the window, I can see my country getting smaller and smaller. Strangely enough, I don't mind leaving. Russia and the school I've just come from haven't felt like home in a long time. My parents lived in Siberia. They saved up for years and years to send my brother to get an education. When he joined the army instead, the opportunity to learn how to read and write fell to the next son. Me. I was five years old. Since then, there's been no news of my family. I barely even remember them.

There are three of us on our way to the States. Vladec is almost eighteen and the oldest. This is his third trip, as he reminds us often enough.

Ivan is seventeen, four months older than me. It's his first time too, but at least I didn't throw up nine times before the plane was even in motion. I hear he cried when they told him he was leaving with us. Russia is everything to him.

Me, I'm the youngest, and I don't really care about America. They keep telling us what a great honor this is, but I can't say I feel it.

Vladec, turning away in disgust from Ivan who's throwing up again, nudges me.

"So, Aleksei, any regrets? Feeling homesick yet?" he asks, only half teasing. I shrug.

"Not really. It hasn't sunk in that I'm really leaving."

He smirks.

"It will. Don't worry. You get used to it. How's your *angliiskii* coming along?"

I shrug again, not answering this time. My English is fine. I just don't feel like being lectured on my accent again.

"It needs to be good enough that you can blend in. Americans get suspicious of foreigners easily." He pushes, insisting on an answer. I don't want to talk. I'm tired and worried about whether or not I was the right choice to be sent on this mission. There are others, much stronger and surer than I, who would have made much better candidates. Vladec, for example, may be bossy, but he's perfect. He would sell out his own mother for the Cause. He's already done it. Twice. She was released at first. The second time, he was ordered and did shoot her himself. I know. I was there.

Even Ivan is a better choice than I am. He'd give his life for a chance to serve the Cause.

"Practice, Aleksei. Take Ivan's mind off of how sick he's feeling."

He sits back, snapping open a magazine and burying his nose in it. I sigh, knowing an order when I hear one. Luckily, our companion has run out of air-sick bags and fled to the bathroom. We barely see him for the rest of the trip.

A few minutes before landing, Vladec shakes me awake. It's time, once again, to go over the plan and procedures for what to do when we see our host families.

"Remember, we met only today, on this plane. We are not from the same school. I am from Moscow…" he says the last part in English, waiting for us to answer in the same way.

"I'm from St. Petersburg." I say, not bothering to switch from Russian. Angry, he smacks me on the back of the head.

"*Pridurak!* Moron! We speak only English from now on, got that? Do it again!"

I roll my eyes, muttering insults under my breath. I duck as he goes to smack me again.

"*Da! Da! Havtit uzhe!* Enough already! Leave me alone! God."

"English! *Now*, Aleksei."

I comply, but not before calling him a few choice names and getting smacked again.

"Ivan, now you. Tell me, where are you from?"

"N-Novgorod? *Da?*" he stutters, wincing in anticipation of receiving the same treatment I got. Instead, Vladec smiles.

"Good. You both know what you're supposed to be doing, right?"

We nod. Of course we know. We've been reminded over and over, a hundred thousand times. We collect information, learn their weaknesses, win over a few more to the Cause, and go home. Simple enough, in theory. The hardest part will be not to let their ways change us. I'll never admit it aloud, but I'm nervous. All my life, I've heard horror stories about Americans, stories of others who let themselves be won over to their bad way of life. Traitors who abandoned home and country for a burger. The shame their families had to suffer through is beyond words. Rumors around school say also that Americans are lazy buckets of fat who let themselves be brainwash   have no patience for stupid peop   o values to cling to. I pray I won't   getting sent back in disgrace.

Funny

The seat belt sign con   through the plane as they let d   e green again, but the flight atter   thhroom. Involuntarily, my own h   another tremor jolts us. It's the first time in the six years I've known him that I hear Vladec laugh.

"Calm down, Aleksei. We're not going to crash. You're being as bad as Ivan."

I squeeze my eyes shut, ignoring him as best I can. I hate heights more than anything else in the world, and this landing is unpleasant enough without having to deal with mockery on top of it.

The second we're allowed up, Ivan rushes back to the bathroom. I almost join him, but the condescending look in Vladec's eyes stops me. The last thing I need is for him to think I'm weak. He'd make my life even more of a nightmare than he already does.

"Remember," he hisses to us in Russian as we file out, "We don't know each other, and we tell them nothing true about our great country or the Cause."

I nod, swallowing nervously. What if Americans are awful and stupid and fat like the rumors said? I wonder if I can change families if we don't get along. Probably not. With an inward sigh of resignation, I hoist my pack higher on my shoulder and push my way through customs, trying hard to fight down panic. Vladec is already gone, striding confidently toward a small group of people. The woman hugs him tightly, looking overjoyed. To my surprise, he returns the gesture, going so far as smiling at them. He catches me staring and gives me a dark look. When their backs are turned, he draws a finger across his throat, letting me know clearly what will happen if I tell anyone what I just saw. For some reason, it makes me smile. Luckily, he doesn't see it, and I quickly turn away to try and find my own family.

One by one, people find those they've been waiting for and leave. Even Ivan is gone, though not happily. I feel sorry for him. He gave me a last, desperate glance as he was dragged away by screaming kids.

Within twenty minutes, the hall is empty, save for me. I've been forgotten. So with a sigh, I simply dig through my bag, take out a book, and sit on the rim of a fountain.

A long time passes. Passengers come and go, some looking panicked, others relaxed and laughing. No one comes for me. A sick feeling begins to build in my stomach. Maybe I really was put on the plane by mistake. Maybe no one will ever come and I'll eventually get sent back. The disgrace would be terrible. I'd be shunned, cast aside, maybe even sent back to Siberia, to a family I can't remember knowing. What should I do? Call Vladec? He'd kill me for disobeying orders. We aren't supposed to text each other until the school year has started in two weeks. No contact allowed before then. I glance at my watch and swear under my breath. An hour already. I almost get to my feet, ready to find someone who can perhaps call the Americans I'm supposed to be staying with to remind them of my existence when something catches my eye. A family of four is standing near the gate where I came in, looking excited. No planes have landed there in a while though, and they stick out, alone as they are. Curious, I listen in discreetly.

"Do you think we're early? You checked the time, right?"

The woman asks her husband, suddenly worried. It's strange to hear so much English being spoken all at once. I have trouble following as they argue back and forth. The little boy, bored, turns to stare at me. I pretend not to notice, buried behind the pages of my book. Releasing his mother's skirts, he comes toward the fountain casually. When I look up again, he's standing right in front of me, curious blue eyes staring at me.

"What language is that?" he asks, pointing at my book.

"Russian. Why?"

"I dunno. Are you Russian?"

"Yes."

"Cool. We're waiting for someone from Russia. Are you waiting?"

"I was, yes."

"Who for?"

"You are very nosy."

"I know. Does it bother you?"

"Yes."

"Oh."

He grows quiet, surprised, I think, by the directness of the answer. After a moment of reflection, he starts again.

"I'm Sam. What's your name?"

I sigh.

"Aleksei."

His eyes grow wide, and he scampers back to his parents, tugging on their sleeve and pointing at me, confirming my suspicions. The relief is almost too strong.

The woman strides toward me.

"Aleksander?"

I nod, rising and extending my hand. A huge grin illuminates her face, and she embraces me so tightly I swear I can feel my ribs cracking under the strain.

"We're so happy you're here!" she squeals, doing an odd little dance step. I choke, struggling to extricate myself. What is it with these people and hugging? The others come up to me too, laughing.

"Let the poor kid breathe, Molly, he's turnin' purple." Her husband says, patting her on the shoulder. She lets go abruptly, and I stagger back, praying for my ribs to be all right.

"I'm sorry, I'm just so glad to finally meet you!" she beams.

"*Da*, yes, I…I am happy too." I cough, trying to get my breath back. I say nothing about the fact that they're so late. No need to make things awkward.

There is another boy, about my age. At first, I'm cautious around him. Back in Moscow, at school, the boys who seem nicest are the ones who get you beaten. As we walk across the tiled floor of the airport to the stuffy parking lot, his attempts to be friendly start to seem more and more genuine, which surprises me. His name is Charlie. The little boy, he tells me, is Sam, his nine-year-old little brother.

"Do you have any siblings?" he asks as we reach the car. It's not said in any suspicious or prying tone, but it throws me off nonetheless. I've been told to beware even innocent-seeming questions, so I pretend not to understand.

"I...don't know this word."

"Oh, well, it means brothers or sisters, ya know. Other kids your parents had."

I settle in the seat, taking my time before answering. In the end, I decide not to tell the truth.

"*Nyet*. No one but me."

I'm so tired all of a sudden. Almost against my will, my head falls against the window, my eyes start to shut. It's been a long trip. Charlie's question has disturbed me though, keeping me awake. It shouldn't. I don't remember my siblings, as he called them. The facts, the details in my file, that I have an older brother and a sister, that much I do know. But the people themselves, including my own twin, are a mystery, lost in time. I don't understand why now it bothers me when it never did before. Maybe because of everything that's happened lately, maybe it's being surrounded by a complete family for the first time in thirteen years. I don't know. All I can do is hope it won't bother me for too long. I have to be able to focus on my mission.

———

When I wake up, we've stopped in front of a small, pale-blue house. Compared to the apartment buildings in Moscow, it looks cheerful. I sit up, blinking away sleep, to find them all staring at me, awaiting a response.

"Is...your home?" I say, uncomfortable. The mother nods.

"Yeah, wha'd'ya think? You like it?"

I nod politely, feeling strangely as though I'm being tested. She looks happy with my answer.

"Well, come on then! Let's not sit here all day. I'll show you around."

Sam drags me to the house. Inside, I'm struck by how cluttered everything is. Things that seem very useless lie in every corner, making me feel claustrophobic. Where I was raised, we had very little in our dormitories. Just beds and cupboards, really. We weren't allowed to own more. Anything extra brought from home was confiscated, even our civilian clothes. It taught us that we belonged to the Cause, not ourselves.

The Americans navigate the flow of mess perfectly, leading me around, pointing things like the bathroom out.

"This," Sam tells me, "is the TV. It's really fun, and you can watch people on it."

My grip tightens on my pack, but I control my temper.

"I know what TV is, yes." I say coldly, raising an eyebrow. His eyes grow big, and he backs away. I've seen that look before, on the faces of new recruits on their first missions. I've scared him, which is not good for my cover. I force my expression to soften, rubbing my eyes.

"Sorry. Just tired. I did not mean sounding angered."

"'s okay," he mumbles, still not coming any closer. Vladec is going to kill me if he finds out things have started out this badly. With a sigh, I crouch to his level and pull candy from my bag, handing him a piece, plastering on the best smile I can manage under the circumstances.

"Apologies?" I say, praying it's the right word and I didn't just swear at him. Luckily, his own grin comes back, and he accepts my offer. Still, there's a reluctance to his movements that I don't like. It's as though he doesn't fully trust me anymore. He doesn't eat what I gave him either.

Thankfully, none of the rest of the family noticed anything odd in our conversation.

The house is small, so the tour is over fairly quickly, and at last they show me my room and leave me to settle in, in peace. I like the place. It is cool now, even if the upstairs is boiling hot from the August sun. This room they call the basement, and really, it is good. I have privacy at least. With a contented sigh, I let myself fall back on the bed, closing my eyes for a blissful second. Of course, my phone chooses this moment to alert me to the fact that I have a new text.

I groan, cursing to myself in Russian. All I want is one moment of peace so I can sleep.

Surprisingly enough, it's from Vladec.

Change of plans. Meet tmrrw @ 1:00 east prk.

I frown, confused, and read it again. There are directions to the meeting place attached in a file. But I don't understand. After all those times he warned us against contact before school starts he wants to meet? Why? I suppose it could be a trap to see if we'll break orders. Then again, if I don't go, that could be very bad too. I decide to obey the message, but not blindly. I'll go early, scout around, make sure of things before Vladec and Ivan get there. I'm not stupid. I've been serving too long to still be naïve enough to believe this unplanned meeting could mean anything good for me.

CHAPTER 2

"He's asleep, poor kid. Looks exhausted. Let's start eating, and I'll take something down later." Molly stated, seating herself at the table. The other two dug in obediently, but Sam merely picked at his food, looking troubled.

"'s 'a matter with *you*?" Charlie asked, noticing his brother's behavior. The boy shrugged.

"Nuthin'."

"Well it's gotta be *somethin'* if you're not eating. You're *always* hungry."

"I just..." he hesitated.

"Just what? Come on, tell me. I won't repeat it, I promise." Charlie whispered.

"I don't like Aleksei. There's something weird about him."

He explained quickly about the TV incident, the cold hatred and anger he'd seen in the Russian's eyes, how it hadn't quite gone away even when a peace offering was made. Charlie thought about it a moment.

"Yeah, he is a little creepy, isn't he? I haven't seen him smile once so far. Maybe he really was just tired though. I say give him some time to adjust. When school starts, he'll lighten up."

Sam remained unconvinced.

"I don't think so. I'm telling you, he's hiding something. I bet he lied when he said he didn't have brothers and sisters."

"What? Why? Why bother? You can't just judge people like that. It's wrong. He was tired from the trip, and maybe he got upset that you were treating him like he's some sort of uncivilized moron. I would."

"How was I supposed to guess they had TV in Russia too?"

Charlie rolled his eyes. "'Cause the whole *world* has it, you idiot. Geez, what're they teaching you kids in school?"

"Boring stuff."

"Fair point."

The topic of conversation moved on, but Sam couldn't chase the uneasy feeling from the back of his mind. Something about the Russian was wrong, and sooner or later, he'd figure out what.

———

I crouch in the stairwell, listening to the conversation as best I can. I'd been right. The kid suspects me. This early on, it isn't a good sign. I'll have to work extra hard on being pleasant and friendly to change his mind. If I fail…well, it's better not to think on the possibility. I wish briefly that it was already tomorrow, that I could talk to Vladec about it. But I know even if I do see him at the meeting spot that I won't mention it. He'd have me shipped back to Russia faster than I can say, "*Vozgasly.*" Oops.

I won't let that happen. Either Sam lets himself be convinced, or I'll have to find a way to be rid of him. Permanently.

I'm not heartless. Killing a little kid isn't exactly high on my list of things to do to gain glory. The Cause is bigger than anyone's life, and that's all there is to it. I won't be forgiven if Sam is a danger to the mission and I don't report it or better yet, do him in. If he keeps seeing through my lies, I'll have no choice.

When I was a child, they beat me for every mission in which I showed mercy and failed to pull the trigger. After the third time, I stopped hesitating. Painful as it was to be punished, it taught

CHAPTER 3

Nightmares plague me that first night. I'm in a dark room. Lights flash on and off. Somewhere out of my line of sight, someone is screaming. The urge to run is strong, but I can't move my legs. Whoever said you can't feel pain in dreams was wrong. A cut on my face stings terribly, and I can taste blood. My chest heaves, my heart feels as though it's tearing in two. More screaming reaches my ears, and I realize suddenly that it's coming from me as much as the stranger.

I wake in a cold sweat, still yelling. I can't stop shaking. I bury my head in my lap, breathing hard, trying not to sob aloud. This nightmare, I've had it many, many times. Almost every night of my life. I don't dream otherwise.

It's always just as disturbing as the first time I had it. When I was younger, it used to send me into such terrible fits that the other boys, risking punishment, would be forced to alert the guards to take me away. For a long time, they tried to beat the bad dreams out of me, but it never worked though I did learn to control my outbursts a little better.

The warmth of the room becomes suddenly unbearable, and I have to get up and open the window. Thankfully, the cool air helps clear my mind. The burning feeling of panic recedes, leaving only a sick taste on my tongue. I touch my face, fingers searching for blood, a scar, anything. As always, there's nothing but smooth skin.

I'm lucky no one upstairs heard me. There's no need to make the situation with Sam any worse. I let my head drop against the wall, shutting my eyes. Why can't I just get some decent sleep for once? One night. One night is all I'm asking for.

"*Proklyatie!*" I hiss to myself, rubbing savagely at my eyes before the tears can fall. It doesn't stop them in the least. I don't understand why this upsets me so much. I've stood strong where grown men have broken down to their knees sobbing. I try in vain to convince myself that it's all the trip's fault, that the stress has worn me out. But deep down, I know there's more to it than that. And I hate myself for being so weak.

Eventually, my body relaxes, the tears dry out, and I can crawl back into bed and try to get some sleep. By the time dawn light starts seeping through the window, I'm still wide awake. I last another hour or so before giving up and deciding I might as well get dressed and head out.

Upstairs, everything is perfectly still. A clock's steady ticking can be heard. The refrigerator hums quietly in its corner. A faucet drips. I slide silently across the kitchen's wood floor to the carpeted entrance and slip my shoes on before unlocking the front door and easing myself out. I figure I'll get a head start on locating the park and scouting around for possible traps. It's unlikely anything is in place this early, but I need to be doing something, and walking will soothe my nerves.

It only takes me about ten minutes before I spot the place. A high fence surrounds a play area for little ones, with benches and trees scattered strategically about for parents. The park is small, so it shouldn't be too hard to find the others this afternoon. I'm about to start heading back, when movement catches my eye, and I duck down behind some bushes to observe.

Two men dressed in dark suits and sunglasses get out of a black car.

"This the place?" one asks, sounding bored. The other nods, hands deep in his pockets.

"Yup. Guess so. I'll post a lookout just in case anyone decides to show early. Your guy say anything about what they'd look like?"

"Nah. Wouldn't give a whole lot of details. Just that they're pretty young."

They move away, out of earshot. I frown, trying to make sense of what I've just heard. I don't like it. For one thing, it seems far too convenient that I just happened to be here in this spot right in time to overhear something so suspicious. Either I'm being set up or the Cause is testing my loyalty. In any case, Vladec needs to know about it. I take my phone out carefully and text him a message.

V. Weird things happening. Text back! Aleksei."

He responds almost immediately. I'm apparently not the only one suffering from jetlag.

What weird?

Men with suit/glasses. Tlkin' bout us i think."

There's a long pause, and I can almost feel him thinking hard.

Run! Get out of there!

I stare at the words, surprised. He's never advocated cowardice before. A split second later, I'm off and running as fast as my legs can carry me back to the house and hopefully safety. I don't make it. Before I've so much as gone around the corner, one of the men is blocking my path.

"In a hurry, are we? How 'bout you explain why you were hiding before I let you go?"

I should panic, be afraid. I know if I speak, he'll hear my accent and figure out I'm Russian. What exactly that would mean, I don't want to find out. Besides, if I blow my cover, getting away won't matter. There would still be Vladec to deal with. At the same time, it's good to be back in action, treading familiar waters so to speak. Here at least, I know what to do.

Before the man can have time to think, I deliver two swift punches, first to his stomach, second to the jaw. Within moments, he's on the ground, stunned. There's no time to hesitate. I run for it, not looking back. He's after me faster than expected though and bawling for his partner's help. The first swing, as he materializes in my path, takes me by surprise, and I'm slow to duck. His fist crashes into my face, sending me reeling back in shock and pain. I pray it doesn't bruise too badly. Raising suspicion in my host family is the last thing I need.

Both men face me now, leaving me little choice but to fight. Luckily, it's something I'm rather good at. I duck, strike, dodge, always moving left, right, forward, back, fast, faster than they can keep up. Then not giving them so much as a millisecond to react, I disappear, leaving the men bloody and confused. Technically, all I did was roll away behind a tree, but they don't know that. From their shouts, I gather my vanishing act worked, and I take off, hurrying back to the house. By cutting across yards and jumping a few fences, it takes me less than five minutes. Still, I'm out of breath, sweaty, and more than likely bruised. I need a shower badly before anyone catches sight of me. Unfortunately, I never get the chance. The instant I set foot in the door, I find myself confronted by four upset Americans demanding to know where I've been for the past hour. Apparently there was something of a panic when the mother went to bring me breakfast and found me gone. I shrug away their concerns.

"I go for walk. Explore. Is okay, I don't go far." I explain as best I can.

"No, it's not okay. You have to tell us when you leave, Aleksei. Your parents trust us to take care of you. What would they think if something were to happen?" the mother scolds.

I'm surprised. Her concern for me seems genuine. Usually, when I get yelled at, it's because I embarrassed my superiors or broke a rule. I shrug again, uncomfortable with the attention.

"My parents, they send me away when I'm five years old. They not care 'bout this."

A cold shiver crawls up my spine as the words leave my mouth. I hate the pity that suddenly appears on their faces. They don't understand. I like my life. I like what I do. Of course, I can't say it aloud, but it's true nevertheless.

"Oh…well…I'm sure you…write to them often and call, right? Just because they sent you to school far away doesn't mean they don't love you, I'm sure. Speaking as a mother myself, I know I wouldn't want anything to happen to my sons because they wandered off in an unfamiliar place."

Her ignorance makes me furious. How dare she assume things about what my parents would want? I control my anger with great difficulty and force myself to stay polite.

"I am sorry about leaving. Next time, I promise to be asking first." I manage to say before turning to head toward the stairs leading down to my room. She grabs my shoulder and holds me back.

"I'm not mad, Aleksei. It's just that you really had us worried. We care about you."

Her tone is gentle and soft. It stirs an unfamiliar feeling in my gut, one that I have trouble naming. I would almost rather she yell at me, hit me. I'm not used to adults doing anything else, and I don't like it. I don't like not knowing how to react.

The others, with the exception of Sam, are nodding in agreement. The kid is just staring at me with a strange mixture of pity and understanding.

"Come on, let's eat breakfast, and then we'll take you out and show you around town. That sound good?"

She leaves me no choice but to nod and let her steer me toward the table. The food served is strange for morning. Sausages, milk, and some potato thing they call hash browns.

To my relief, no one asks about the bruise. Conversation is pleasant, only about trivial things. They ply me with questions about Russia, and I quickly find that for most answers, it doesn't matter whether I lie or not since they ask nothing of importance.

At first, I try not to say too much, nervous that something vital might slip. After awhile though, I relax. These people are harmless civilians and actually interesting to converse with once I got to know them. I'm even genuinely laughing at some of the jokes before too long. Sam too softens, warming up to me easily enough.

When everything has been cleared away, I head back downstairs to shower before leaving. A new text from Vladec brings me back to the bitter reality of why I'm here. This family, these people—I cannot let them become anything but my enemies, no matter how much I'd rather not. I don't want to have to kill them for getting in too deep.

Still breathing? Vladec sends.

Da. Bruised but alive. Wat's goin on?

I wait a long time for an answer. When none comes, I go to join the others in the car. All I can do is pray we'll be back in time for me to get to the meeting.

———

Vladec yawned deeply, stretching. He hadn't slept all night, and the morning's incident with Aleksei hadn't helped relax him much. Someone knew about their mission, that much was obvious. Worse still, they'd known about the park. Was there a traitor in the government? He knew every message sent was being read, every conversation listened to. It certainly wasn't one of the boys.

They feared him too much. Especially Aleksei. Vladec grinned to himself, recalling their first meeting, six years previously. He'd been twelve, nearly thirteen. Aleksei, having just turned eleven, had been transferred into a higher class because of his unusually high grades.

CHAPTER 4

It was snowing outside. In the upper dorm rooms, the air was so cold the boys could see their own breath. No one dared complain though. Getting a whipping in this weather meant hospitalization at the least. More often than not, the hospital meant death.

Vladec lounged on his bed, book in one hand, cigarette in the other. He was only half listening to the other boys' talk, most of which's content involved various girls they'd supposedly met.

He was the youngest of the group but had forced his way into a somewhat leader-like position, and so was left mostly in peace. In this room at least, he was respected, listened to. Something which the rest of the school, in his opinion, had yet to learn.

"*Vnimanie! Mest!* Guard coming!" The shout rang through the room, sending the boys into a sudden frenzy. Magazines were shoved under mattresses, cigarettes put out with a few choice curses until in a matter of seconds, the room appeared neat and tidy. When the guard stepped inside, buttons glinting, heels clicking, every boy stood ramrod straight at attention, salute firmly in place. The man surveyed the scene a moment; then satisfied, he yelled out a command.

"*Zdes'!* Come!"

A small, dark-haired, surly looking boy entered reluctantly. He had a canvas army bag slung over one shoulder almost carelessly. Vladec bit back a smirk. Finally. Someone new who would have to learn respect. It had been too long since he'd had an excuse to dish out regular beatings. Not that one was really needed, it just added to the fun.

"Men, this is your new comrade, Aleksander Mihailovic. I expect you to treat him with the respect befitting a fellow soldier, despite his youth."

As the guard's lecture droned on, Vladec's attention wandered. He noticed suddenly that the new boy was staring at him with something akin to defiance. It was as though he'd already pinned who he'd be getting a beating from first. Vladec frowned, unsettled slightly by the way the black eyes seemed to pierce, unblinking, into the older boy's thoughts. He shifted uncomfortably. Was that the trace of a grin on the child's face? Strange.

At last, the guard finished, saluted, waited a moment for the gesture to be returned, then left. For a long moment, nobody moved.

"All clear!" the lookout shouted as the last trace of adult presence disappeared around the corner.

Vladec, followed closely by the others, moved leisurely toward the new victim.

"So…promoted you, did they?"

The boy shrugged. "*Da.* And you're going to beat me up."

"Of course. It's our special way of greeting newcomers."

He sighed, dropping his bag in readiness. "Come on then, get it over with."

Vladec paused, surprised.

"You actually want a pounding?"

"No. I'd much rather be left alone. I just didn't think I had much choice."

There were stifled chuckles from the others. Vladec held up a hand, and they quieted. A sense of eagerness filled the room, radiating from every boy present. They knew what was coming as their leader lowered himself so as to be eye level with the victim.

"Well, aren't you a brave little boy." He hissed, anger masking his unease.

"Comrades," he said, straightening, "I say we give him what he wants."

A cheer of approval greeted the words. Two of the biggest boys leapt forward, grabbing the child by the arms, pinning him to the wall. But Vladec did not move to strike. A brilliant idea had just come to him. He turned back to face the crowd.

"On second thought, comrades, perhaps our new friend deserves a special sort of welcome." He paused, letting the tension mount a few notches. "Get me a rope."

The order was obeyed instantly and without question.

"Now tie it around his middle, hands behind his back."

To Vladec's immense satisfaction, the first hint of fear appeared on Aleksei's face. The kid could handle a beating, obviously, and had known to expect one. Anything else, he was unprepared for.

"Make sure it's tight enough. We don't actually want him to die. Good. Now someone go open the window."

A rush of freezing wind and snow blew into the room, making them all flinch and draw back.

Vladec dug into his pocket and drew out a pack of cigarettes. He lit one casually, pretending not to notice the impatience of his crew.

"Let's hang the laundry out to dry, boys. Teach it some respect for superiors."

Aleksei screamed as dozens of eager hands reached for him, dragging him forward.

"Nyet! Otpusti! Please! I'll do anything!"

Vladec held up a hand again, halting them.

"Really? Anything? Not scared of heights are you?"

Aleksei shuddered, nodding his head vigorously.

"Please not the window. Please."

"Would you rather get a beating?"

"*Da!*"

Vladec raised an eyebrow in surprise.

"As you wish. But you know something? I'm feeling generous. So after we hang you out the window, I'll be more than happy to pound you. Hoist him." He ordered. Aleksei's screams were drowned out by the others' cheers as they lifted him up and out.

CHAPTER 5

Vladec was jolted out of his pleasant memories by a knock at the door. He opened it to find a tall, red-haired girl waiting for him.

"Cassy, hello! What do you need?" he asked politely. She was his host sister, and on the surface, he kept up the appearance of being good friends.

"Hey, Vlady. We're gonna head out, meet a couple new families with exchange students. Wanna tag along?"

He considered it for a moment. It would be easier to meet with Aleksei and Ivan if they were all invited to the same place. People wouldn't get suspicious if they saw the boys talking. He nodded.

"Sure, I'll come. Any new Russian kids this year?"

Cassy shrugged, leading the way down the narrow stairs.

"I think so, yeah. A couple at least. You'll have to ask Mom to know for sure."

He agreed and changed the subject. There was no need to appear too interested or as though he knew more than he let on.

"So, Cassy, you get boyfriend over summer?" he asked, teasing. She laughed.

"You ask every year. The answer's still no, sadly. How 'bout you? Any Russian girls in your life yet?"

Vladec plastered a grin in his face, forcing a chuckle.

"*Nyet*. You know you are the only girl for me!"

It was a long running joke between the two of them and had been going strong for three years. Yet every time, just saying the words made him want to gag. Cassy was far from pretty, with her red hair and freckles, and she was far too skinny. Russian girls, with their blond tresses and pale blue eyes, were much more to his liking. Besides, she was American, and soon enough, she and all her people would bow to the supreme will of Russia. His heart glowed at the thought. It filled him with an indescribable feeling of pride and patriotism. He craved moments like these. Moments when he could be certain of the future of this and all other countries. Only through a miraculous effort of will did he manage to keep his thoughts to himself.

———

The instant I see the look in Vladec's eyes, I know something big has happened. The last time he looked this excited, a bomb went off at the US Embassy in Moscow and killed forty people. I've always suspected him of setting it off but can't ask without getting smacked. Apparently it's top secret, and I'm too nosy.

My new family has taken me to a party for exchange students. I spent the first hour being alternately bored out of my wits and attempting not to strangle Sam, who has apparently gotten over his fear of me. His questions have yet to run out.

"But why don't you like ice cream?"

"Because not everyone must be like you."

"But why?"

"Because that is life!"

"Why?"

I grit my teeth and bend to his level.

"I warn you once, okay? Talk to me again in next hour, I rip out all the little fingernails one by one, got that?"

He considers the threat for a moment before deciding I'm kidding and running off, screeching something about having to catch him first. I curse him under my breath, fighting with great difficulty the urge to break cover by pulling out my gun and shooting the little brat. Before I can follow through, a hand lands on my shoulder.

"Already killing people in your mind, Aleksei? You've only been here two days."

I shove him away.

"Get lost. I'm not in the mood to handle your authority issues, Vladec."

I stalk away before he can have time to retaliate. It's the first time I've dared speak to him so harshly. Even as a child, I was bold, but never disrespectful. Anger is a powerful thing, crouching in your belly, crowding fear and reason from your mind, giving its strength. People say rage is a hot, burning thing. It's not. It's ice cold, as unforgiving as the frozen steppe of Siberia, rousing as gripping the trigger of a gun.

I leave Vladec standing slightly in shock and take refuge inside the building. My knees go weak all of a sudden, and I have to lean against the wall so as not to collapse. What have I done? He's going to kill me for my brief lapse in respect, or worse, send me back to Moscow. Barely two days in and already I'm in over my head, done for. To calm my frayed nerves, I focus instead on my surroundings.

I'm in a long, low-ceilinged room. Glass cases with various bugs, plants, and stuffed animals are strategically placed. At the far end, I can spot shelves of books behind a wooden counter. There's a girl too, looking around. I hadn't noticed her before, though from the way her head is tilted in my direction, she's seen *me*. Good. Vladec can't beat me up in front of a witness. I make my way casually toward her, one eye on the double glass doors in case Vladec decides to come bursting in.

"Hello. My name is Aleksei." I say, holding out a hand. She turns, an amused glint in her eyes.

"I'm Cassy." She answers, taking my offered hand. She's very pretty, with green eyes and hair as red as flames. I've never seen such a color before on a person's head. It suits her.

I stand awkwardly, hands in pockets, not sure what to say. My experience with the female kind is rather limited. Luckily, she seems to understand this.

"Are you from Moscow?" she asks, genuinely curious. I almost answer yes, catching myself just in time.

"No. Um … Saint Petersburg, you call it?"

"Yeah, I've heard a lot about it. The exchange student living with us, he's from Moscow, but he's visited there, I think."

A nasty feeling of suspicion builds in my gut.

"Maybe I am knowing him? What is name?"

Cassy opens her mouth to answer, but her gaze falls on a point behind me. Her face goes a deep red, and she grins.

"Vlady! Have you met Aleksei? He's from St. Petersburg apparently. See? I told you there would be other Russian students."

I have to stifle a laugh as I turn and see the look on *Vlady's* face. No one in their right mind who knows Vladec would dare give him a nickname. Not to his face at least. He looks about ready to kill me, and I'm extremely grateful for the girl's presence.

"We've met. Briefly."

There's an awkward pause.

"Well, I should be going now. Very hungry, *da*?" I say, forcing a chuckle and inching discreetly toward the door. Vladec grabs me around the shoulders in a mock friendly hug before I can make it.

"No, no, stay. We are simply *dying* to know all about St. Petersburg. Are we not, Cassy?"

I don't like the emphasis he put on the word *dying*. It doesn't bode well.

"Uh, yeah, sure. I mean, if he wants to go eat, that's fine too. I wouldn't mind another hot dog myself."

y. He's losing control, I can
in, he might even let some-
ray he holds on to his self-
 the room.

s something, yes? I need to
tions, and we come find you,

ed at being bossed around.
a her." I pipe up, praying she
ezing my shoulder painfully

ry funny! But we must talk
Sorry, Cassy. We be quick,

o protest passes her lips. She
of suspicion in her eyes.
nt the door has shut behind
of the exhibits, knocking the

alk to me like that, huh? You
und you? In Siberia, with no
me again! I'll see you back in
' He shouts, slapping me hard
ences. I shove back, rage in my
at.

do! I'm not a child anymore,
et to push me around here and

Infuriated, he leaps at me, trying to land a blow to my stomach. I block easily, twisting his wrist and pushing upward, making him grunt in surprise and pain. I let go, and he backs away,
breathing hard.

"You—" he gasps, pointing a finger at me, "I'm your superior! You owe me respect. Loyalty. I'll tell Moscow about this. I'll tell them how disobedient a soldier you are."

"Go ahead. See if they listen. I'm not afraid of you anymore, *Vlady*. And you've never been my superior. Why do you think I was promoted to your class? Why do you think I was sent on this trip? Go on. Call Moscow. See what they tell you. Or better yet, admit to them that you can't control me."

To my surprise, he barks out a harsh laugh.

"Is that what you think? My God, you're so naïve, Aleksei. Look at yourself. You may think you're all grownup and mature, but inside, you're still that shrieking little boy I dangled out of a window. I'm going to give you one last chance now. I'm going to forget about today. But the next time you make even the slightest mistake, I'll kill you, understand?"

I hesitate, then nod reluctantly. My cheeks burn with indignation. It's not fair. It's not right that he should always win. I want to run after him, beat him to a pulp. But I stay where I am, humiliated. What use is being this smart if I can't even beat an idiot like Vladec? It's not right, and I hate it. What choice is there though? I lied when I said I didn't care about being sent back to Siberia. I do. More than anything. The Cause is my life. I've served it for as long as I can remember. There *is* nothing else out there for me. No future. If anything, it would be more merciful to shoot me. I let myself slide to the floor, wallowing in self-pity. How could I have been so stupid as to fight back?

"You okay?"

I jump at the sound of a voice. Cassy crouches down in front of me, looking worried. I groan and pass a hand over my eyes. Just what I needed.

"You heard?"

"Well yeah. I came back in when I heard shouting. Obviously, I don't speak enough Russian to have understood any of it, but…I did *see* a rather different side to Vladec. Can you tell me why he hit you?"

I shake my head.

"No. And if I was you, I would not let him know what you see today."

"Yeah. I kinda figured. Come on, let's go back outside. Your family'll be wondering where you went off to."

━━━━━

By the end of the day, I've made my first real friend in years. For the only time in memory, it feels as though I can be myself around somebody. I don't have to hide anything but my past, and I like it. Don't get me wrong. I don't trust her, not completely. She's still the enemy as far as I'm concerned. But it's good to have someone to talk to who doesn't know anything about me. If she knew I was a killer, she would run away as fast as her legs could carry her. As far as she knows though, I'm just a shy exchange student looking to make a friend.

We part with a promise to meet again and with each other's cell phone numbers.

I saw Vladec and Ivan talking discreetly on the side but did not join them as I normally would have. I don't have the stomach to bear more humiliation on Vladec's part.

Later that night, as I lie in bed thinking over the day's events, my so-called superior sends me another message, giving me my new orders. A text is risky, but I suppose he didn't want to talk. Things are moving faster than expected. It's starting to look as though we won't be here a full year before everything is in place. Good. I don't like America anyway.

CHAPTER 6

I see her again only a few days later. I'm busy trying to teach Sam Cyrillic when the doorbell rings. I prick my ears at the sound of voices, trying, out of habit, to make out the conversation. I'm surprised when the mother comes into the room, grinning.

"Aleksei, there's someone here to see you."

I don't have time to ask who before a red head pops into the room, decidedly happy to see me.

"Cassy! Hello! What are you doing here?" I ask, confused for a moment. I'd been expecting Vladec or Ivan. There aren't many other people here who know me.

"I volunteered to help show you around the city. There's a whole bus of students going on tour, and since Vlady's being lazy and staying home, I thought maybe you might like his spot." She answers cheerfully. I nod, smiling. At least it'll be less frustrating than trying to teach Sam an alphabet he doesn't understand.

"Good idea. I am happy to come to visit your city." I reply, polite as always. For once, it's not too hard. Sam leaps to his feet eagerly.

"Me too! Me too! I wanna come!"

His mother and Cassy exchange an amused glance. They were expecting this, so of course, permission is granted straight away.

Cassy doesn't seem to mind. Happy, she takes my arm and leads me out to the bus idling on the driveway. It's a horrible yellow color and very loud inside, mostly because of a variety of languages I can't understand, but we settle in the back and, despite Sam's constant interruptions, manage to have something of a conversation. I learn that she's younger than me, only sixteen, even if she'll be in the same grade in school as me and has both a brother and a sister.

"I skipped kindergarten." She explains proudly when I ask about the grade difference. I answer something about my being impressed, I think, but I'm not really paying attention. Her bright red hair is a constant distraction. The way it catches the sunlight, the way the curls bounce. For some reason, I find her even prettier than the first time we met.

Our first stop is a museum. We manage to lose Sam and the rest of the group in the gift shop, making our own way around the exhibits. I'm surprised by how much she knows.

"You come often here to have learn so much?"

"As often as I can. Most people don't like museums, but I love getting lost in all the history and the weird exhibits. You must have visited places like this in Moscow? Oh, sorry, St. Petersburg."

I shrug.

"Not really. School takes up all time. I do not do much other than study and train."

I could bang my head against the wall for my stupidity. How could I have let that slip?

Cassy frowns.

"Train? What for? Do you play sports?"

Relief at the easy way out she's given me seeps through my blood, relaxing me.

"Yes." I nod. "Sports. Look, what is this? It looks like monkey."

As I hoped, she launches into a long explanation that I barely listen to. It was a close one. I can't mess up again. I'm in danger of forgetting who I am and why I'm here. Another mistake could cost me my life and perhaps hers as well. I'm edgy the rest of the day despite my efforts to hide it. The incident has rattled me. I let myself in much too deep. Never again.

Our next stop is a little ice cream shop. I pretend to have trouble with the English alphabet, so she picks flavors for me. She has good taste as it turns out.

Several times as we walk, I catch myself genuinely laughing at some of her jokes. Each incident makes me edgy again, and there are other times when I have to force myself to smile and not reach for the gun I have strapped under my jacket. If she notices anything, she doesn't say it. But near the end of the day, as we rejoin the bus and Sam, she takes my hand and gives it a reassuring squeeze, letting go again quickly.

"Where've you guys been? You missed the most awesome stuff! Did you see the dinosaur skeletons? Aren't they cool?" Sam squeals, running toward us, going off on a ramble about prehistoric animals and how they could kill you with one bite. As the bus reaches home, he leaps off, jumping in excitement and beginning all over again as he vanishes inside.

"You want come in?" I ask her, feeling awkward. She shakes her head.

"Nah, I gotta get home or Mom'll worry. But I had a good time. Thanks for coming."

Before I can react, she's planted a quick, nervous kiss on my cheek and run off back to the bus. It takes me a moment to recover my senses. I should never have gone with her. She's gotten herself into something she doesn't understand, and trouble could come of it for both of us. In the end, I decide to shrug it off. I will be back in Russia soon, and she will forget easily as will I.

———

The months pass quickly. Each day, I feel more and more confused about these people. They are nothing like what I was told. At first, I thought it must be an act, a game they play to hide their true selves. But they go so far out of their way to make sure I'm comfortable and happy, it's starting to look as though everything I was ever taught…is wrong. Even I would not go so far to protect my cover.

As for those men from the first day, they've vanished without a trace. I thought they would at least look for me. In a way, I'm disappointed. I expected more. At least I'm far from bored, with Cassy visiting often with some excuse or other. We never talk about what happened after the bus ride, but I can tell it's on her mind. I decide to ignore it and hope it goes away. She's a nice girl, but she is American, not Russian. *She is still the enemy*, my head reasons. Deep down though, I'm beginning to like her, think of her as friend, and it scares me.

School starts around the middle of September. The hardest part is making myself appear to be an idiot. I could find harder classes in my underpants. So far, Americans' biggest weakness is stupidity. There are no military training classes, no strategy rooms, nothing. They'll be easy to conquer at this rate.

Vladec is making a point of ignoring me every time we cross each other in the halls. Cassy, at least, speaks to me whenever she can, and reluctantly, I admit it's a relief, not being completely alone. Our mission and observations are going very well though, better even than Vladec predicted. So we won't be friends very much longer.

"Hey, I never asked, how are you finding America so far?" Cassy asks, breaking my train of thought as she hurries to catch up with me in the crowded hallway. I shrug.

"Is okay. I miss Russia. Classes are very hard. Especially as my English is not so premium."

My face heats up as she laughs.

"What? What I say wrong today?"

"*Premium* isn't exactly the right word."

"Sorry."

I push past Vladec quickly, not looking him in the eyes. Cassy doesn't notice the deadly glare he sends my way, but I do. It means the end of a short period of peace.

As expected, he grabs me as I come out of the building, dragging me into a secluded spot. Instead of a beating though, he lets me go as Ivan joins us. I know that look on his face.

"It's time!" Vladec whispers eagerly, eyes alight. I can barely contain my own excitement. At last! Something to do for the Cause!

"You both know what to do."

We nod, too eager to voice our opinions.

"Comrades," he says, saluting, "I wish you luck. If all goes well, the next time we meet will be at home."

Ivan and I return the gesture, pausing for a brief moment before moving off to our places. Vladec stops me.

"Aleksei...no hard feelings about what passed between us? After all, we are both working toward the same goal, even if I am your superior."

I hesitate.

"I don't forgive easily, Vladec. But for the sake of our country and something much greater than we, I'm willing to try."

He nods, understanding. It's the first civil conversation we've ever had. It's strange. He doesn't usually miss a chance to make me feel inferior.

——

Then the time of action is upon us, and all else is forgotten.

"Can I speak with you, sir?" I call out, rushing forward to intercept the target. The man turns, surprised.

"Of course. Aleksei, wasn't it?"

"Yes, I have question." I answer, trying to distract from the fact that I'm reaching into my belt, grasping my weapon. It's far from elegant, but it'll do the trick. Before I can act, a voice sounds behind me, chilling my blood.

"Leksei, wait up!"

What is it with that girl and nicknames? I ignore her, pretending not to have heard. I keep talking, leading the man away from the crowd. When we're out of sight, I draw my weapon, plunging the needle into his arm. He drops unconscious instantly, cut off midsentence. I have to act fast now. Soon, his disappearance will be noticed. I must be certain Ivan is ready before I move on.

"Aleksei—"

I spin around, gun ready. Cassy stares in shock, her mind trying in vain to process what she's just witnessed. I curse her silently for being stupid enough to follow me. This is what I was afraid of. It's the only thing that this stupid friendship could have resulted in. I'm just as much at fault as she is for allowing it.

"Don't move. If you scream, I kill you. Got that?" I hiss, forcing her up against the brick wall. Vladec is not going to like this, and neither is Moscow.

———

Vladec had no trouble knocking out his own victim. Within moments, she was drugged, tied, and ready to be shipped to Russia. He dusted himself off, pleased. There was a bit of trouble shutting the trunk, but after dislocating her shoulder, she fit fine.

On the way to the airport, he was extra careful not to speed or burn red lights, no matter how eager he was to get this mission over with.

On reaching the terminal, he turned right, straight onto a parking lot. His contact was meant to be waiting near a service door. It took him a few minutes of driving through the maze of parked cars before he finally spotted a tall figure, dressed in black, leaning against a pillar. Vladec swallowed nervously, praying his fear wouldn't show. They'd sent one of the few men in the world who terrified him.

He stopped the car, getting out quickly to greet his superior.

"Luka! It's been a long time, friend. How are you?" he called, extending a hand. Luka ignored it.

"I'm not your friend, Vladec. And I don't want to be. Where's the woman?"

"In…in the trunk. She wouldn't fit, so I had to…force a little. Other than that, she's unharmed, I swear it."

Luka tossed him a folded wheelchair. Vladec caught it clumsily, letting it clatter on the ground.

"Not my problem. You can take it up with Moscow when you get back. Put her in that and scram."

"Okay, okay."

He dragged his victim out, nearly dropping her in the process. Luka let out a snort of impatience, lighting a cigarette and shoving him aside.

"Now leave before you miss your plane. Government won't pay for another ticket. Don't take the car."

"But—" Vladec opened his mouth to protest, shutting it quickly as he saw the look in the other's eyes. Luka let go of the wheelchair, taking slow steps toward his subordinate. Vladec backed away, excuses sticking in his throat.

"Are you…arguing with me, little Vladec? Are you…questioning my orders? You wouldn't really be that stupid, would you?"

Cold sweat ran down the teenager's spine.

"No! No, of course not. I would never disobey you, Luka, you know that!"

Luka blew a cloud of smoke into Vladec's face, a mocking smile playing on his lips.

"Of course, you wouldn't. You haven't got the guts. All you'll ever be capable of is picking on those smaller than yourself. No backbone, no nothing. Passion, yes, I see that, but it is useless in a coward like you. Shame, really." His last words seemed to be more to himself than to his victim. Then he turned and left, pushing the wheelchair carelessly in front of him. Vladec could hear it bumping into walls, scraping against trashcans, long after the service door had shut.

He stood there a long moment, calming his pounding heart. Luka was a madman. Everyone said so. He was completely unpredictable, one second laughing, the next trying to slit your throat. It was rumored the government had experimented on his mind, turning him insane when he was still a child. Then again people also said he ate raw meat and painted himself with the blood of his victims. Truth was a difficult thing to discern with a man like that.

Suppressing a last shudder, Vladec began to make his way toward the exit. He knew he wouldn't feel safe until he was on the plane. He never made it.

"Vladec!"

He turned, surprised. There was a bang followed by two sharp bursts. He was dead before he hit the ground, a permanent look of astonishment on his face.

CHAPTER 7

I've come to a conclusion. I hate airplanes. I hate the people, hate the smell, and the turbulence. If I never have to set foot on one again, it'll be too soon. Plus, the passenger on the seat next to me isn't exactly pleased to be here. Or she wouldn't be, if she were conscious. Fortunately, she's up to her neck in drugs and not about to wake up. Ivan is two rows away, taking care of his own sleeping prisoner. I haven't had the guts to tell Vladec yet about Cassy. I don't know how Moscow is going to react either. They can probably hold her for ransom, but will they bother? What was I supposed to do, leave a body for the American police to find? At least now she can disappear quietly.

I don't sleep well this time round, and the trip seems to take years. A few hours before landing, a flight attendant comes down our aisle, proposing drinks. She casts an amused glance at my companion. "Long trip?"

I give her a pained smile.

"*Da*. My friend is very tired. Please, careful not to wake."

"Who is she?"

"I told you, a friend."

The question has put me on my guard. I don't like the attention. "Aleksei. Who. Is. She?"

I swallow, understanding suddenly who I'm talking to.

"A mistake, *devrochka*. I had no choice."

She scowls, obviously unhappy with my decision-making skills.

"We'll talk about this later. Just leave her here when you exit. I'll deal with it."

I nod, breathing a sigh of relief. At least she'll be out of my hands. For some reason, the last couple hours seem to take twice as long as the entire trip. When we finally land on firm ground, I shoot out of my seat, shoving past Cassy as quickly as possible.

"Leksei?"

The barely audible whisper tears at my heart. This could easily be the last time I see her. I stop reasoning for once and crouch in front of her.

"I am sorry 'bout this, Cassy. I really am. Maybe we will meet again someday. I hope you will have forgiven me by then."

I reach up and brush her cheek with my fingers. She's so beautiful. For the first time in my life, I wish things were different. I wish I wasn't serving the Cause so I could stay with her. Reality shatters the feeling quickly though, and I draw away, a soldier once more. I don't look back again as I exit. It's best to forget her once and for all. She's probably going to be killed anyway. No matter how I deny it though, my soul is heavy with guilt and regret.

"You all right, comrade?" Ivan asks, shuffling along next to me in line. He's not such a baby when Vladec isn't around.

"Yes. I'm fine. Happy to be home."

"Mmm. Me too. I've missed Russia. It was too hot in America."

"*Da*. California is very warm for so late in the year."

An awkward silence settles between the two of us. We've never had such a long conversation before. He's usually cringing and whimpering, not daring to disagree with anything we say.

"Any idea who we're supposed to meet?" Ivan asks suddenly, worried.

"No. Vladec was supposed to tell me. He hasn't texted yet."

"That's because he's dead."

We both turn at the unfamiliar voice and immediately snap to attention at the sight of the slick uniform.

CHAPTER 8

The man is tall. His white-blond hair hangs slightly in front of his eyes. Eyes so black, it feels as though one is staring into an empty, bottomless pit. Something about the way he's looking at me causes my stomach to churn. I take an instant dislike to him. If he notices, he doesn't show it. I glance quickly at Ivan to see his reaction. He's reverted back into a frightened child, hands shaking visibly.

"At ease, boys." He says casually, half smiling. "I'm Luka, your new commander. I'll be debriefing the two of you and sending you on new missions."

I frown.

"What about Vladec, sir? Is he really dead?"

"His body was found next to his car. His host family was also murdered, though I believe one escaped."

There's no emotion, either in his tone or in the glance he sends my way. I can't bring myself to feel sorrow over Vladec's death. I will not miss him. The only loss is for the Cause. He was loyal and a good soldier. I am sad about his family, but I really only knew Cassy, not the others.

"So what now?" I ask Luka, more boldly than I feel. For a split second, I think I see emotion cross his face at last. It's gone so fast though, I can't be sure.

"Come with me." He orders, striding away. Ivan gives me a panicked look, like he's about to pee his pants in fear. I shrug, following Luka. Orders are orders, no matter who gives them. I had to learn that the hard way. Ivan trails behind reluctantly, looking dejected. Somehow, I expect he's not feeling much remorse over Vladec's death either. Still, he could at least try to look a little happier.

Luka leads us to a long black car with tinted windows, motioning for us to get inside. I'm liking this less and less, but I don't question it. Besides, at least it's warm inside the car.

"The two of you are going to be sent on separate missions." He tells us after a few minutes, pulling files from his bag. Ivan whimpers in apprehension, looking very much as though he'd like to disappear. I elbow him sharply in the ribs, warning him not to mess around. We don't know what sort of things our new boss does and doesn't tolerate yet. With Vladec, he would've gotten smacked and lectured. Luka, however, shows no sign of having heard.

"It's been decided that you are now both old enough and experienced enough to go solo. Aleksei, you're being sent on the more difficult one."

He hands me my file.

"I trust you can handle it. As for Ivan, it is an easy task, but a crucial one. I will shoot you myself if you fail."

"Like you shot Vladec?" I blurt, regretting the words instantly. There's never been a doubt in my mind that he's the one who did it. How else would he know? He gives me a strange, searching look, almost as though he's disappointed I could suspect him of such a thing.

"I didn't kill him. He was a valuable agent, and we could have used him a while longer."

"If not you, then who did?"

He sighs.

"I don't know, and to be honest, I don't care. He's dead and of no more use to anyone."

I'm not convinced but let the matter drop, focusing instead on the details of my new mission. It's not what I was expecting.

"You're sending me to Siberia? Why? What could there possibly be of any interest in an already-conquered territory?"

"Are you questioning your assignment? There is much there that threatens our beloved Cause."

"No, no of course I'm not questioning. Just curious, that's all."

"Good. Respect for authority is essential to being a strong soldier."

I nod, agreeing. He's right. I shouldn't voice my opinions. If those in charge didn't know what they were doing, everything would fall apart. My esteem for Luka rises a little, replacing the earlier unease. As we speak, my sense of respect continues to grow. The man has more passion for his country and the Cause than anyone I've ever met. His words light a fire in my heart that I'd thought long extinguished. He inspires my imagination, rekindling in my soul a desire for glory. The way he paints the future under Russian rule is magnificent. There will be no more suffering, no more ignorance. All will be united under one idea. Luka shares the same hopes and dreams I have always cherished.

By the time we reach the station, where I'm to board a bus to my next destination, I'm both sorry to go and eager to serve. I feel light, light as a feather, and yet strong as a bull, ready for anything. No one has ever inspired me so much, not even the generals at the school with their speeches.

"Comrade," he salutes as I leave, "good luck."

I return the gesture gladly. Perhaps I only imagined the glint of pride in his eyes, before the car door shut. I'd like to think not.

The bus's features are hardly luxurious. The seats are worn, and the windows don't open. I sigh. Travel is quickly becoming my least favorite part of missions. The end goal is worth it though, and I put aside my longing for comfort with some disgust. America has made me weak. The whole trip should take about two days, providing I make it there in one piece.

I settle myself as best I can into the uncomfortable seat as the bus sputters to life. It shakes so much, I know I won't be able to sleep. So instead, I study my mission file, memorizing details, planning out exactly how I'm going to go about accomplishing this. I fill page after page of blank paper with ideas and concepts, each more unrealistic than the last. But I can't seem to focus. My mind keeps going back to my conversation with Luka, to Cassy, and, strangest of all, to my host family. Vladec's was killed. Isn't it possible that mine was too? I don't want them dead. Toward the end, we were becoming good friends. And Cassy. Is she even still alive? The look on her face when she saw me with that gun still haunts me. In my heart, I know it always will. I betrayed her, lied to her about nearly everything. If we did meet again, I don't think she would ever forgive me.

Luka said not a word to Ivan as they drove on. He didn't like the boy. Besides, neither had anything to say really. The quivering little coward was nothing like Aleksei. He followed orders out of fear, not loyalty. The instant someone stronger came along, he would cringe and cower in exactly the same way, not caring what cause was served. Children such as he were to be held in utter contempt.

"M-may I...ask a question, sir?" Ivan suddenly piped up timidly. Luka sighed.

"I suppose."

"Does Aleksei know?"

He frowned, not liking the turn the conversation had taken.

"No. Why should he?"

"Because everybody does. Sir."

"Do they now? And what exactly is it that "everybody" thinks they know?"

Ivan shrank back, regretting having spoken at all. The way Luka was looking at him was far from friendly.

"Well? You started something. Finish it, boy. What are they saying about us?" He snapped.

"That…merely that…greatness…seems to be genetic."

For the first time, Luka smiled completely.

"Da. I suppose it is. You're not as stupid as you look, comrade. But if you tell him anything, I will kill you."

Ivan swallowed nervously, nodding. He had no doubt Luka would follow through on the threat. They grew quiet again, thinking. Luka recalled the last time he'd seen Aleksei. The kid had barely come up to his knee, though they were only three years apart.

CHAPTER 9

"Luka! Luka, wake up!" The eight-year-old ignored his brother, turning over with a groan. The feel of icy little feet slipping under the thin blanket startled him awake.

"Not again, Aleksei! Go back to bed." He hissed. Five-year-old Aleksei stuck his thumb in his mouth and made his black eyes go wide and sorrowful.

"I had bad dream," he mumbled, rubbing a fist over his face.

Luka sighed. If he didn't agree, there would be no end of trouble.

"Fine. But this is the last time, okay?"

Aleksei nodded solemnly, curling into a ball in an attempt to keep warm. It was freezing in the tiny house. An icy wind blew through the cracks in the wall, chilling the very marrow in their bones. Luka would never admit it, but he was secretly glad of the warmth his brother brought with him. Even if he snored and took up too much room, it was better than being cold and alone.

The boys had just managed to fall asleep, when a third visitor presented herself and her frozen feet.

"There's no room, Tati! Go away!" Luka grunted, kicking to make her leave.

"I'm cold!" she whimpered, kicking back so viciously it made him squeal with pain.

"Wanna stay wiv Leksei," she complained, crawling over Luka to bundle herself against her twin. When Aleksei slept, very little short of a nuclear explosion could wake him.

"Don't you dare start sucking your thumb!" Luka warned, slapping her hand away from her mouth. Tatiana had the notorious habit of being a very loud thumb sucker.

"No hitting," she scolded, slapping back.

"Stop! I'll wake up Mama if you don't go away!"

"You go! You smell," she sulked, trying to shove him out of bed. He resisted, getting angry. Tatiana bit him savagely, making him wail in pain. Satisfied, she turned around, snuggling close to Aleksei.

"Mama! Mama, she bit me!" Luka shrieked at the top of his little lungs. A long minute later, a soft light appeared, moving closer to the children's tiny room. A woman came into view, her eyes still full of sleep, her long blond hair tied back in a loose braid. She'd been beautiful once. You could still see a few traces left. Poverty and worry had lined her face though, aging her before her time.

"Luka, *detka*, what happened?" she asked softly, stroking away the tears.

"Tati bit me, Mama. She won't let me sleep," he sobbed. The mother sighed, not fooled by her only daughter's feigned snoring.

"Tatiana."

The child opened her eye a crack, shutting it again quickly at the accusing stare.

A loud banging at the front door made them all jump. Aleksei, finally awoken, began to wail loudly. His mother gathered him up in her arms, quieting him.

"*Da?* What is it? What's happened?"

They listened intently as the father opened the door. Even Tati abandoned her pretense.

"Police!" a loud voice stated. There was a pause. The mother, frightened, held Aleksei closer. Luka and Tati crept close to her side, burying their faces in her nightgown.

"Police? But…we've done no wrong, sir. My family is loyal, I swear it."

"We are not here to arrest anyone. You have children, do you not?"

"Yes…two boys and a girl. They are very young though."

"How old is your eldest boy?"

"Eight. Only eight. Why? What do you want with him?"

"Bring him here."

Luka cringed, whimpering as the sound of hesitant, shuffling footsteps drew near. The father appeared, black hair messy, a baffled look on his face.

"Senka…they want…they want to see Luka."

She took a deep breath, putting her free arm around her son.

"Are they going to take him?"

There was no mistaking the fear in her voice.

"I don't know. I don't know."

He shook his head, as confused and frightened as she. Aleksei wriggled free of his mother's grasp, clinging instead to his elder brother.

"No! No! Luka stays," he stated, patting the woman's arm reassuringly.

"I don't wanna leave, Mama. Please don't make me go with them!" Luka sobbed, eyes wide with terror. He'd heard enough stories of other taken boys to know what to expect. But there was little choice in the matter. The men, in their tight uniforms and gleaming black shoes, took one look at the little boy and, without a word, tore him from his family, tossing him into the back of a truck. Senka's screams filled the air as they began to drive away. The father had to hold her back to stop her from running after them.

"There's nothing you can do! Stop it! You'll frighten the children!"

But she could not stop.

"My baby! My baby! They took my baby! Let me go, I want my baby!" she screamed again and again. No one noticed Aleksei in all the commotion. He ran after his brother, stubby little legs struggling to keep up.

"Luka! Come back, Luka! Don't go!" he shrieked, tears blinding him. A small hand reached out from a crack in the truck's wooden slats.

"Aleksei, don't leave me! Take my hand, don't let them take me!" Luka pleaded, stretching his fingers desperately.

"I can't! I'm sorry, I can't reach!"

The toddler fell, exhausted. He lay on the dirt road for a long time, too spent even to cry. He did not know that a year later, it would be his turn to be in the truck, blood running down his face from a guard's blow, reaching desperately for his mother.

CHAPTER 10

Luka shut his eyes tightly, fighting hard to block out the memories. He didn't want to remember. For so many years, he'd striven to erase all traces of his past from his mind. It wasn't fair of the government, pairing him with Aleksei like this. They could at least have given some sort of warning before telling him to take charge of the boys. The shock of finding his little brother standing in front of him in a Moscow airport had been hard to hide. On the plus side, he could now feel great pride in how loyal the boy was to the Cause. He'd answered every question perfectly and with a passion that warmed Luka's heart just thinking of it. There, now. The awful memory buried itself deep beneath the new, more pleasant one. It was gone.

"Are you all right?" Ivan's annoying voice broke through his thoughts.

"*Da*. Of course I am. Stop asking foolish questions."

It was true. He'd managed, once more, to kill his feelings. A slipup would not happen again.

My fingers are freezing through the black wool gloves. The weather has been miserable so far. Half rain, half snow—it soaks me to the bone, dripping down my neck, making me shiver.

I've been crouched on this rooftop for over an hour and can't even feel my legs anymore. My target is late. For a whole week, he sticks to the same routine. Of course, today, he decided to do something different. I curse him under my breath, checking for the millionth time that everything is in place. Where *is* the traitor bastard? I blow on my hands, rubbing them together to keep from getting frostbite. I am not liking Siberia thus far. It's filthy, poor, and I haven't been able to shake the chill from my bones since I came a week ago. My hotel room also has a cockroach infestation and a window I can't close. I tried, and the entire wall nearly came crashing down. Even my dorm room in Moscow wasn't so bad, and I had to share that one with Vladec. Still, there's a strange familiarity to it all. Almost like coming home. Not that that makes it any more comfortable.

I should be headed back to Moscow by now, to a better, more important mission. But no. He had to be late. Bastard. I'm actually looking forward to killing him now. That hasn't happened since I got to nail the man who butchered one of my few friends when I was ten.

If my target doesn't show soon, I'm going to have to go look for him, and that will be unpleasant for us both. I don't like using knives. Too messy. Sadly, I'll have no choice if he doesn't make an appearance in the next ten minutes. A thought occurs to me. Maybe someone tipped him off, told him I was coming. I get to my feet, stretching my aching bones. His office is right across the street. Maybe his secretary will be able to tell me where he's vanished to.

It only takes me a few minutes to dismantle the sniper and put the parts carefully back in my bag. This rifle, a knife, and two handguns were waiting for me in my hotel room. Good thing too.

All I had on me was my own pistol, which never leaves my side anyway. It wouldn't have been of much use.

A quick trip down the stairs, across the street, and I'm in the building lobby. It's one of the richest places in town, with a high vaulted ceiling and thick carpet.

"Hello." I say, walking up to the receptionist. She glances up, a bored expression on her makeup-coated face.

"What do you want?"

I ignore her rudeness, miraculously managing to stay polite and smiling.

"I'm looking for Dr. Fyodor? I'm doing a report for school, and he said I could interview him today."

She yawns in response.

"He's not here right now. Even if he was, I doubt he'd have time for you. The doctor is a very important man."

I give her my sweetest smile.

"Okay, okay. I get it." I raise the gun then, pointing it at her Barbie face.

Her jaw drops, a panicked look suddenly in her eyes.

"Where is he?" I ask, losing the smile.

"I…I don't know! He never came in this morning."

I click my tongue impatiently, cocking the revolver so she can hear the click.

"I know that. It's not what I asked. Don't make me ask you twice."

"I told you! I don't know! I swear I don't! Upstairs, go upstairs. Third floor. His secretary will know. She'll talk!" the woman squeaks, hands raised in surrender.

"*Spasiba*. I hope I don't have to come back."

She nods emphatically, also hoping for the same thing.

I put the gun back in its holster and head toward the elevator. It's a good feeling, being taken seriously again. Dealing with pathetic, underpaid employees is always fun. They scare so easily.

The door slides open as I reach the third floor, revealing a long, carpeted hallway. I step out cautiously, scanning the row of wooden office doors for a clue as to the right one. Number four has "Doctor Fyodor, Pediatrician" written in large, gold Cyrillic letters.

I try the knob, entering carefully, one hand on my sidearm, ready to draw. If he's been warned, he could be ready for a fight.

The place is empty. No patients and no secretary. I don't like it. It's too quiet. My heart sounds loud to my ears, pounding against my chest.

I check every room, behind the front desk, even in the bathroom. There's no sign of anyone, and judging by the layers of dust, they haven't been here for a long time. The whole situation is starting to make me nervous. Every morning for the past seven days, I've watched him come to work. What has he been doing here if not curing people, namely, his job? The file said nothing about this. That means that either Moscow herself doesn't know or they didn't think I needed to. In any case, something has probably already gone wrong.

A sudden clatter of falling objects makes me jump. I pull out my gun, moving quickly toward the sound. Hurried footsteps rush into the other room, and I plaster myself against the wall, peeking out only briefly. It's him. I recognize the duck-like walk. But where did he come from? And how did he get in without being seen by me? He's limping slightly too when yesterday he was fine. My curiosity is stronger than any fear. I decide to get to the bottom of this once and for all, tailing him carefully, not wanting to be noticed. What I witness surpasses all expectations.

The doctor, obviously in a hurry, pulls out drawer after drawer, tossing the contents carelessly, muttering to himself. At last, with a cry of triumph, he pulls out a small wooden box. I can't see it very well, but it looks to be beautifully decorated. He opens it carefully, almost reverently, taking out a magnificent pistol. My breath catches in my chest at the sight. The handle appears to be made of pearl or ivory, inlaid with gold. It seems very old. What I wouldn't give to hold it in my hands. The feeling vanishes as the doctor fires, narrowly missing my ear.

"Come out! I won't miss next time!" he yells, his voice trembling audibly. I step out slowly, hands up, gun visible.

"Okay. Just calm down, all right? Look, I'm not going to hurt you. See?" I drop my weapon, kicking it across the floor to him.

"A boy!" he moans to himself, "They send a boy to kill me! Why? Why?"

As expected, his eyes drop down, following the gun's path. I take full advantage of his temporary inattention, darting across the room. A quick blow to his windpipe, a kick to his kneecap, and he's on the floor, breathing hard. Before he can recover, I step on his fingers, forcing him to release his own weapon. I pick it up gently, cradling it in my hands a moment before aiming it at his head. It feels as though it had been made to fit my hand perfectly. In comparison, my gun is clumsy, ugly.

"Beautiful, isn't she?" the old man croaks, jerking me back to earth. I nod, turning it over in my hands.

"*Da*. Where did it come from?"

"It has been in my family for many generations."

"Ironic, then, that I'm going to kill you with it."

His eyes squeeze shut, and his whole body trembles. "Please. Please don't shoot me. I'll take you to her. I'm the only one who can."

I frown, confused.

"Take me to who?"

He glances up, surprised, a faint glimmer of hope in his eyes.

"Your friend, the girl from America. Cassiopeia. Strange name, but she claims to know you. I know where she is kept."

I swear my heart skips a beat at the sound of her name.

"Cassy? She's alive?"

He nods eagerly.

"Yes! Yes! Alive, very much so. She said you would come. Many times she warned me."

I hesitate, knowing I should pull the trigger but unable to. As much as I'd like to see her again, as much as I'd like to know if she's forgiven me, I know the Cause comes first. I've been ordered to kill this man, in spite of conflicting emotions. Of course, I can still shoot him later, but what if he gets away? What if this is a test to see if I'm loyal? For the first time, an emotion stronger than love for my country pushes me, tugs at me. I have to find her. I have to. After all, I got her into this mess. I should be the one to get her out of it.

"Take me to her," I order, letting the old man get unsteadily to his feet.

"And...you'll let me go?"

"If she's alive, maybe. I'll certainly be more open to the possibility." When did lying get so easy? He nods absentmindedly, only half paying attention. His wrinkled hands travel carefully over the back wall, searching.

"I warn you, if you've been lying to me—"

My threat is cut short by a low mechanical whirring as the entire wall slides back to reveal stairs leading the way down.

"This way," he mutters, motioning for me to follow as he totters away. I hesitate a second, apprehension building in my gut. It's not as though I have much of a choice now. I go before he vanishes from sight, keeping my gun aimed at the back of his head. The slightest hint of a double-cross, and I'll blow his brains out.

He leads me down a long corridor, past metal doors until we reach one with the number nineteen above it. The doctor pulls out a keycard and slides it into the slot, casting me a worried, furtive glance as it opens.

"You first," I snap, pushing him in front of me, making him stumble inside.

A light blinks on as we make our way further in. At first, I see nothing but a chair with what might be rags on top. Then I recognize her.

"Cassy!" I shout, forgetting the old man, forgetting the Cause. I run to her, dropping my gun to push the matted red hair from her face. She's bruised and battered, barely conscious.

"Cassy, it's me, it's Aleksei. I am going to get you out, promise," I whisper, praying there's enough of her mind left to hear me. Fumbling with my knife, I cut through the plastic restraints on her wrists and feet. She tumbles forward into my arms, weak as a rag doll. I cradle her head in my hands, not bothering to try and control the swell of emotions rising up in me. I never should have put her on that plane. It's my fault she got hurt. My gaze falls suddenly on her right arm. They've torn away the sleeve, and I can make out puncture wounds.

"What have you done to her?" I hiss, burning with hatred and fury. The doctor merely shrugs.

"Only what I was ordered to, same as you. We are both serving something greater than ourselves, boy. I cannot allow you to stand in the way of that."

My blood runs cold as he raises the gun I dropped, aiming at me. Putting Cassy down carefully, I get to my feet.

"You don't want to do that. Just put it down, walk away. They'll send others after you. None of whom will be as kind as I was. It won't end here."

Even from this distance, I can see his hands are shaking. I hide the knife behind my back, ready to throw it if he panics or doesn't heed my warning. In the silence that follows, you could have heard a pin drop. Cassy whimpers, breaking the tension, startling us both. To this day, I don't know whether his finger slipped, or if he pulled that trigger deliberately. All I heard was the bang. Before the bullet even reached me, I'd thrown the knife, straight and true to his heart.

I reel back in pain as a burning agony tears through me. The shock of it is so great , I don't so much as cry out. For a moment, the pain is so awful, I'm not sure where I've been hit. A fog envelops my mind as I try to stay awake. For Cassy's sake, if not for my own. I fall to my knees beside her, senses focusing on the tiniest, most insignificant details. Her ragged, uneven breathing, the *drip, drip* sound of drops of blood falling to the ground, splashing against the tiles. My blood. My pain. I've been hit before. There are the scars to prove it. He had good aim, that doctor. If I hadn't moved to throw the knife, he would have been the one standing over my corpse. As it is, I think he missed any vital organs. Once more, I got lucky.

I clutch my side, trying in vain to keep the blood from pouring out. What began as a trickle has soaked my shirt and sweater in seconds. Suppressing a groan, I tug up my clothes to take a look at the damage.

It's bad, bad enough to make my stomach heave, but really, it could have been much worse. My problem now is that I'm quickly bleeding to death. Shuddering at even the smallest of movements, I manage to tear a strip of fabric from my shirt, bunching it into a ball and pressing it to the wound. The pain my actions bring nearly makes me pass out. I have to bite my lip bloody to keep from screaming. It takes nearly all my strength to rise, and I fall back against the wall, breathing hard. Under normal circumstances, I'd call for help or drag myself back to the hotel where someone would eventually find me. I don't think Luka would approve of my risking so much for Cassy though, and I'm not about to leave her behind again. My problem isn't getting out of here. That I could manage well enough. But I can't carry Cassy, or drag her, without killing myself in the process. So what now? My head swims, my limbs grow heavy. I fight against the darkness again, pushing myself to stay above the surface of consciousness. I fight…I fight.

CHAPTER 11

Luka tapped the edge of his pencil impatiently on the desk. He was having a hard time focusing on his work. There had been no word from Aleksei in far too long. He would never admit it, but he was worried. His brother had a perfect record, both on the field and off. He'd never been late reporting in before. Now, nothing. Not so much as a text in two days. The doctor's body had been picked up without a hitch. They'd found Aleksei's knife lodged squarely in the old man's heart. The boy himself, however, had vanished.

Luka cursed, throwing a mug against the wall in frustration. It shattered loudly, bringing his secretary running.

"Are you all right, sir?" she asked, worried. He rarely ever lost his temper in public.

"I want Aleksei found! I don't care what it takes, but you'd better get those lazy bastards moving if you value your job," he hissed, chest heaving. She took a step back, frightened.

"But—"

"Don't give me excuses!" he shouted, sweeping everything from his desk in a rage. "I want results! I want *him* here, standing in front of me explaining where he's been, not *you!*"

The girl cringed, swallowing nervously, head bobbing in agreement.

"Get out!" Luka snarled, a dangerous look in his eyes. She gave a loud squeak, ducking for the door as a stapler flew at her head.

"Out!" he yelled again when she didn't move fast enough. "And shut the door!"

He sank back in his padded leather chair, passing a hand over his weary face. Stupid cow. Why couldn't Moscow have sent someone competent? All she had to do was make a few phone calls, blackmail a little, and get the results he wanted. Even if Aleksei was dead, at least he'd know what had happened. An idea came to him suddenly, and he sat up, a sick feeling of dread washing over his bones, making his blood run cold. What if…no. No, Aleksei was loyal to the Cause, he knew that. He'd seen the light shining in his brother's eyes the last time they'd spoken face-to-face. The same that burned in his own heart. Wasn't it? But the girl…he'd obviously cared for her. Could her pull on him have been so strong as to push him to desert? No. Surely not. Besides, they had nowhere to go. But it *was* strange that she'd gone missing at the same time. She could have kidnapped him if he'd been injured. A lot of blood had been found at the scene, so it was a possibility.

Luka rose from his chair, mind awhirl with new ideas. If his brother had been taken, there would be hell to pay. The girl was as good as dead.

———

Sometimes, waking up can be pleasant. On Saturday mornings in America, for example, when you come to slowly and you know you have nothing to do that day. This time, however, is not the case. I wake up screaming, my body awash in wave after wave of agony. Everything hurts. I can't see. Can't breathe. Can't think through the fog of pain that envelopes my mind.

A cool hand strokes my forehead, soothing the burning a little. My screams fade to whimpers. Still I don't dare open my eyes. I'm afraid of what I'll find.

"Sleep, little one, sleep. All is good. All is safe." A voice whispers softly in Russian. She starts to hum quietly, a vaguely familiar tune. I can feel myself starting to drift back off to sleep.

"Cassy?" I struggle to ask. "Where—is she ok?"

"Your friend will live, just as you will soon recover. Now sleep. Everything will be better in the morning."

Her voice grows more and more distant, eventually fading away altogether to be replaced by cool, reassuring darkness.

———

The next time I come around, the pain is much less. I'm able to open my eyes and sit up slowly to take in my surroundings. It's poor, but clean, better than the hotel. Colored pieces of glass hang from the low ceiling, reflecting light over the white washed walls. There's a small wooden chair in a corner next to the mattress I'm lying on, but no other furniture. Crude curtains cover the window, and a shaft of sunlight filters in. The only sound to be heard is a sort of snuffling coming from the foot of the bed. I rise slowly, leaning against the wall for support. My side is bandaged neatly, and someone has dressed me in a warm sweater. I walk slowly, carefully. My wound still hurts quite a lot, but I can handle it now. The sound, I discover, is coming from a large black dog. Its fur has turned gray in places, and it doesn't stir as I creep forward toward the door. Some guard dog. At school, it would have been put down a long time ago. We keep only young, useful dogs. They're trained to be aggressive and bite intruders. Human or animal, you're only kept around so long as you can make yourself valuable. The thing stays asleep even when I turn the handle and head out into a low, dark hallway.

I find myself in a cozy little kitchen with a warm stove and a tiny table in the center. In a corner, a small, round old woman is busy. From behind, she reminds me of a *matriochka*. She has the same patterned dress and apron and a scarf on her head.

"*Privet, babushka,*" I greet her politely. She turns, looking surprised.

"What are you doing walking around like a *myagkie mal'chik?* Crazy fool! You'll undo all my good work and kill yourself! *Pridurak!*"

She charges toward me on her short legs, brandishing a rolling pin. I back away quickly as she jabs it in my direction, forcing me back to the room I just left.

"*Babushka!* Calm down, please. I meant no harm." I say, trying to pacify her. She doesn't listen, driving me relentlessly down the hallway, where the ceiling scrapes my head. I would disarm her, but the pain is getting worse again.

"Okay, okay! Look. I'm going, see? I'm going!" I push open the door and let myself drop onto the mattress. The dog glances at us curiously before giving a huge yawn and settling back to sleep.

"I'm okay, really. I've had worse," I tell the woman as she pulls the covers up to my chin, grumbling to herself. Her expression softens.

"I know. I'm old, but not yet blind. I saw the scars when I was tending your wound. It's not an easy life you've led. But you are safe now and must rest if you wish to heal."

There's so much tenderness in her voice, I don't dare object, and lie back obediently. She plops herself down in the chair, a faraway look in her small, gray eyes.

"They took my sons, you know. All six of them. I never saw them again," she says after a pause. I can't find words to answer her. Regardless, she goes on.

"My youngest would be an old man by now. Thirty-seven on his next birthday, my Fedya. He was five when they stole him from me, ripped him from my arms. There are some scars, boy, that can't be seen. But they hurt more than the others. What poor mother lost you, I wonder?" she muses, more to herself than to me.

"No one lost me, *babushka*, my parents sent me to school. They paid for me to get to Moscow and have a better life." I explain as gently as I can. She gives me a crooked grin.

"Is that what they told you? I suppose it makes sense they would lie."

Before I can protest, she's risen, heading to the door.

"I will check on your friend now. She does not heal so fast as you. Get up again, and Sobaka will bite your head off."

At the mention of her name, the dog glances up, a confused look on her fat face. I doubt she could do anything to stop me if I really tried to go.

"Wait, please. I want to see Cassy," I say, trying to follow the old lady. Sobaka gives a low sort of moan and shifts her enormous weight onto the bed, right across my legs. Despite my attempts to wriggle away, there's no getting her off. I'm pinned. Already my toes are going numb from lack of blood circulation. The old woman chuckles at my frustration.

"Sobaka does not need to bite you to keep you in place. She has more gentle methods. After all, she was once a mother too."

The dog wags her tail contentedly. I swear there's a smug look on her face.

I give in eventually, deciding to simply lie back and wait until the thing gets hungry and leaves. I sleep, on and off, bored, but grudgingly glad for the rest. I wish I knew how we got here. What the old lady said about my mother losing me makes me uncomfortable. She's lying, obviously, but why? Is she just crazy, or is there more to it? I wasn't lost, I was saved. My parents saved me from the miserable life of a peasant. I know that. It's what I was told, what's in my file. They wouldn't lie to me. Not about something like this. So why do her words bother me so much? The last time I wake, night has fallen, and the dog is finally gone. There's a bowl of food next to the mattress, with a spoon and glass of water placed carefully next to it. I drink the water in one gulp, immediately wishing for more. The food, however, I hesitate before eating, despite my extreme hunger. It smells all right, but one has to be cautious around peasant meals. What's edible to them might not be to me. I taste a little, just to see. It's tasteless, but not too awful. I've had military meals that were much worse. In any case, I'm hungry enough to eat it all, if not to lick the bowl clean.

After a moment of careful listening, I decide it's safe to rise and see to Cassy. She's somewhere nearby, and wound or no wound, I intend to find her.

Sobaka, I quickly discover, is asleep in front of the door. I step over her, holding my breath. She keeps snoring, much to my relief.

Once again, I follow the hallway down to the little kitchen. It's empty this time and cold without the stove lit. I half wish I'd brought my blanket. Wherever we are, it's still Siberia, that much is certain. Even Moscow was never this bad. There's a door on the other side. I've almost reached it when a stabbing pain wrenches through my gut, making me double over in agony. I bite back a cry, clutching my side. My hands come away wet with blood. I curse under my breath, fighting down panic. A reasonable person would go back or at the very least call for help. I'm not one of those. We can't stay here. Sooner or later, Luka will track us down, and when he does, things won't go well for Cassy. I might get away with a beating, but he'll kill her. I can't help but wonder why they kept her in the first place. What use did they have for my girl? The thought makes me pause for a moment. Is she "my girl"? I'm not even sure I want her to be. Only one way to find out really. I open the door and step inside. Her room is smaller than mine, more of a closet than anything else. She seems peaceful, asleep like this. Only the bruises break the illusion. Truth be told, they're not half so bad as they used to be. I must have been out a long time. Too long. Every second wasted is a second

Luka gets closer to finding us. I can't let that happen. I won't. Blocking out the pain in my side as best I can, I kneel down next to her mattress.

"Cassy," I whisper, taking her hand. She's cold to the touch and doesn't wake. I say her name again, shaking her shoulder gently. This time she gives a faint whimper and her eyelids flutter briefly. I sigh, holding her icy hand in my warm one.

"I am going to make all better, promise," I say, using English for the first time in weeks. A frown creases her face.

"You're an idiot, Aleksei."

The mutter is faint, but the words clear. For some reason, it makes me smile.

"Yeah? Why's that?"

Cassy pulls away, opening her eyes at last. The look she gives me is far from friendly though.

"You…drug me…you…kidnap…me, and you let them torture me and…expect…to be forgiven? Stupid." She hisses, faltering, her voice sounding like someone about to cry. I sit back against the wall, thinking of an answer to give.

"You think I had choice?"

She turns away, hiding her face.

"I don't wanna talk to you."

"Cassy, if I had not done this, you would be dead. Vladec would have shot you."

"Vlady—he's my friend. He wouldn't!"

She's really crying now, sobs shaking her body. I want to comfort her, but I don't know how.

"You did not know him, Cassy. A man who could murder his own mother could easily have got you too."

There's a long silence. As I rest, the pain lessens slightly, and I relax.

"You're lying. He wouldn't do that."

"I'm not. I was there. Looked her right in the eyes, your Vlady, and shoot her. He was beating *me* many times." I try to explain as gently as possible. She shifts again, this time to face me.

"You lied before. How am I supposed to trust you now?"

"Because…I come back for you. Because I am tired of lying to people." I stop myself before giving the third reason. I'm not ready to tell her yet.

"Fine. You saved my life, I saved yours. We're even. I just want to go home, Aleksei. I don't want to be here, I never did."

How am I supposed to tell her she no longer has a home to return to? In the end, I say nothing. She hates me enough as it is.

"It was you, then, bring me here?" I ask. She shakes her head.

"No. I got you out of the building, that's it. Mashka, the old lady, she found us and brought us here. I thought you'd died, you were bleeding so much. I wasn't heartless enough to leave you for Luka to finish off."

"Why not, if you are hating me now?"

Cassy hesitates before answering. I can tell she's not comfortable with where the conversation is leading. I push for a response though. I want to hear it for myself.

"Because…in the end…you did come back."

I don't stay long at the babushka's house. It would be poor repayment for me to get her killed. I know my value. The government won't let me go easily, and the cost for hiding deserters is a high one.

As soon as I'm able to get out of bed without bleeding to death, I pack some food and a few clothes and get ready to go. The old woman doesn't seem surprised at my decision, just as she wasn't surprised to find me asleep in Cassy's room. She does not scold or question or even try to persuade me to stay, and I'm strangely grateful for it. It feels as though the slightest argument would convince me not to leave, and I know, deep down, I have no choice.

"You should take more food."

I glance up from my packing. It's still early in the morning and weak sunlight shines on the colored glass hanging from the ceiling. The colors play on her face and hair, making her seem as though she's appeared from another world. I try to smile.

"Do not worry. Mashka has given me enough to go from Moscow and back. I will be fine."

I can't say I expected her to come with me, but it hurt when she told me she was staying.

"I'm not worried. Really. I know you'll be okay. You just…be careful out there. Don't do anything stupid."

"Me? Stupid? Psh. Never! I don't do stupid," I reply, giving her my best angelic grin. Cassy can't help but smile back.

"You'd better not. I won't be there to save your butt this time."

Our "friendship" has taken a cautious turn. I explained about the school, the Cause, why we were in America, everything. Even, eventually, her family. She took it well enough or, at least, didn't show me her grief. I suppose after awhile, you go numb from all the bad that happens, and it doesn't hurt so much anymore. Most surprising was that she believed all I told her. Being tortured by Russian officials demanding to know if you're a spy has a way of opening one's mind. Apparently, she also had a few unpleasant encounters with Luka. He's the one who gave her the bruises. It's hard to keep admiring him after hearing about his work in detail. Reluctantly, I'm also starting to question the good of the Cause. My faith is wavering.

"Are you certain? About staying, I mean?" I ask her one last time, hoping for a different answer. Cassy nods mutely, not meeting my eyes.

"Then this is last time we are meeting," I say, moving closer instinctively. She bites her lip, tucking her hair behind one ear and nodding again, more grudgingly.

"Yeah. Guess it is."

Before she can back away, I lean in and plant a soft kiss on her lips.

"I am sorry things could not be different," I whisper in her ear, hoisting my pack onto my shoulder. I head out the door without so much as a glance back, the image of her face imprinted so clearly in my mind, I really don't need to turn.

CHAPTER 12

Cassy stayed where she was for a long moment, rooted to the spot by surprise and slight shock. He'd kissed her. She raised a trembling hand to the spot, hardly daring to touch in case it turned out to be a dream. But it wasn't. Aleksei had kissed her. Without knowing quite why, she suddenly burst into tears.

Mashka, alarmed by her sobs, rushed to her side, taking her in her arms and grumbling in Russian.

"He's gone! He left, and I didn't even say I forgave him!" she wailed, burying her face in the old woman's shoulder. Despite the language barrier, Mashka understood. She saw more than the children knew and knew more than they saw.

She led Cassy back to her room, whispering soothingly.

An hour later, they stood side by side in the kitchen, laughing at Sobaka's attempts to catch a mouse. The girl held back a sniffle, trying hard to focus her thoughts on anything but Aleksei.

"*Privet, dorogaya,* the wonderful smell of your cooking has drawn me in."

The voice sent cold shivers down Cassy's spine. She did not turn for fear of what she knew she'd see. Mashka had no such qualms. She spun round, brandishing her rolling pin. He switched to Russian, obviously trying to calm her down. The words rolled off his tongue like honey, quiet, charming. Mashka lowered her weapon, reassured.

"Cassy, do you forget me so easily?" he asked softly, as though hurt that she hadn't yet turned to greet him.

Hiding her trembling hands under her apron, she faced him.

Luka stood, leaning casually against the doorframe, a triumphant smirk on his pale face. Sobaka, sensing tension, let out a low growl, baring her teeth. He ignored her.

"Babushka," he said to the old woman in their language, "would you leave me a moment with the young lady? We have much to discuss."

Mashka hesitated, unsure. Finally, she nodded, shuffling out past him, the dog trailing behind her. When she'd gone, Luka turned to Cassy.

"Little girl, when last we met it was under difficult circumstances. Perhaps *this* time we may get along better, *da?*"

To her horror, she found that the more he spoke, the more she wanted to listen. He had a voice that could have charmed honey from wasps.

Luka came slowly toward her, pinning her against the sink.

"I will not hurt you. Not if you tell me what I want to know."

"I don't know anything. I swear."

His smirk did not match the cold fury in his eyes. She shuddered and squeezed her eyes shut as he traced a finger across her cheek, letting it rest near her chin.

"I think you are lying to me, little girl. That is not wise," he hissed in her ear, hand traveling down to her throat. Cassy, in a last attempt at bravery, swatted him away, trying to push past to get to the door. Before she could get far, he grabbed her by the neck, choking her. She struggled, unable to draw enough breath to scream for help.

"You should have taken me seriously, little girl." Luka snarled, "Now tell me. Where. Is. My. Brother?"

Tears streamed down her face as she clawed desperately at his grip.

"Tell me!" he yelled, throwing her to the floor and kicking her as she tried to rise.

"Where is he? Where's Aleksei? Tell me!"

"I don't know!" she sobbed, shielding her face with her hands as he kicked her viciously.

"Do you *want* me to kill you, huh? *Do you?* I swear to God I'll shoot you if you don't talk!"

"Luka. Stop." A calm voice broke through the shouts.

"Aleksei? You're here? I thought—" he paused, confused.

"I know what you thought. She didn't harm me. She saved my life."

Luka backed away slowly, trying to make sense of the situation.

Aleksei, controlling the urge to run, stepped cautiously to Cassy's side, keeping his gaze fixed firmly on the other. He raised her to her feet, holding her close. Behind him, Mashka looked on.

"It's over, Luka. I'm done. I don't want to fight anymore," he said, in Russian this time.

"But…you can't. We…we're brothers, Aleksei. We're supposed to fight together, side by side, the greatest force in Russia, in the world. Please. Don't do this."

Aleksei sucked in a shuddering breath.

"Brothers?"

Hope shone on Luka's face.

"Yes, it's the truth. I swear it on my life. You weren't supposed to find out, at least, not yet. Please. Stay. You and me together, we'll rule the world, little brother. We'll get our family back. Mama will have rich clothes. Papa will get a good job with his carpentry. And Tati…do you remember Tati? She'll be so happy to see you again. We'll buy her pearls and jewelry, and we'll all be together, just like the old days. Except better, because we'll never be cold or hungry again. What do you say, little brother? Will you come with me?"

Luka reached out a hand, beckoning. The look on Aleksei's face spoke volumes. The temptation was almost more than he could bear. His grip tightened on Cassy's shoulder.

"What about her?" he asked, his voice threatening to break. Luka shrugged.

"I can do nothing for the girl. She must die to serve the Cause. What does it matter? We'll find you another one, I promise. A better one."

With those words, he lost his brother completely. Aleksei took a deep breath.

"A week ago, I would have taken you up on that offer in a heartbeat."

Luka's smile faded slightly.

"Today, I realize I can't anymore. I came back here because I found out I couldn't leave her again. It took me a whole hour to figure it out, but I did. And I can't let you hurt her again. I'm sorry, Luka. But I'm done."

He held Cassy close as though afraid he might lose her if he let go. Luka's jaw tightened, his eyes flashed dangerously.

"This is your last chance. I don't want to, but I will kill you if you force my hand. Don't do it, Aleksei. She's not worth your life."

"She is to me."

"Then…you leave me no choice."

Luka drew his gun, aiming between his brother's black eyes. Before he could fire, something shot across the floor, nearly bowling Cassy and Aleksei over. Sobaka, snarling viciously, grabbed their attacker's leg in her powerful jaws. They all heard the crunch of bone. Blood poured out as Luka screamed in pain, vainly attempting to free himself. His shot went wild, burying itself in the wall instead.

"Come quickly, children, come! I know a safe place!" Mashka ordered, shoving them out the door as fast as possible. Luka's shouts and curses followed them as they ran.

"Over here!"

The old woman led them into a small shed. She flipped on a light switch and tugged a heavy tarp off a small mound, revealing the last thing they could have expected.

"A motorcycle? Babushka, where did you get this?" Aleksei asked, dumbfounded, forgetting for an instant the danger they were in. She shrugged, looking saddened.

"I lied when I told you I never saw my sons again. They came back a few times. This was my youngest's. It is made for snow, so you shouldn't have any problems. I keep it filled with gas regularly. All you have to do is head north, into the forest. The people will help you if you say Mashka sent you."

Aleksei translated as best he could for Cassy, then turned to argue with the old lady. They couldn't take her only means of transportation away. She cut him off.

"Don't argue with me, boy! There's no time! It's go or die."

He nodded, understanding.

"Aleksei! I'm going to shoot you like I shot that damned dog! Then I'll kill your girlfriend and that thick-headed old woman too! Come out and show yourself, coward!"

The shout jerked them into action as instinct took over. He leapt aboard the bike, Cassy clinging to him from behind.

"Thank you, babushka. I won't forget your kindness," he said, before revving the engine and bursting out into the open. Shots rang behind them as Luka stumbled out, one leg in bloody tatters. But Aleksei was an expert, well trained in dodging bullets, and they sped off into the distance, unharmed.

Luka stood there a long moment, chest heaving. Then he turned and caught sight of Mashka.

"You," he snarled, an ugly grimace distorting his face. "This is all your fault! You turned my brother against me, hag!"

Mashka stood calm and firm in the face of his fury.

"I did nothing. His love for the girl and freedom were stronger, that's all."

"You poisoned his mind! Turned him from the right path! Love had nothing to do with it."

He raised his gun. The old woman stared him down, unflinching. Dignity radiated from her bent form. Luka fired. Once. Twice. Four times. She crumpled to the ground, the snow about her head turning crimson. He turned from her body. It was time to go hunting.

CHAPTER 13

The icy wind burns my cheeks as I speed through the dense wood, branches whipping at us. Mashka had said people would help me. I don't know who, but I hope they show up before we freeze or starve or get eaten by wolves. Despite the cold, maybe because of it, I'm all too aware of Cassy's hand on my chest, her head leaning against my shoulder. I pray Luka hasn't hurt her too badly. My throat constricts at the thought. I have a brother. I betrayed my only family. He has every right to hate me.

"Aleksei…"

Cassy's voice breaks through my thoughts. It's hard to hear her over the wind and roar of the engine.

"What?" I shout.

"Why did you come back?" she yells, louder this time. Of course. She didn't understand when I explained. It's harder to tell her than it was Luka.

"I…I couldn't leave. Again." I stutter, trying to find the right words in English. She's quiet a while, thinking. Before either of us can break the silence, a wrenching pain tears through my gut. I've done too much, it reopened the wound. I lose focus for a precious instant, gasping in pain. The motorcycle goes spinning, crashing to the ground and throwing us apart. I manage to skid to a halt a split second before my head smacks against a boulder and curl into a fetal position, clutching my side.

"Aleksei!" Cassy shouts, staggering over to me in a daze. She's got a nasty cut above her eye, but otherwise looks fine.

"I'm okay. I'm all right. No worries." I groan, not wanting her to see.

"I'm not an idiot, you know. Stop treating me like a child and let me help!"

Her reply takes me by surprise. It shouldn't. I ought to have realized she's stronger than she looks.

"It hurts." I moan, letting go of all pride and dignity, like a child with a scraped knee. "It hurts so bad, Cassy. Please. Make it stop." I plead, at the same time hating myself for being so weak.

"I will, I promise, but you have to let me look, Aleksei. You have to try and relax."

Her words don't register in my pain-clouded mind. I can hear, but not obey.

"Luka…" I gasp, "He'll be after us. Have to-have to go. Run."

I'm babbling, not making sense.

"Calm down. You're going to be fine. I can't help if you panic in Russian, okay?"

But it's as though all the English I learned has vanished. She keeps trying to pry my blood-stained hands away from my side, but I fight her.

"*Ruki uverkh!*"

I stop struggling at the sound of a strange voice from some-where above me. Everything goes dead still. Cassy raises her hands above her head.

"We're friends." She says slowly, "Friends, okay?"

In a whisper, she asks me a quick question. "Leksei, what's the Russian word for *friend*?"

I answer automatically, without thinking.

"*Druz'ya.*"

She repeats it several times aloud. Her accent is terrible. I can only hope that whoever is pointing the gun won't be offended. A pair of boots land near my head. Small boots. A child's. I force myself to look up.

To add to my surprise, it's a girl holding the rifle. She can't be more than seven or eight years old and looks more confused than anything else. If only I wasn't wounded, I'd be on my feet, grabbing the gun out of her hands.

"Valentina!" someone shouts in the distance. "What in God's name are you doing with that weapon? *Pridurak!* You're going to kill yourself. Get back here!"

The little girl turns, a pained look on her face. I can't help but laugh, though it hurts terribly. Cassy, on the other hand, doesn't look reassured.

"What's going on?" she asks in a whisper. I shake my head. I don't know any more than she does. The boy who yelled steps into view. He takes one look at me and confusion spreads across his face.

"What is this? What's happened?" he demands of the girl. I'd like to ask the same thing. He looks like a smaller version of Luka, except his face isn't as pale and his blond hair is close cropped. The girl, Valentina, shrugs, obviously mystified.

"Go get Tatiana. She'll know what to do," he orders, taking charge. I let my head drop back, not caring what happens anymore. I just want the pain to stop once and for all. I want it to be over. I barely even notice that the boy has come to kneel next to me. He's trying to ask Cassy a question, which even if she understood she wouldn't be able to answer. I focus just long enough to form a coherent reply.

"*Druz'ya.* Mashka...sent us. She said...you would help." I breathe out. The pain is both worse and fading. My mind wanders between darkness and dream. Reality becomes a blur. I can't tell what's real and what's not anymore. It seems as though a rush of people pass me. Faces blend into each other. Sometimes I think

I see flashes of Cassy's red hair. I want to reach her, be with her the last moments of my life, holding her close to my heart, but my arms won't obey.

A long time passes, I think. It's hard to tell for sure. I sleep and wake, sleep and wake. Once, it sounds as though some person close by is crying. I can't tell who or why, but it breaks my heart to hear. In the end, darkness wins, and I know nothing for what must be an eternity.

———

It's dawn when I wake fully for the first time. My side aches a little, but no more than that. My sweater is gone, and all there is covering me is a warm blanket, and a clean white bandage around my middle. I sit up and peel it carefully back. The scar is still bright red, not completely healed, but well on its way. It won't reopen again, that much I can tell. I rewrap the cloth and swing my legs over the edge of the cot. My bare toes land on a worn rug, and I take a hesitant step forward. The tent canvas above my head glows in the faint dawn light, crinkling in an unfelt wind. I grab the blanket and wrap it around my shoulders just in case. There's a lantern flickering in a corner, and I pick it up, pushing back the cloth doorway.

A few small fires dot a makeshift campsite, with tents circling one large fire pit. Mine seems to be the biggest, so I suppose it must be the infirmary.

There's no one about yet, no sound of people laughing or arguing. It gives the whole place an eerie feel. I shiver, hugging the blanket more tightly. I'll have to find my shoes before heading out to explore. Going barefoot through the snow is not a pleasant prospect. I'm given no time to plan any further. A shout from a figure emerging from one of the tents soon brings more faces peeking out curiously to see what he's pointing at: me. I back inside quickly, uncomfortable with the attention. Soon, though, they've swarmed around, yelling very loudly and happily in

Russian. I smile back nervously, wondering what's going on. A tall girl with long, dark hair and even darker eyes pushes her way through the crowd to stand in front of me, hands on her hips. Everyone quiets, waiting. It's strange, but she looks oddly familiar. Then, without warning, she gives a loud, piercing squeal of joy, nearly suffocating me as she wraps me in her arms in a bear hug. She's as strong as one too.

"I missed you so much, big brother! Welcome home!" she squeaks in delight. I frown. Big brother? Who is she? The crowd seems to understand though, and they roar their approval, clapping madly.

"Vodka!" someone shouts, eliciting general laughter from the rest. His cry is taken up by several others.

"Drinks outside!" the girl yells over the noise. I've never seen a room emptied so quickly.

"Good. That should keep them busy for awhile." She states, satisfied. "Mama wanted to be able to talk to you alone. Aleksei, you do remember me, don't you? You know who I am?"

I hesitate. A vague idea is forming in my mind, but I don't dare put it into words yet. Finally, I nod.

"You're Tatiana? Tati. You…you're my twin sister?"

Tears well up in her big, black eyes. My eyes. My face. No wonder she looked so familiar, she's me. Tati nods, biting her lip to keep from bawling.

"Luka…he…mentioned you," I add, embarrassed. She stops crying, surprised.

"You saw him?"

"Yeah. Right before he tried to kill me and Cassy. Cassy! How is she? Is she alright? When can I see her?"

My sister holds up a hand to stem the flow of questions.

"Your friend is fine. She learns fast. Before I let you see anyone, Mama wants a word. Please, Aleksei, whatever you do, don't mention Luka."

I would ask why, but the look on her face is enough.

"Wait here. I'll be right back." A grin illuminates her features. "Oh, Aleksei, I'm so happy! We have so much to talk about."

She squeezes my hand tightly before turning and vanishing outside. I sit back on the cot, slightly overwhelmed. I have a sister, a mother...a brother. Am I dreaming? It can't possibly be real. A month ago, or however long I was out, I had nothing, no one. I was alone in a world that would have had me embrace death with joy. Here, they seem as though they'd rather take pleasure in life than die for a cause. It is a strange, but good thing.

A woman enters the tent, interrupting my thoughts. My breath catches in my chest. Something in me recognizes her, knows who she is. Never in a thousand years could I doubt that she really is my mother, not here, and not if I'd just crossed her on a busy street.

"Mama," I whisper. She opens her arms, and I run into them, feeling like a child again.

"My baby. My Aleksei," she chokes, over and over, stroking my head though I'm taller than she is.

"Mama. Mama," I cry. Both of our faces are wet with tears.

"*Mo ïmal'chik!* How I prayed for this day. You've grown so much."

She cradles my face in her hands, radiating happiness.

"I missed you, *Mat'*. Why did you send me away?"

Her smile fades, and she shakes her head in confusion.

"What are you talking about, *lyubov?* They took you from me, in the dead of night, tore you from my arms." She pauses, then, "Come, sit down. We have a lot to talk about, I think."

I let her lead me to the cot, numb with shock. Mashka was right. They lied to me. My mother grasps my hand tightly in her callused ones. She explains what happened the last time she saw me, how with my father, they chose to go into hiding when they found she was pregnant again.

"We weren't going to let them have anymore of our children," she says, her voice cracking slightly. She goes on, telling about how desperate they felt, with Tati being so small, and a new baby on the way. Mashka found them just in time. Together, they built up the camp. As time passed, more and more refugees joined the group. Children were born. First Marko who is now thirteen, then two small babies who didn't live long. I listen to everything without interrupting, drinking it in. It feels so strange, knowing I have siblings, a whole family who loved me and wanted me. My mother has a hard time speaking of my father. Apparently, after the last baby's birth, he decided he wouldn't wait any longer for the government to fall. He would rescue his missing sons. He never came back.

"A better man than your father there never was. Alive or dead, he is still the only one I could ever love. I never remarried. And that's it, really. That's the whole story up to now. When Marko and Valentina found you in the woods, I didn't dare believe it. They told me they'd found a boy who looked like my Tati with shorter hair. I thought at first they were playing tricks again or were mistaken. Thank God they weren't. And I praise him for giving you back your life. You slept so long, I was afraid you'd never wake," she finishes. I note she was careful not to mention Luka or Cassy. Then the dreaded question comes.

"And you, *detka*, what happened to you?"

I shake my head.

"Please don't. Don't ask. You don't want to know, believe me."

"Of course I do, Aleksei. No matter how terrible, we've both had our share of hardship, and I want to know."

So I tell her. I leave out the more traumatic parts of my childhood, like being suspended out of a window by Vladec, but try to be honest all the same. Even the softened version is hard to give though. Painful images resurface, flashing through my mind. The beatings, the terror of being punished for a misstep, shooting down men, women, and children in the name of the Cause and being glorified for it. Mama stays silent a long time when I finish. There's pain in her gaze, as though she can feel my agony.

"I don't like talking about it." I mumble, pulling away. Noticing my unease, she changes the subject quickly.

"Are you hungry, *lyubov*? We have meat cooking outside."

I give her a weak grin. "Starving."

She reaches under the bed and pulls out a pair of sturdy boots.

"Come join us when you're ready then." She kisses my forehead and leaves. I pull on the shoes and follow her out, eager and a little nervous about meeting the rest of my family, even if I did already talk to Tatiana a little.

As I step out into the wind, wishing for a sweater, a hand grabs me by the folds of the blanket and drags me behind a tent.

"Cassy! What—"

She doesn't let me finish. Before I can so much as blink, her arms are around my neck, her lips on mine. Surprise fades quickly, and I close my eyes, returning the kiss. Warmth fills me despite the cold. I let my hand run through her hair, trusting instinct. Time slows to a standstill. The moment both lasts an eternity and is too short. I have to come up for air eventually, breaking it off and immediately wanting more. Cassy buries herself in my arms, head leaning on my chest. I can feel her heart beating against mine.

"I thought he'd killed you." She breathes, sounding scared.

"What, and leave you all alone to be kissing some other Russian boy? Not likely." I tease, stroking a strand of red hair from her eyes. She laughs, pushing me away playfully.

"There's too much of a language problem for that, Aleksei. I would have to be able to communicate first."

I pull her back to my side, wrapping her in the blanket with me. We start walking back toward the smell of food cooking.

"Cassy, I think you communicate very well enough. Not sure I survive any more communication, *dorogaya*."

She scoffs, pretending to be offended. From the color of her face, it doesn't seem to bother her much in reality. I can't help but grin sheepishly at the whistles and cheers that greet us as we come into view. Two long tables have been set out, along with a few stumps for chairs.

"Here. Put this on before you freeze to death,"Tati says, handing me a thick woolen sweater. I pull it on gratefully.

"*Spasiba,* little sister."

She beams, leading us to the seats of honor at the head of one of the tables. We sit, feeling awkward. Cassy reaches discreetly for my hand, holding it tightly. I realize this must all be terrifying for her. She's surrounded by people she doesn't understand, who don't have a clue who she is, or what she's saying. All the poor girl knows is that a couple hours ago, the only person capable of translation was dying a few feet away. I give her hand a squeeze, trying to smile reassuringly. For better or worse, we're in this together now. I won't be leaving her again. She smiles back, but I can tell hers is forced too.

"Listen up everyone, quiet please."

My mother steps between the tables, waving her hands for silence. They obey, and calm descends on the camp.

"My friends, today is a glorious day."

I lean over, translating quickly for Cassy.

"Today we celebrate not only thirteen years of freedom from oppression, but also the return of my son, Aleksander."

A few cheers rise tentatively. My face burns. I wonder suddenly if it's possible to die of embarrassment. Cassy raises an eyebrow, mouthing my full name. I roll my eyes.

"Nobody calls me that." I grunt, going even redder. She giggles.

"Today we forget our troubles for a little while as we eat, drink, and enjoy the life that has been given back to us." She's about to add more, when a man at the far end gets to his feet. He doesn't look happy.

"How can we trust him, Senka? He claims to be one of us, but is he really? As far as I'm concerned, he's a dirty spy! We can't trust him. If I were in charge, I would have ended his suffering with a bullet to the brain. And what about that girl at his side? She speaks no Russian, supposedly, but other than that, we know nothing of her. I say kill them both before they bring trouble down on us."

Tati leaps to her feet, furious.

"Nobody asked for your opinion, fat man!" she yells. My mother silences her with a glare, and she sinks back onto her seat, fuming visibly. I stopped translating for Cassy awhile back and shake my head warningly when she presses me. I knew it was too good to be true, too easy. I glance at my mother, wondering what she'll do. Interestingly enough, it seems she was expecting the outburst. She lets him finish ranting without interruption. At least now he's mostly yelling at my sister. When he's run out of steam, she addresses the issue calmly.

"Enough. Tati will apologize for her behavior. I understand your fear. The consequences of being found or worse, betrayed are more terrible than we could ever imagine. But my son is not your enemy. I have spoken with him, and I know he will not bring us harm."

The man laughs derisively. "He is trained to lie. They all are! How do you know he isn't deceiving you?"

"He's my son. I trust him."

"You said the same thing about Luka, and remember what he did with your so-called trust? He murdered half the camp!"

A pained look contorts my mother's face. The subject is obviously a sore spot. Several people boo at the accusation.

"Unfair! Leave the bastard out of this!" someone shouts.

"That's like blaming her for the devil!"

"Well, she spoke up for the devil, how is that any better?"

I cast a worried glance at Tatiana, but she's clutching the table, knuckles glowing white with the strain of restraining herself from joining in the fight. If this goes on much longer, punches are going to start flying. The same thought has obviously crossed mother's mind because she yells for silence, ordering them back to their seats.

"This is not a day for arguing, my friends. The council and I will discuss this tomorrow in private. For now, let us eat, drink, and enjoy the moment. Please."

Reluctantly, they all grumble their approval, giving each other dirty looks.

"More Vodka!" someone shouts, breaking the tension. I relax as laughter erupts, sitting back. Discreetly, I take my hand away from the carving knife I'd been ready to throw. I hadn't even realized I was gripping it. Cassy gives my arm a worried squeeze.

"What was that all about?" she asks. I don't answer, still feeling tense.

"Aleksei, tell me. I'm not a child. You don't have to protect me." She insists. So I give her my warmest, most comforting grin.

"Is nothing, promise. No worries. Just relax, eat. Meat is good."

She remains unconvinced, eyeing me suspiciously.

"No worries?"

"None. Promise."

Thankfully, she lets the matter drop. I can tell she isn't happy though and refuses to talk or even acknowledge my presence for the rest of the meal, despite my best efforts.

"Come on, Cassy. Do not be like this. I don't treat you as child. Promise. Fight had to do with Luka, not us. Come on, please talk," I beg, as she leaves the table.

"I'm only going to the bathroom, Aleksei. You don't have to follow me like the lost little puppy you are," she snaps, not bothering to turn and face me. I let out a frustrated snort.

"Fine. I go and talk to Tati. Maybe she is less moody than you."

"Fine by me."

"Okay, fine! Good! I go."

I stay where I am though, hesitating, watching her as she vanishes into the trees. Women. I'll never understand what's wrong with them. An hour ago, she was kissing me, and now she is angry for no reason. I don't get it. I'm about to head back and ask my sister for advice, when a piercing scream stops me in my tracks.

"Cassy!" I shout, running toward the sound, suddenly gripped by the fear that someone has taken her from me again.

CHAPTER 14

Luka was not the sort of person who took failure well. Those who knew that stayed well out of his way. Those who didn't usually ended up in body bags before they could figure it out anyway. To be summoned up to his office when he was in a bad mood was like a death sentence. The man now standing in front of him knew it well, made obvious by his trembling.

"*Da*, of course, sir. Of course. I can get you dogs. Any kind you need, sir."

Luka nodded, pretending not to notice the man's fear.

"Good. That's what I like to hear. I need tracking dogs, blood hounds. I'm looking for someone, and they vanished into the forest on a motorcycle. Can your dogs handle that?"

"Oh, yes, no problem. I've trained them to follow the smell of exhaust fumes. They can do it if the trail isn't too old."

"Well, it has been a few days. Almost a week, in fact. Will it be an issue?"

"No, no sir. At least…it shouldn't be. Traces can sometimes last weeks, depending on the weather. Snow and such."

"Fine. I trust you will do your utmost to ensure that there are no…how shall I say it? *Glitches*."

The man nodded, eagerly promising he would allow nothing to stand in his way.

"That's good. Very good. I'm glad of your cooperation. You have family?"

Coming from anyone else, the question might have been harmless, polite small talk. Luka, however, was not one to ask pointless things. The man swallowed nervously.

"Yes. Yes, sir. A wife and two grown children."

"I thought as much."

Luka paused, letting his victim squirm. Then he leaned forward, his black eyes sparkling with malice.

"Your daughter…she's expecting her first child, is she not?"

"Y-yes."

"A boy, if my sources are correct."

"Yes, sir. They are."

"It would be a shame for him to be taken from his mother's breast at the moment of his coming into the world. But, sadly, duty calls, and the army could always use more boys to train. So many die at war."

"Please sir, don't—"

Luka held up a hand to silence him.

"The army recruiters do sometimes make mistakes. Overlook certain candidates…you never know, you could get lucky. Now, before you go, I have one more question ."

"Anything for you, sir."

He gave his best demonic grin, sending shivers of terror through the cowering man.

"Your dogs, how vicious are they exactly?"

Luka's new assistant was the latest in a long line. The others had all gone under rather mysterious circumstances. She was the youngest by far, only about fourteen or fifteen. The job had only recently become hers, her predecessor having been found with her skull smashed. The police had declared it suicide, as usual, but everyone knew differently. Besides, it was hard to see how she could have done the deed herself.

Katya was none too pleased about where she'd been placed, but the Boss knew best. As it turned out, he'd been right. Barely a few days into the job, and she'd already found out enough to destroy Luka and the government for good.

"Not yet," the Boss kept telling her whenever she expressed her impatience over the phone. The timing had to be right; otherwise, all their efforts would come to nothing. They'd already gotten rid of a serious thorn in their side by killing Vladec. She hadn't been there when it happened, but rumor had it that the Boss had done the job himself.

Katya leaned her head on her hands, allowing herself a precious moment to daydream. In her fantasy, the Boss's life was in terrible danger, and she alone could save him. Of course, she always arrived just in time to prevent tragedy. He would sweep her into his arms in a magnificently romantic gesture and profess his long hidden love. He'd look deep into her eyes and say—

"Where's my coffee, girl?"

Katya gave a little jump, coming back to reality with a thump. She blinked, confused.

"What?"

Luka snorted in disgust.

"Are you deaf as well as stupid? I said get me my coffee!"

"C-coffee? Oh, yes. Of course. Right away, sir. Forgive my slowness, I beg you," she said, bowing low, at the same time thinking about how her real boss would never have spoken so harshly. Luka sighed in frustration.

"Just go. And hurry back. It's not like I'm asking you for the moon."

Katya scurried away as fast as she could, thanking God he'd been in a forgiving mood. There were days when he seemed ready to kill for much less. At this rate, the Boss would have to rescue *her*, and that would never do. It wasn't nearly romantic enough. Down the stairs, past a few doors to the kitchen to fill a mug with his personal brand, which no one else was allowed to so much as look at, and back up quickly to his office. She knocked timidly at the door.

"Come," the order sounded. The girl went in, careful not to spill a drop of hot liquid.

"Set it down there," he said, not bothering to look up from the papers he was reading. She obeyed, then backed away hurriedly, wanting to get as far from him as possible.

"Wait," he ordered again, still not granting her so much as a glance. Katya stopped, suddenly nervous. At last, he put down his pen and looked at her curiously, his keen eyes studying her every move. She squirmed, not liking the way he seemed to be able to see what she was thinking or the way he stared.

"Are you frightened of me?"

The question took her completely by surprise.

"I…I suppose everyone is, sir."

He clicked his tongue impatiently, then controlled himself, leaning back in his chair. A strange look came over his face, like a snake eyeing a fat mouse.

"Yes, I know that. It's not what I asked you."

Katya stared down at her shoes, wishing her Boss could be there to protect her. Luka would kill her if she answered incorrectly. The gun was right there, close by his hand.

"I don't…I don't know what you mean, sir."

He startled her with a clear laugh. It sounded nothing like the villainous cackle she'd always heard before.

"It's a simple enough question. Yes or no, are you afraid of me?" he caught her glance and smirked, picking up the weapon and dropping it into a drawer. "I want an honest answer, child. So let me reassure you. No harm will come of your response, no matter what it is. This little chat is, as our American friends would say, 'off the record.'"

Katya frowned, thinking hard. If she said yes, it would flatter his vanity, but he had the uncanny ability to tell when he was being lied to. If she said no, however, he might get angry and shoot her. Then she would never find out if the Boss really loved her. She took a deep breath and looked him straight in the eyes for the first time.

"The truth is…I don't know. I haven't made up my mind about you yet. I think you pretend a lot so that people will respect and fear you."

She stopped, worried she'd gone too far. But Luka merely smiled as though the snake had just swallowed its meal.

"Little girl, you are very honest with me. Brutally so. I appreciate that. Had you lied, I would have killed you. I don't enjoy shooting children, but it is sometimes…necessary for the common good of all. You understand this, I think. Do you know why I hired you, young as you are?"

"Because you like pretty girls?" Katya blurted without thinking. The turn of the conversation was making her edgy. Luckily, he laughed again.

"Good observation, but no. You're a little young for me. Perhaps in a few years, if you're still alive. No, normally I like to bring in women closer to me in age. I can have my way without any fuss, and nobody cares when I kill them. It's quick, clean, and best of all, no paperwork. Problem is, I'm forced to hire only stupid ones, otherwise they might betray me. I'm tired of being surrounded by giggling fools. You, you're young, innocent, unpolluted by prejudices and vague ideals that demand your loyalty. You can be molded, and you seem a bright girl on top of everything. The time is coming when I'll need brains equal to my own fighting at my side. I had thought—" He halted abruptly, mid-sentence, as though an unpleasant image had crossed his mind. Luka shook his head, casting whatever it was that troubled him aside. "The point I'm trying to make is that very soon, I will ask you to make a difficult choice, and I hope that you will be ready to answer when that day arrives."

Katya's mind raced. Was she supposed to decide now? Luka, however, dismissed her with a wave of his hand.

"Sir? M-may I…take the rest of the day off to think on this?"

It was a daring thing to ask.

"Take an hour, go for a walk, clear your mind. I expect you back by two. Have an answer for me in the morning."

She breathed a sigh of relief, thanked him, and rushed out into the crisp Moscow air. She had a phone call to make, and it was better done in private.

———

Later that night, as she headed back to her little apartment, she couldn't help but feel sorry for the others who'd had her job. Luka was not easy to keep happy. After demands for more coffee, being sent to run on errands halfway across the city, and following the man's every fickle whim, she was exhausted. At least he'd let her get her own place. With a tired yawn, she pushed open her door, switched on the light, and went to make herself a sandwich. When she turned back from the refrigerator, the shock of having someone standing calmly in front of her made her drop the packet of ham. He was tall, handsome, with dark hair and clear, intelligent gray eyes. Even in her daydreams, he hadn't looked this good.

"Hello, Katya. Do you know who I am?"

The girl nodded mutely, not trusting herself to speak in case it made her wake from the dream. He had the voice of an angel too.

"You—you're…you're the Boss," she stuttered at last, hardly daring to believe it. He laughed, and it was like music to her ears.

"Yes, but let's not go too much by titles. You wouldn't want me to address you as Soldier, would you?"

She shook her head dumbly, too astonished to reply. The Boss extended a leather gloved hand.

"You can call me Ivan."

CHAPTER 15

By the time I reach Cassy, she's managed to take care of the problem very well herself. The scream came more from him than from my girl. A man lies at her feet, groaning in pain.

"What happened? What did you do to him?"

Cassy, still breathing hard, tries to explain.

"He was shouting all this stuff—in…in Russian—and waving a knife like he was going to gut me or something. So…so I kicked him. In the groin. It was self-defense. He scared me!"

I can't help it, I have to laugh. She gives me a half-confused, half-disgusted look.

"Cassy, I am sorry. Forgive me for ever thinking you helpless."

Pure relief mixed with adrenaline has me doubled up with laughter. It's catching, and soon enough, she's cracking up too. After a minute or so, I manage to calm down enough to get down to the man's level and ask him why he was trying to attack my girlfriend. All of a sudden, it hits me. I've seen him before. He was the one shouting we were spies not an hour ago.

"Friend, why did you try to hurt the girl?" I ask as gently as I can. He glares furiously at me and tries to spit on my shoe, missing by a centimeter.

"I am no friend of yours, boy! Traitor! You betray your country and your people by being here. Mark my words, Luka will hear of it!"

I raise an eyebrow in disbelief.

"Oh, will he now? And you call me a traitor when you're working for such a bastard?"

"Traitor to the Cause, you and I were born to serve, yes! Traitor to everything you once fought for, bled for, *killed* for. There is no worse kind of scum on this earth than you. Trash. Pure trash. *Da*, and the girl too!"

I let him have his rant. He's right, in a way. Somehow though, it doesn't matter anymore. I have Cassy, I have my family—or most of it anyway—what more could I need? His words bounce off harmlessly. I don't care what he says or thinks. I'm at peace with myself for the first time. Quickly, I translate for Cassy.

"You have to go find my mother and the others. I stay and guard him."

She gives me a skeptical look.

"How am I supposed to do that when I don't even speak Russian?"

I smile up at her. She blushes, tucking back her hair self-consciously.

"What? What is it?"

I shake my head.

"Nothing. You're beautiful, you know that? And clever too. I trust you. I know you can do it."

It's pure manipulation, but she falls for it easily.

"You…really think I'm pretty?"

"Not pretty, beautiful. To be smart on top is little wonder I fall for you."

She bends down and gives me a kiss.

"You're sweet, Aleksei. But I'm not falling for it."

I grin, getting to my feet.

"No. I did not expect you to. Just kick him again if he is moving. I'll be right back."

It only takes a few minutes for me to alert everyone, but by the time we get back, it's too late. The spot is empty. No Luka's henchman and no Cassy. Any other situation, I could easily have kept my cool. This time, I panic.

"Cassy!" I shout, sprinting away in the direction their footprints lead. Tatiana, close behind, yells at me to slow down, but I'm beyond being reasonable. I am tired of losing her all the time. I can't let it happen again. I won't. Over and over I shout her name, till my throat burns. Over and over, only silence answers. Tati finally catches up, tackling me from behind and knocking me to the ground. I fight her off, desperate.

"Aleksei!" I stop struggling a moment, hardly daring to believe my ears.

"Aleksei, it's okay. I'm here," Cassy calls, a few strides away.

Tati lets me scramble to my feet. I run to her, alternately holding her close and checking her for bruises. She's got several and a few scratches from brambles, and she's shaking slightly, but otherwise seems unharmed.

"I'm ok, Leksei, I'm fine. Stop panicking, you big baby." She says, trying to sound stern. I feel my muscles relaxing, my breathing slows to normal.

"What happened? Did he try attacking again? I'm going to kill him if he is hurting you."

Cassy shakes her head.

"No, no, he didn't hurt me, he just ran. I tried to follow, but I lost him. I'm sorry, I tried. I really did. I tripped on a branch, and he got away. I'm so sorry."

I cup her face in my hands and smile, brushing some dirt from her cheek with my thumb.

"It doesn't matter. At least you are safe."

"It *does* though. He'll go back to Luka, he'll give us away. He won't let us escape this time, you know he won't. He'll kill you. I don't know what he'll do to me, but I'm sure it won't be very pleasant. He gives me the creeps, Aleksei. I don't think I can face him again."

"You can! You're stronger than you think. Besides, I am here. I protect you, *da*?"

She giggles.

"*Da!* That you do."

"Aleksei."

I turn at the sound of my mother's voice.

"He got away, Mama. You should move your camp as quickly as possible before he brings Luka. Cassy and I are leaving too. It's my fault this happened. I don't want to bring any more trouble."

Mama sighs as though she's used to this. Now that I think about it, Luka probably sends spies on a regular basis.

Tati starts to protest, but my mother stops her with a warning glance.

"I understand. I do. But I think perhaps it would be best to convene the council first and hear their thoughts on the matter. Is that all right with you?"

I nod reluctantly. Truth be told, I'm in no great hurry to leave. I've only been awake a few hours, and already I feel more at home here than I ever have anywhere else. Also, my side is aching again. There's little choice though. I won't stay to see them all killed because of me.

As we make our way back, I translate events for Cassy. She's not particularly happy about my decision, but after giving it some thought, she agrees it's for the best. To my relief, she doesn't speak of the possibility of her staying if I go.

———

Katya leaned her elbows on the table, head in her hands, absorbing every wonderful word that came from Ivan's lips with adoring attention.

"So you agree with me then?" he asked, slightly unnerved by the devotion. Ever since he'd shown up the night before, the girl had barely spoken a word. She seemed much more intent on keeping him talking, which was strange in itself since she never actually listened. Not that he wasn't used to girls acting strangely around him. They all did at first. This one was bordering on the extreme though. The way she just…stared. It sent shivers down his spine.

"Katya, do you agree?"

The girl blinked dazedly.

"Yeah, I agree, absolutely. Whatever you say."

"Good. So you'll do it? I admit I'm impressed. The risks are big."

"Do what?"

Ivan sighed, rubbing his eyes wearily. "Kid, I don't know what's going through your head, but I have a girlfriend. Besides, you're only about, what, twelve? I'm sorry. It just wouldn't work out."

"Fifteen."

Katya's voice shook, her lip wobbled dangerously, big blue eyes filling with tears.

"Please don't cry. At least I'm honest with you! A lot of guys would lie to you and trick you because you're pretty. I'm not going to. Listen, I came to see you because when we spoke on the phone, you sounded like a very smart girl. One I could trust with a very important mission. No, don't cry. You'll meet someone, someday, I promise. Someone better, closer to you in age. Please stop crying, Katya. We can be friends, can't we?"

Eventually, after much coaxing and reasoning, he got her to calm down.

"There we go. All better?" Ivan asked tentatively, handing her a box of tissues. She nodded, blowing her nose loudly. He breathed an inward sigh of relief. Finally they could get back to the business at hand.

"All right, let me give you the mission again. You're to stay close to Luka, learn his secrets, pretend to be on his side. Don't lie outright because he'll know and shoot you. Half truths work better. I know he's after Ale—after a friend of mine, but I need details. I need to know what he knows the instant he knows it. Can you manage that?"

Katya sniffled mournfully.

"Yes. I think so. It shouldn't be too hard. He trusts me. When he notices I exist at all."

Ivan leaned forward across the table, an urgent light in his eyes.

"Don't *ever* assume anything like that again. Do you understand me? Luka trusts no one, not even his own brother. He lures people into thinking they're trusted, makes them give up their secrets, and then kills them. He enjoys it too. Don't *ever* assume *anything* about Luka. It could mean your life. Got that?" he hissed, slamming his hand down so hard she jumped, startled.

"Okay, okay. I'm sorry. It's just…the way he spoke to me…"

"Yes, he's very good at that. For a while, even I believed he wasn't so bad. Then he murdered my baby sister to punish me and made me bury her. I was nine years old. He doesn't remember, but I do. He'll draw you in with his words, make you believe in all sorts of magnificent possibilities for the future. It's all lies. Why do you think he's so good at figuring fact from fiction? He's a master of words. Be careful not to get caught in his web, Katya."

There followed a long, tense silence. The girl looked shaken. Good. Better she know. It would keep her alive at least a little while longer, and he needed her. The whole plan rested on her frail little shoulders. Without Katya, he would never find Aleksei, and without Aleksei, there would be no defeating Luka. Failure meant death for them all.

"I…I should go. He'll be suspicious if I'm late," she stuttered. Ivan nodded.

"*Da*. Go. No need to take unnecessary risks."

He stopped her as she reached the door, putting a hand on her shoulder.

"I trust you, Katya. I know you can do this. Just…be cautious, all right? I don't want to lose you."

To his relief, a faint light of hope and enthusiasm, previously extinguished by tears, reignited in her eyes.

"You can count on me, Boss. I promise I won't let you down."

———

Luka watched his assistant's every move like a hawk. There was something different about her this morning, more subdued. He was no fool. He knew exactly who she'd been talking to. And so far, it was all working perfectly according to plan. He could almost feel the trap closing in on that traitorous leech. Then she would see him for what he was. Not a hero, but a manipulating coward who had tossed her to the wolves. Not yet though. Not yet. Let Ivan believe a while longer that they had him fooled. He was patient. The carefully woven net would soon be in perfect position. The whole operation would come tumbling down around their clueless heads. Victory and the girl would be his. First, a crucial piece of the puzzle was missing: Aleksei. He would be found soon enough. His girlfriend would die, supposedly at Ivan's hands, and the boy too would turn back to the right path. Then it was only a matter of time before the government fell and the world was his. His brother would make a fine second in command, providing he cooperated. If not, well, there were always the mines. A personal slave didn't sound so bad either. Come to think of it, he rather liked the idea.

CHAPTER 16

I trudge through tall drifts of snow, wishing for daylight. My mother, as it turns out, didn't take kindly to the idea of me leaving after all. She ignored Cassy completely. All through the council meeting, she kept trying to convince me to stay. Not openly, mind, but I got the subtle messages all the same. I tried the same method to find out exactly what Luka did to them and failed miserably. In the end, it just seemed better to leave without causing any fuss. So when night fell, I packed a bag with blankets and food, woke Cassy, and we made our escape.

"Aleksei, wait."

I stop, half-annoyed. She's been dragging behind, walking slowly in the snow, calling for me to pause every couple feet. I almost tell her that she's driving me mad but stop when I see the look on her face.

"I think someone's following us," she whispers, more excited than scared. I feel rather proud of her then. The soft, pliable little girl from America has been transformed into a strong, almost-Russian woman, ready and eager for a fight. I decide to indulge her this once. After all, I do want to encourage her fighting spirit. It'll be a good start to my plan for her training too. Then I hear it. Footsteps, dogs whining.

Putting a finger to my lips, I motion toward a clump of trees where we can hide in wait. She nods, understanding, and climbs into the branches after me.

We crouch in the darkness for what feels like an age. Really, by my watch, it's only three minutes or so before we hear the sound of snow crunching under heavy boots. Cautiously, I peer out from behind a branch. It's a shame we're in the middle of winter. There are no leaves to help conceal us now. I don't like what I see.

A sliver of moonlight illuminates the scene. The man and his three dogs stop just a few feet from where we were a minute ago. The animals are sniffing around, digging their noses through the snow. Bloodhounds. Not particularly friendly ones either, judging by the size of those teeth. Luka must have sent them. There were no dogs back at camp, and even if there had been, I don't think Mother would go so far as to get them to chase after us.

I motion for Cassy to stay low and inch my way carefully up the thick branch for a better look. So far so good. They're turning around in circles, whining and whimpering, looking to their master for help. I would laugh if the situation weren't so serious. If they're quality dogs, they'll find our trail sooner or later. I pray for later. For once, it would seem that God is listening to me. There's no time to waste though. I look back at Cassy, shivering in the cold. How to get out of this? An idea begins to grow in my mind. It's risky, but do we have any choice? At first, she doesn't understand my motions and gives me a strange look. Then it dawns on her. She shakes her head, incredulous. Before she can protest further, I pick her up, letting her legs drape over my arm. She wraps her hands around my neck, biting her lip to keep from protesting aloud and buries her face in my shoulder. I guess there's still a part of her that hasn't changed after all. I take a deep breath, steadying my nerves. If I miss or slip, the consequences will be much worse than broken bones. I jump before I can change my mind.

We make it to the next tree and the next. On the third, I almost lose my balance, righting myself just in time. Cassy sucks in her breath, clinging tighter in alarm. I pry her off before she chokes me to death, setting her down gently.

"Don't *ever* do that to me again," she hisses, regaining some of her bravado. With a grin, I bow low mockingly and jump backward, out of the tree onto solid ground. We're far enough now that the dogs won't find our trail for at least a few hours.

"Aleksei? Where are you?" Cassy whispers, a slight note of panic in her voice. I keep forgetting she can't see as well as I can in the dark. We'll have to remedy that when we're safely away.

"Here. Jump. I catch you!" I hiss back, stretching out my arms. She hesitates, but the sound of dogs barking in the distance decides her. She lands in my arms, winded but unharmed.

"See? Was not so terrible, was it?"

———

Luka tried hard to hide his fury. He really did. It simply got away from him a little bit, and by then, nothing could have saved the man anyway, so what did it matter? He strode out of his office, rage still burning, hot and fierce, in his chest. He needed to shoot something else.

"Katya, clean up this mess. Then I want you to call the army, tell them to keep an eye on a pregnant woman. She's expecting a boy. When you're done, call the pound. Have them take those dogs to my summer house. You hear me?"

She nodded, terrified of what he might do next. Even on his worst days he'd never been this angry.

"Good. And contact the troops. Tell them the plan is going ahead a little early. I'm tired of waiting. Moscow will soon know of my power. It's time to teach those cowardly bastards the real meaning of fear."

He left, slamming the door behind him. Katya, somehow managing to keep her panic under control, did not call the army first. The instant the sound of Luka's footsteps had faded down the stairs, she dialed Ivan's number.

"And you're sure of it?" he asked after she'd explained the situation breathlessly.

"*Da, da*, positive! He was really, really angry that Aleksei got away again!"

"All right, don't panic, whatever happens. Just follow his orders and you'll be fine. Any news on Aleksei's location?"

"Yes, he yelled something about Siberia and a forest. The man with dogs said something about a little house too and a dead old lady before Luka shot him. That's all I know. Does it help?"

There was a pause. Ivan muttered a word that sounded like *Mashka*, then said quickly, "Okay, I think I know where he is. Stall Luka's plans if you can, but don't risk anything, not your life and not your cover. Good luck." He hung up abruptly, leaving her holding the receiver, slightly in shock.

"How do I do that?" she wondered aloud, feeling faint all of a sudden, betrayed and frightened. Luka would kill her the instant he thought he saw something odd in her behavior, especially now, when he was at his most paranoid. Already he saw imaginary spies everywhere.

Reluctantly, Katya had to admit that what her Boss was asking for was impossible. For the first time, she found she simply couldn't obey. It made her insides churn. How could he? How could he have just left her like this after all she'd done and been through? There was nothing to do now but follow Luka's orders and pray that the world would survive. She'd never felt so alone.

CHAPTER 17

A few moths later,
the middle of Siberia.

I put my gun to the back of the intruder's head, making sure he can hear the click.

"Drop your weapon and turn around slowly," I order with a snarl. Cassy and I have walked through the snow for days on end until we were sure of no one being able to find us. We'd even started building a shelter, figuring we would wait out the rest of the winter before moving back toward civilization. That is until this rat came snooping around, carrying a gun in his belt. Cassy went out to check our traps for game hours ago. She should be back just in time to keep watch while I interrogate our prisoner.

"Don't shoot, Aleksei. Please."

I frown, confused. I know that voice.

"Turn around," I order again. The spy obeys.

"Ivan? What are you doing all the way out here? How did you find us? Did Luka send you?"

Ivan let out a sharp, barking laugh, so unlike his usual cringing that it takes me by surprise.

"Luka? Send *me*? As if. If I hadn't gotten out of Moscow when I did, his soldiers would have killed me. Things have changed since you were last in the world, Aleksei, especially in the last couple weeks. I swear to you, I'm here as a friend and ally. Will you let me speak?

I hesitate, then lower the gun slowly. There's something different about him, though I can't put my finger on it. Since when has he been this confident?

"Fine. Say what you must. I warn you, one wrong move and I'll shoot."

He lowers his hands, a relieved grin spreading across his face.

"Is there someplace we can sit? It's a long story."

I shrug and then nod toward two stumps. We settle down as he begins his story.

"I, like you, and many others, was taken from my home when I was very young. Certain…events…created in me a hatred for Luka and all he stood for. He forgot me while I vowed to destroy him. Slowly, my plans began to take shape. I gathered strength, ready to strike when the time was right."

He pauses as though his next words are hard to force out.

"And?" I prompt. "Did you?"

He sighs.

"No. We waited too long. He moved forward with his plans much earlier than we believed he would. He put things into motion so fast; there was no time to react. A lot of my people died trying to stop him. The rest are like us, in hiding. Soon, though, there won't be any safe places left. His armies have already taken control of half of Europe. They infiltrated the governments years ago, just waiting for his word. Moscow was first to fall."

There a long, heavy silence as his words sink in. Finally, I have to ask. "So…all this time…you were pretending to be a whiny little brat? Why?"

"It was the best way to avoid suspicion. Worked on you pretty well. Worked on Vladec too, right up until I killed him."

"That was you? But…I thought—"

"You thought Luka did him in or someone working for him. That was part of the plan, to shift blame somewhere else. And before you ask why, let's just say…Vladec was a loose end. I don't like leaving loose ends."

I consider this revelation quietly for a moment. It's something I was never expecting to hear, not from Ivan anyway. There's another thing that's been bothering me for some time, and I have to ask. "Those men at the park, the ones who chased me, was that you too?"

He looks suddenly embarrassed. "Yeah. They uh…they weren't meant for you. That was a mistake. They thought you were Vladec. I called them off when I found out. Not that they were willing to give up, but I pulled some strings. Forget about it, okay? It's in the past."

Taking the hint, I drop the subject. Sometimes, it's just better not to know.

"Why come to me then if you have so many other options? What can I possibly do to help?"

Ivan leans forward, an eager, almost crazed look in his eyes. "Because you're the only one who has the strength and guts to face him! We need you, Aleksei. We need your planning skills, your ability with weapons. We're all trained, yes, but nowhere near what you have. If anyone can defeat Luka, it's you. Besides which, you're good at speeches, even better than he is. You inspire, give courage where there is none! I know. I've heard you. We need you! Without your help, the world is lost forever to Luka's madness. Please. Will you come? Will you help us?"

He's so desperate, so sure, I can't bring myself to say no. I want to do it. I want to fight. The problem is Cassy. What will she think of all this?

"Ivan…do you remember that girl from America? The one on the plane?"

He blinks in surprise at the change in subject.

"Sure. Why?"

"Because I sort of...rescued her. She's with me now, and I won't leave her behind."

To my astonishment, instead of being perplexed or embarrassed, he laughs heartily.

"I heard she escaped, but I didn't know it was your doing. Why not bring your girlfriend along? Another ally, especially a bilingual one, is always welcome."

I smile.

"Good. Allies it is then. Any particular plan in mind for taking down my brother?"

At that moment, Cassy appears, holding a brace of snow hares over her shoulder. It takes awhile to translate to her what's happened. When she's been filled in, she doesn't hesitate before agreeing to help take down Luka. After all, he was the one to murder her family in revenge for Vladec's death, Ivan tells us.

We shake hands, making a pact. Together, the three of us will fight. We will win, or die trying.

"To the death." I say, gripping his shoulder. He nods, the light of battle in his eyes.

"To the death, brother in arms," he answers solemnly. So our great quest began, and a journey that would bring us to the very gates of death.

PART TWO

Dmitri's Cause

CHAPTER 1

Aleksei raced down the hallway, boots ringing on the metal walkway. He pushed through the panicking crowd, heart pounding with fear. Fear of not arriving in time, fear of what he might find, or worse, not find. He cursed himself for having left them alone, for not having seen the trap until it was too late. The lights overhead flickered as another explosion rocked the building. People screamed as they were thrown against each other. Aleksei fell to the ground, smacking his head so hard on the floor he saw stars. Groaning, he staggered to his feet, clinging to the wall for support. Blood dripped into his eyes from a gash on his forehead. His mind reeled with shock and pain. He was aware vaguely of someone shaking him by the shoulders, shouting his name. Darkness obscured his vision momentarily, sound fading to a buzz. Then everything came back in a rush of blinding lights, colors, and noise.

"Ivan...where's Cassy?" he asked, focusing on his friend's anxious face.

"I don't know! I thought she was with you. Have you seen Maïa or my daughter?"

Aleksei shook his head, regretting it immediately as pain lanced through his neck.

"No. And I lost Teo in the crowd."

"We'll find them, don't worry. We've been through worse and survived."

He shut out the pain as best he could, trying desperately to believe his friend's reassurances. It was true they'd all had their close shaves in the past six years, ever since Luka had taken power. There had been happy moments too of course. True, his wedding to Cassy had been far from glamorous, but whether in a cave or a cathedral, it had been the best day of their young lives. At least until Teo's birth. Now they were both missing, and he knew Luka was likely somewhere near, watching. Had his brother already taken them?

"You should be with the medics, Aleksei. I can send them to you when they're found."

The younger man would not listen to reason.

"Medics are busy enough as it is without me adding to it for a scratch. I'm going back to the apartment to find Cassy. Are you coming or not?"

Ivan gave in with a sigh. Folly or not, he had to admit it was their best chance of finding their families.

By sticking close to the wall, they were able to avoid the worst of the screaming crowd. People ran every which way, colliding, falling. Most were not as lucky as Aleksei. They were trampled underfoot by the terrified mob, never to rise again. It struck him suddenly. He'd been stupid not to realize it before, really.

"He's blocked them," he breathed, horrified.

"What?"

"The exits, Luka's blocked them. That's why no one is leaving! He wants as many as possible killed in the chaos before opening fire. We must have really made him angry this time."

Ivan scowled, doubtful.

"How can you be so sure?"

Aleksei chuckled.

"Because it's what we learned at school, remember? It's basic tactics. No point in wasting bullets on people who are doing the job for you."

"That's sadistic even for him. What'd we ever do to him?"

"You mean apart from blowing up his mansion twice, poisoning his hellhounds, hiding refugees trying to escape his rule, and wrecking his plans of world domination?"

"Don't forget turning a dozen of his men to our side every week."

Aleksei would have answered, but a shrill scream, rising above the roar of the crowd, made him pause, heart pounding.

"Did you hear that?" he asked, hardly daring to breathe lest he miss it again.

"Hear what?"

Aleksei shushed him, holding up a hand to stop his friend.

"That's Teo's voice…I swear it is! But where is it coming from?"

Ivan scanned the mob carefully. After a tense second, he found him.

"There! On that window ledge, you see him?"

Before Ivan could stop him, Aleksei had plunged into the chaos, fighting like a wounded bear to get to his son. The other tried to follow but was rejected by the tidal wave of people.

"Papa! Papa!" the shriek became louder as Aleksei neared his goal.

"I'm coming, Teo! Papa's coming. Just hang on!"

He could see him as well as hear him now too, clinging desperately to the narrow ledge.

"*Mne strashno*, Papa! I'm scared!" the child wailed between sobs. Then he was there, stretching out his arms to catch the boy just as the ledge gave way. Teo buried his little head in his father's shoulder, shaking with terror. His tears soaked the thick woolen sweater. Aleksei held his son close, whispering soothing words and stroking the dark hair that was so like his own.

"Papa's here, *detka*, don't cry, I'm here. Hush now, hush. It's all over, *malyutka*, you're safe now. Papa's got you."

Over and over, he whispered the words, stroking and rocking gently until the wrenching sobs lessened and the child grew calmer.

"Are you hurt, Teo?"

"Da." He sniffled sorrowfully, clinging to his father's neck.

"Show me where, *detka,* show Papa where they hurt you."

Teo popped his thumb out his mouth just long enough to point to a spot on his elbow.

"There. Got a bruise 'cause I falled," he complained. Aleksei fought back a smile. Feigning concern, he peeled back the sleeve and pretended to inspect the so-called injury.

"Is it bad, Papa?" the boy asked, suddenly anxious. Aleksei kissed the top of his son's head, thanking God silently that there was no worse harm done.

"I think you'll live. Shall we go find your mama so she can tell us for sure?"

Teo nodded, sucking his thumb again. It worried Aleksei sometimes, the boy's refusal to break the habit. He was so small for his age too, no bigger than a three-year-old. At least Teo seemed to have inherited his father's intelligence, even if he didn't like to use it. They'd been trying to teach him to read and write, and he could do it coherently when he applied himself. His vocabulary wasn't bad either.

The crowd was starting to calm a little. There hadn't been any explosions in a while, and most of the screaming had abated. Crossing back was much easier than before, though they still had to hurry in order to avoid being trampled. The calm, however, only served to heighten Aleksei's fear. Luka had been searching for their base for six years. He wasn't about to let them off easily.

CHAPTER 2

"**D**mitri!"

I jump to attention at the sound of my father's voice. He doesn't tolerate laziness, and I don't relish the idea of another beating added to the two I've already suffered today.

"You're on watch, not on break! What do you think you're doing sitting down?"

I swallow nervously. "I'm sorry, Father. My legs got tired," I mumble, lowering my eyes in shame. He smacks me hard across the back of my head. It doesn't hurt as much as usual though, so I figure he's in a good mood. He should be. We've just destroyed the rebels' hide out. There can't be many left alive inside.

"You're a soldier, Dmitiri, not a weak little child. Act like one for a change. You think I took you in out of charity? Because I love children so much and my wife can't have any so I was heartbroken?"

His sarcasm stings bitterly. It hurts just as much as he meant it to, if not more.

"*Nyet*! Never! I took you because you showed strength and intelligence beyond your years. I took you because I need to be certain there will be someone strong to rule after me. You might want to start thinking of proving to me you are worthy of such a task!"

I know better than to argue. No one disagrees with my father and lives to tell about it. He's very brave and fair, but he has to be stern with me often. It makes me a better man. I may be only eight, but I already have a grand future ahead of me thanks to his efforts. I'm to be his heir, take over after he dies. I know he'd rather have children of his own in my place, but there's something wrong with his wife, and in six years, she hasn't given him any. So it's a great honor to have been chosen. Many would kill for it. That's why he beats me and yells a lot, to make me tough enough to face my enemies without fear. I keep my eyes carefully trained on the ground. I'm not allowed to look up at him without permission. Nobody is.

"Yes, Father. I understand. It won't happen again, I promise," I tell his boots.

"It had better not. I won't have you embarrassing me." At that moment, an officer comes running. I glance up discreetly, watching. He keeps his head bowed, hands behind his back, like me.

"Speak," my father commands.

"Emperor Luka, sir, we're ready to enter the building and deal justice to those traitors within, and the prisoners are secured."

Father gives a curt nod, pleased for once.

"And you put the redhead far from the others?"

"She's being transported to your home as ordered, sir."

"I imagine she didn't like that."

"No, sir, she didn't, but it was difficult for her to really fight us."

Father raises an eyebrow in surprise.

"Oh? And why is that?"

The officer hesitates, uncertain of what the reaction will be if he answers.

"Speak!"

"Sir, she's…quite heavy with child. She was reluctant to cause harm to her baby by resisting."

A delighted grin spreads across Father's face, giving me shivers. It's never a good omen when he smiles.

"Indeed? Well, well. My brother *has* been busy. Here I was, thinking he only lived to make my life difficult. Take good care of her, officer. We can't have her losing her health and harming the child. I get the feeling Aleksei wouldn't forgive me for allowing such a tragedy to take place."

It's the first time I've ever seen him genuinely happy. He's actually giggling, like a child with a new toy.

"Is there something special about her, Father?" I ask as humbly as possible.

"She is the key, my son. The key to destroying my brother once and for all. Without their leader, the so-called rebels will be lost, and we will have won at last."

A flutter of excitement runs through my veins. It's been all he talks about for so long. To see the end near is almost too good to be true. Emboldened, I dare ask a favor. I want my father to be proud of me and may never get another chance.

"Father, I'd like your permission to join the raid. Please. You spoke earlier of my proving myself. I only ask for a chance to be a good soldier and a good son."

He gives me a curious look as though weighing my worth. Finally, he gives a cold smile.

"That was well said, Dmitri. We'll make an orator of you yet. Why not? As long as you obey orders and conduct yourself well, I have no objections. Now come. We have work to do."

I follow eagerly, my heart pounding wildly against my chest. Visions of glory flash through my mind. I see myself capturing the famed leader of the insurgents, Aleksei. The feeling of basking in my father's pride is so tangible I can almost taste it.

No one pays me much attention as I scurry to find a position in the line of soldiers. Before I can, someone shoves me hard from behind. I fall face first into the mud. Angry, I get to my feet and turn to confront my attackers.

"Who did that?" I hiss, balling my hands into fists. A group of teenage soldier boys snicker condescendingly.

"Get lost, kid. This war is for men, not babies. Go back to your mama," one of them sneers. The others laugh, adding insults.

"How dare you speak to me like that! Don't you know who I am?"

They only laugh harder at that, slapping their knees in mirth.

"Who cares? I said get lost!" the leader shouts again, this time throwing a rock at my head. I shriek in pain and shock as it hits my jaw. As more missiles fly, I'm forced to duck and flee for my life. Tears of rage burn my eyes. I wipe them away savagely. Hurt, humiliated beyond bearing, I slink away to hide my shame. At least Father didn't witness any of it. He would never forgive me my weakness.

CHAPTER 3

Aleksei loaded his rifle with expert ease. He'd refused to let the medics do more than bandage his head. Ivan stared at him.

"What do you think you're doing?" he asked, incredulous. His friend did not so much as glance up.

"Getting ready to fight Luka. What did you expect?"

Ivan sighed. "You really think he'll come? It's been quiet for hours. The lookouts said the coast is clear. No army coming to attack us."

Aleksei snorted disbelievingly. "I know my brother. I've been fighting him for six years, remember? He wouldn't give up so close to his goal. It's either a trap or he's trying to make us lose our nerve."

"I've been fighting him too, and I don't think he'd do something this predictable. If, *if,* he comes, it won't be now. Maybe a few days, probably not for another week. Are you even listening to me?"

Aleksei shrugged, not answering. All he knew was what his gut was telling him, and it had never led him wrong before.

"No, Teo, I said no guns. You're too young," he snapped suddenly, not bothering to turn around. The boy let out a moan of disappointment, dropping the pistol he'd been trying sneak out.

The thing was almost as big as his head, barely fitting under his shirt. Discretion was not a strong family trait.

"But I can shoot! I shoot good like you, Papa. Want gun too!" he complained, latching himself onto his father's leg. There was no smile on Aleksei's face this time as he lifted his son to eye level, sitting him down on a metal table.

"I know that. I taught you, remember? But I can't afford to be worrying about you every minute if there's a battle. I don't want you getting hurt. Your mama would skin me alive if I let anything happen to you. And we don't want to make Mama angry, do we?"

Teo shook his head emphatically. "Nope. Mama's scary when she mad."

"That's right. She is. Besides, I have a more important job for you."

The child's black eyes lit up like stars. "I can do it! Promise!"

"Okay, well, I trust you. You have to keep the mothers and other children safe while we fight. Can you imagine what would happen if an enemy got past us and found them without a big, strong soldier to protect them?"

He considered it seriously for a moment, thinking hard. Finally, he sighed and nodded solemnly, with the air of one shouldering a heavy burden with great humility.

"It'd be bad. I get small gun to protect, okay?"

At last, a grin forced its way onto Aleksei's face. Teo could always make him smile, no matter how bad a mood he was in. It was a gift he'd inherited from his mother. Cassy knew his weaknesses all too well.

"Yes, it would be bad. And no, you don't. No guns."

As Teo scurried from the room, Ivan dared ask a question. "Are you doing this because there's still no news of Cassy?"

He nodded, unable to voice the fear in his heart.

"Maïa and my little one are missing too. I trust your instincts, Aleksei, so if it comes to a fight, I'll fight with you. But only until I get my family back. After that…I'm done. I'm tired of this war, tired of having to fear for their safety every minute of every day. You understand, don't you?"

Silence fell heavily between the two men.

"What about Luka and your revenge? You want to just let him win?"

Ivan shrugged.

"It was always going to be you who'd kill him, not me. We've both known that from the start. It bothered me at first. I wanted so badly to be the one who put a bullet in his head."

"And now?"

"Now…now it doesn't matter anymore so long as the job gets done. Besides, it should be you. It's much more poetic that way. People love a tragic ending, Aleksei, and what's more terrible than a man killing his brother? It makes for a good ending. People will remember that. I don't fit into it. Whether or not I fight doesn't make a difference. You'll win this, with or without me."

Aleksei leaned forward, planting his hands on the table. He shook his head. For a moment, Ivan thought he was angry. When he looked his friend in the eyes though, there was only understanding.

"Six years is a long time. We made a good team, the four of us. I'll be sorry to see you and Maïa leave," he said at last. The awkward moment was dispelled at the sudden entrance of a scout.

"Sirs!" he said, saluting smartly. The friends shared an amused glance. The boy was shorter than they by at least a foot, and his helmet kept slipping in front of his eyes. He was maybe ten or twelve years old, filled with the importance of his mission.

"Go ahead, speak." Ivan said, not unkindly.

"The watchtower commander sent me to tell you that he saw something strange and wants you to come. Sirs." The boy's face was almost purple from the speed at which he'd delivered his message.

"You might want to think about taking a breath between words. It helps when you don't want to suffocate. Come on then, lead the way."

He went from purple to deep red, rendered speechless by the fact that he'd been addressed directly by the great Aleksei himself.

The three of them walked in silence awhile, down the now deserted hallways. Aleksei tried hard not to show how worry pressed on his chest like a boulder, making it hard to breathe. He had to stay strong for the sake of the people fighting at his side and for Teo. *Especially* Teo. He had to show his son what it meant to be a leader.

———

My hand trembles as I take the gun Father hands me. He found out about my humiliation much faster than expected. I should have known. He sees everything.

"Shoot them."

The order comes, cold and devoid of any emotion. I wish I could be like that. Then I wouldn't be so afraid. I've never killed anyone before. The teenager closest to me glances up, and our eyes meet. He's scared too. Scared of dying. Scared of what will happen if I can't pull the trigger. Scared of me, a little boy he wronged. Kneeling next to him, hands tied behind his back like the others, his companion isn't making much of an effort to hide his feelings. Great tears pour down his face, and whimpering sobs are heard occasionally.

"Dmitri, I'm not going to wait forever. These boys wronged you. They hurt you. They must be punished. Now shoot, or I will."

Only the leader, the one who started it all, shows not the slightest hint of fear. He stares ahead, as emotionless as my father. How do they do it? And why can't I?

"Please, sir, why?" he asks boldly. Father ignores him, motioning for me to continue. Knowing I have no choice, I take a deep breath, steadying my nerves.

"Why, sir?" he shouts, louder.

My finger trembles on the trigger. I fire. Instead of the expected bang, there's only a click. I try again, puzzled, with the same result. Confused, I turn to Father for an answer. He's smiling, amused. I feel my blood run cold.

"Because, soldier, a lesson must be learned. Did you really think I was going to let you kill off perfectly good men, Dmitri, just because you aren't capable of defending yourself? Next time you embarrass me, you'll be the one kneeling, and I promise you, it won't be an empty barrel pointed at your head."

Father turns and strides away, issuing orders for the assault on the building as he goes. My determination to prove myself only increases. I already know he'll win against his brother, so what can I do to impress him? Hostages are always good. Father would probably be pleased by that. I could sneak into the compound before the battle starts, find where they're keeping the women and children hidden, and bring one back. Plans begin forming in my mind. I can see myself returning, heroic, praised, and loved.

A strange scene draws my attention suddenly, and I duck behind some ammunition crates to listen in. Two generals are whispering anxiously to each other, casting worried glances over their shoulders.

"You're sure of it?"

"Positive. One of the men managed to send a distress signal before she got to him."

"What do we tell His Majesty? She was supposed to be a crucial hostage. He made it clear enough what would happen if we let her escape! He'll kill us!"

"You'd rather I reported that a pregnant woman bested six of my top soldiers? He'll do worse than kill us! He'll feed us to that devil child. That...*shadow*. You've seen what he can do! We say nothing. For now. We'll talk about it again after the battle."

I've heard enough. Father will want that prisoner back badly. He'll reward me when I bring her back to him in chains, maybe even be proud of me for once. It's my chance to prove myself worthy once and for all. I can't fail again. I won't.

CHAPTER 4

Aleksei was busy checking defenses for the thousandth time when he felt something tug at the back of his shirt. He turned to find Teo staring up at him with worried eyes.

"You can't be here, *detka*. Go back with the others. I gave you a job, remember?" he said, crouching to the boy's level.

"Where's Mama? I want Mama, Papa. Is she fighting too?"

Aleksei, pain tugging at his heart, avoided the question. "Bad men are coming, Teo. I need you to be safe. Please go back now."

"How do you know?"

"I saw them from the watchtower. They'll be here very soon." Teo stuck out his bottom lip, pouting.

"Want Mama," he said stubbornly, crossing his arms.

"Teo—"

"I want her! I want my mama!" he shrieked, tears threatening to spill over.

Aleksei felt his patience draining rapidly. He tried hard to stay in control. Before he could reason with his son, the boy turned and began to run, calling for his mother. It was the last straw. Striding after him, he grabbed the struggling child, pinning him under one arm. Taking Teo aside where they would be out of the way, he trapped him against the wall.

"Stop it! You hear me? Stop it now! What's the matter with you? I want her back too, but she's not here, and there's nothing we can do about it! Now you're going to go with the other children, and you're going to stay safely there, understand?"

Stunned, Teo stopped crying for a moment. His father had never yelled at him before.

"It's bad enough I lost your mother, I won't lose you on top of it," Aleksei said, more gently. Teo sniffled, wiping his nose on his sleeve.

"Wanna go find her," he hiccuped. His father sighed, praying for patience and strength inwardly.

"I do too. We will, I promise. First we have to fight Luka. When this battle is all over, we'll go find her, I promise."

Teo nodded, though he stayed unconvinced. Relieved, Aleksei let him go. Later. There would be time to deal with his son later after the coming battle.

———

Teo toddled down the hall with all the stubborn determination he'd inherited from his parents. If his father wouldn't go rescue his mama, he would. No one would notice he was missing, not for a long time. By then he would have his mother back, and his papa would be very proud of him. He'd see he wasn't too young for a gun.

Crawling out of the window was no easy task, but the boy had been trained well enough. His parents, were, after all, legends. A great many people had been more than eager to teach him about fighting and obstacle courses. Outside, the wind blew through his warm clothes, making him shiver and almost turn back. Almost. He walked forward, hesitant, uncertain which way to go. In the distance, he could see a cloud of dust coming closer and closer. Objects shone and glinted in its midst. Teo thought about it a second. Maybe there were people in the cloud who could tell him where his mother was. In any case, it was as good a place to start as any.

———

I made my move the instant the army moved out. Not that they noticed. I knew which way the prisoner transport truck had gone. I have a good sense of direction, and with my compass, it was easy. Eventually, I come across tire tracks, making things even simpler. I smile to myself. This is going to be more fun than expected.

The crash site is a good mile further, but I reach it without too much difficulty. As far as I can figure, she must have attacked the driver, making him lose control. The truck lies on its side, windows smashed, back doors pried open. She must be quite something if she managed all this while pregnant. More importantly, where could she hide? There are sheer cliffs on one side, and only desolate, empty waste on the other. If she'd gone away from the rocks, it's likely she wouldn't have traveled very far. Ignoring the bodies of the motionless soldiers, I pick my way toward the cliffs. Whether or not the men are dead doesn't matter. They will be anyway by the time Father gets done with them. Besides, this is for me alone. He'll be proud of *me* and no one else.

I scan the area for caves near the ground where she could have taken refuge. Immediately, a crevice catches my attention. There's something moving inside, I can tell by the brief shadow illuminated for an instant by the sun as the cloud cover clears. Carefully, keeping as quiet as I can, I creep toward the spot. My only weapon may be an empty pistol, but the woman doesn't need to know that. Taking a deep breath, I draw my gun and leap inside with a shout. Nothing could have prepared me for what I see.

———

Aleksei fired, reloading instantly. He had yet to see his brother in all the chaos, but then again, the battle was barely begun. Luka was somewhere near, he could feel it. He saw him in his mind's eye, strutting importantly at the back of the ranks, issuing orders while staying clear of any action himself. Rage and the heat of battle made Aleksei's blood boil. This was his chance. It was now or never.

"Ivan!" he shouted above the din of men dying and guns firing. His friend turned, ducking a hail of bullets.

"Cover for me! I'm going after Luka!"

Ivan gave him a thumbs up to show he'd heard. Though it was a hard thing to admit, Aleksei knew they were doing badly. Luka and his army outnumbered them ten to one, and they had the upper ground. The rebels were trapped, with no possible retreat. If Luka was not taken out quickly, they would lose.

Finally, he spotted the enemy. Luka saw him at the same moment. For an instant, time stood still as the brothers stared each other down. They hadn't been face-to-face in over six years.

"You've been busy, little brother! Are you going to shoot me while my back is turned, like the gutless coward you are?"

"No. I'm not you. I fight fairly when given a chance."

The battle raged on around them, unheeded. Aleksei took a few steps closer, gun at the ready. The enemy's bodyguards raised their own rifles but were waved down. One scurried off on a whispered order.

"This can't go on forever, you know. I mean, with me winning one battle, you taking the next, and so on. It has to end someday." Aleksei reasoned, talking to distract his brother until he had a clear shot. The grin that spread on Luka's face made him suddenly uneasy. Too late, he felt the trap closing in.

"You're right as always," Luka said, still smiling. "I believe today is that day, little brother. And you've lost."

The soldier returned, a struggling bundle slung over his shoulder. Aleksei's heart skipped a beat as it was handed over to Luka, and he realized what had happened. His brother held a wriggling Teo by the back of his collar. He held him up, a smug grin plastered on his face.

"*Otpusti menya! Ublyudki!* Put me down!" Teo shouted, trying in vain to free himself. "Papa! Make him let me go!"

Luka chuckled.

"Your son has quite a vocabulary for his age, especially in swear words. I didn't know you had such a large family. A pregnant wife and now a little boy? You should have told me I was an uncle."

Aleksei swallowed his fear, answering as calmly as possible to the obvious threat.

"I swear on all that I hold sacred, if you hurt my family, I'll make you wish you'd never been born. Put Teo down, and we can talk through this like adults."

"Teo, is it? Short for Teodore, I imagine? 'God's gift.' What an interesting choice for such a wild boy. It's funny how much he reminds me of you. Almost like a miniature clone. That's not a compliment, by the way."

"Just put him down."

With his father within earshot, Teo had eased up on the swearing. Now it was more like listening to a sailor instead of a sailor's parrot. Where had he picked it all up? Before either man could find a way to end the stalemate, the boy somehow managed to twist his head around. Quick as a flash, he bit down on his captor's wrist as hard as he could, sinking in his sharp little teeth. Luka, more surprised than hurt, released the boy as if by reflex.

Teo scrambled to his feet, running toward his father. Aleksei, dropping his gun, seeing the danger far more clearly than the five-year-old, charged forward. He knocked his son to the ground, shielding him with his body. The bullet hit his shoulder, digging in deeply. He let out a grunt of pain but otherwise did not let it stop him from trying to get Teo out of the line of fire and to safety. Picking him up with his good arm, Aleksei struggled to his feet, breathing hard. The boy clung tightly, whimpering. The shock of being sent flying to the ground had knocked all bravery out of him. Luka's men were faster though. In seconds, they were surrounded. It was over. They'd lost.

CHAPTER 5

I hold the newborn in my arms, struggling to figure out what to do. The woman is asleep, her red hair still damp from the effort of giving birth. She nodded off after feeding the baby, exhausted. It's funny. It never mattered to her who I am, she never even asked my name. What would Father do? I know the answer, really, but putting it into action is much harder. I'm not like him. I'm not strong enough or cold enough to steal the baby from its mother. I should. I know I should. But after everything that's happened in the last hour, I don't know if can do this anymore. In my heart, I realize Father will never look at me the way she looked at her child when I gave him back to her. What do I do? Do I go back alone to face disgrace, or do I take the baby and face reward? It's obvious who his mother is from the thick red hair already growing on its tiny head. No one would dare call me a liar. The idea of the mother waking up alone repulses me though. Father could do it. I can't. Carefully, as gently as possible so as not to wake them, I put the baby, wrapped in my coat, down on his mother's chest. I won't steal, and I won't go back.

As I reach the entrance to the cave, a quiet voice stops me.

"Wait. Don't go. Please."

I turn, surprised. The woman is awake, clutching her baby tightly. Her Russian is stilted, and she has an accent, but it's not too awful.

"Please. I cannot walk yet. Can you find my husband? Bad men were taking me. He does not know where we are."

An uneasy feeling grows in my gut. I think I'm starting to guess why she was so important to Father. I swallow, clearing my throat so my voice doesn't squeak. It does anyway.

"What's your husband's name?"

She smiles, and her cheeks go red. "Aleksei. He is in charge, back at base. You should find him easy."

It's what I was afraid of. Father's brother and sworn enemy. How am I supposed to find him without getting shot? What if he died in battle? Worse, what if Father has taken him prisoner? I hang my head, ashamed at what I'm about to say.

"I'm sorry. I can't."

A frightened look crosses her pretty features. She knows what's coming, though she asks all the same.

"Why? Why not?"

Because I'm a coward, I almost say, because I'm frightened of my father and I'd rather lie to you than face him. It's not what I tell her. The lie, bitter as it tastes, is better.

"He's dead. There was a battle. F—Luka got him."

Her eyes shut tightly as though that way she can block out the terrible news. Tears squeeze through anyway, and a heart-wrenching sob escapes her. Guilt floods my soul. Too late now.

"And...and Teo?" she asks, her voice trembling. At least this time I can tell her the truth.

"I don't know. I'm sorry."

To my surprise, she suddenly opens her eyes, struggling to her feet. There's such a look of determination on her face it scares me. I back away as she comes slowly toward me, each step causing obvious pain.

"Then I have to find him. Please. Help me to find my son."

Is she insane? Maybe the pain was too much, and it scrambled her brain.

"What are you talking about? Lady, you're holding him!"

She grimaces, shaking her head.

"Teodore. He is my eldest. If Aleksei—" she stops, obviously fighting to control her emotions. "Will you help me? He is little, a little boy, only five. I must find him. Please."

There's so much pain in her voice, it's impossible to refuse. I can't lie to her and then just leave. Father would, but I'm not him. I don't want to be.

"I'm Dmitri," I say, keeping my gaze firmly on the ground.

"Cassy," she answers.

The way she holds her baby close, the glances she keeps giving him—it makes my chest hurt someplace deep down inside. I never knew my own mother or my biological father. The closest thing I ever had was Luka's wife, and she's not much of anything. All she ever does is cower in a corner and try to stay out of his way. He has to hit her a lot to make her do anything, so mostly she just cries. I was growing up alone in the streets of Moscow, with no one to see me the way Cassy sees her son, when Luka found me. When I was chosen out of all the other boys, two years ago, and told to call him "Father," it was like the end of a nightmare. I thought he would love me as a son. Up until an hour ago, I still hoped he would. For so long, all I wanted was for him to be proud of me, to give me a kind word or look. I know I'm weak and a coward, and I know I was never worthy of his attention, but I never did ask for very much. He should have chosen one of the others. Why did he take me? I find myself wishing, all of a sudden, that I could tell Cassy all of this. There's too much at stake though. I can't risk losing the only friend I have left.

———

Aleksei rolled onto his back with a groan. His whole body ached from the blows Luka's soldiers had given him. For a moment, he wondered why he hadn't fought back. His shoulder had been shot, true, but that was no reason. Then he remembered. Teo. They'd taken Teo from him. Luka had threatened to hurt him. Aleksei opened one eye slowly, painfully. The other was swollen shut. His hands and feet had been bound tightly. Looking around as best he could, he thought he recognized the jail. Yes, it was one of theirs, hastily built the first year and solidified over the next five. They'd never had cause to use it as no prisoners had ever been taken. Luka had obviously found good use for it though, and fast too. As if summoned by the mere thought of his name, the man himself appeared, gloating.

"Don't get too comfortable, Aleksei. This is only temporary. I intend to bring you back to Moscow and make an example of you."

The prisoner spat out a wad of blood, staring up at his brother with pure hatred.

"Where's Teo? What have you done with my son?" he snarled.

Luka paid him not the slightest attention.

"It's good to see a menace to peace like you behind bars at last. The chains suit you."

Aleksei scowled. If looks could kill, the enemy would have been nothing but a pile of smoldering ashes.

"What are you talking about? Peace? You've never wanted peace, only power for yourself. I want my son, Luka. Let me see him."

"You should have joined me when you had the chance, little brother. You and I, we would have conquered the world together. Your family need never have suffered either, and your son, dear little Teo, he would never have known the pain of losing his parents. I'll make him watch as I have you tortured in front of all of Russia. After that…well, I've been in need of a good slave ever since the last one died of a simple beating."

To his surprise, Aleksei chuckled. "Good luck with that. He won't make a good slave, I guarantee it. Stubbornness is genetic, and you'll never turn him."

Luka leaned forward, gripping the metal bars. "I'm sure he'll be cooperative with the whip at his back."

"What do you want from me? You've already taken my wife, my son, even my home. There's not much left for you to do. I'd say you could take my life too, but at this point, I really don't care anymore."

"What do I want? I want you to pay. To pay for betraying me. I want you to lie there, helpless, while your wife and children cry out in pain for you to save them. And then I want you to die, slowly, painfully, in front of the whole world and everyone who ever believed in you, so that none dares ever resist me again. *That's* what I want," Luka hissed, eyes bright with cruelty and malice. Aleksei somehow managed to stay calm.

"I'll warn you one last time," he said quietly, "if you hurt my family, if I find so much as a bruise on either of them, you'll have an enemy on your hands that you won't be able to handle. What I did before, blowing up your stupid fancy mansions, poisoning your dogs, it won't compare to the fury I'll let loose on you. I'll make you wish you'd never been born. Whatever you have planned for me, I'll increase by tenfold if they've been harmed in any way."

Luka frowned and then scoffed. "Idle threats. You're hardly in a position to be saying such things." He tried to sound dismissive, but an uneasy feeling was growing in the pit of his stomach. His brother had eluded capture a long time. Despite precautions taken, he was probably smart enough to escape. Being wounded might impede attempts slightly, but not for long. The important thing was keeping the little boy secured. Aleksei had made it clear enough he wouldn't be going anywhere without his son. With one last, condescending look at his prisoner, he turned and left. It was time for a speech.

———

"Fetch my son. I want him by my side when I address the troops," Luka ordered, not turning from his reflection in the mirror.

The slave bowed obediently, exiting. He adjusted his outfit and smoothed back his blond hair. There was something missing.

"Wife! Bring me my coat!" he barked. The girl rose unsteadily from where she'd been sitting in the shadows. Had anyone known her as the fifteen-year-old Katya, they would not have recognized her. She was bone thin, her face bruised and cut. Despite which, Luka noted pensively, she was still quite pretty. He had tried not to hit her face too much. After all, what was the use of an ugly wife, especially one who could not bear children? Unfortunately, being married had not, at first, stopped her from trying to run. He'd punished her first attempts by chaining her ankles together so she could barely walk and then leaving her in a dark cell with little food and no human contact, save for himself, for six months straight. When it had failed to break her spirit and she'd been caught in her fourteenth escape, Luka had flown into a terrible rage. Katya hadn't tried again after the final punishment.

She hobbled to his clothes trunk, pulling out an intimidating black trench coat. The collar was edged in red and gold.

"Bring it! I haven't got all day!" he snapped, impatient. He never just spoke to her; he snarled or he shouted.

She helped him slip it on without a word. Satisfied with his image, Luka turned to her, grabbing her arm before she could back away, pulling her close.

"I expect you by my side for the speech. Pretty as you are," he pinched her cheek in mock affection, "you'll make all the men jealous. Go and put on something a little more formal, hmm, before joining me? I don't want you to be an embarrassment."

Katya squirmed as his grip became painfully tight. Reacting instinctively, she resisted, trying to pull away. It was a weak, pitiful attempt, and she stumbled, nearly falling, as he released her abruptly and strode out without so much as a glance back.

When he'd gone, Katya dressed quickly and followed, silent as a shadow. Luka had taught her that a good wife was little different from a good slave, one, like the other, learned to go unseen. A bad one, one who drew attention, got beaten. Invisible, but ready to serve at the snap of his fingers.

As she tottered down the hallway, hugging the wall, trying not to trip over the red-and-gold-trimmed dress, someone suddenly grabbed her from behind, a hand firmly over her mouth. They needn't have bothered. Even had she been able to scream, she knew better. Frightened, Katya struggled against her attacker, punching and slapping in vain.

"Katya, stop! Stop, it's me, Ivan. Remember, from Moscow? I'm not going to hurt you." He hissed. Surprised and relieved, she stopped fighting.

"I need you to tell me where they're keeping a little boy, Teo. Aleksei'll never let me break him out if his son isn't with me. I know him. He won't leave without the kid."

She shook her head, digging into her pocket for a piece of paper. Ivan gave her a strange look.

"Luka's long gone out of earshot. You can talk."

Katya ignored him, taking out a stubby pencil. Her hands trembled as she wrote. After waiting so long for rescue, it was difficult to have to pause long enough to scrawl something legible.

> All prizenurs were takn to hq thiss mornig. There werent anee childrun tho.

She wrote, handing him the note. Ivan paled as he read.

"No children at all? What about girls? Did you see a little girl about five years old? She has brown hair and grey eyes, like me." He indicated her height with his hand. Katya shook her head, snatching the paper from him.

> Nun. Sory. Only kid ive seen all day is Dmitri. That wuz bad enof.

He frowned.

"Who's Dmitri? And why won't you talk instead of writing everything down?"

They had to duck behind a corner as a group of young soldiers passed by, chattering eagerly about the coming speech. A terrified look came over Katya's face as though she'd only just remembered where she was and what would happen if Luka discovered she wasn't at her post. Ivan took her hand gently.

"Come on, let's get out of here. You're one of us. If I'd known you were alive, I would never have left you. I'm taking you with me, all right?"

She shook her head violently, jerking away in fear. Rescue had come too late. Her terror of Luka was greater than her wish for freedom.

"What? What's wrong? I'm not about to leave you behind again! We have to go!" Ivan whispered, putting a hand on her shoulder, trying to understand.

"Find her! I'll have your heads if she escapes! And where's my son, useless little twerp that he is? I want them found *now*!"

There were screams, and the sound of several objects being smashed either on walls or on peoples' heads. Ivan grabbed Katya's arm, trying to lead her down the hall. But she pushed him away, eyes filling with tears. Her whole body began to tremble, and she stood rooted to the spot, filled with obvious terror as the sound of booted footsteps drew near. Still no sound passed her lips. Not a whimper or a cry.

"Katya, please. We have to go!" he hissed, desperate. Before he could stop her, she'd torn free of his grasp and run out into the open. Immediately, shots rang out as she was spotted. Heart tight with guilt, Ivan took advantage of the distraction to sprint down the familiar path to the cells. He'd often gone there when in need of peace and quiet. Ma⬛a had sometimes joined him. Just the thought of her round, cheerful face made his chest ache. He wanted his wife and daughter back as badly as Aleksei wanted Teo.

He wondered briefly what Luka had done to Katya to change her so dramatically. The thought was put quickly from his mind as he reached the prison door. For the moment, getting Aleksei and Teo out was more important.

CHAPTER 6

Teo had not cried when they separated him from his papa. He hadn't cried when they hit him or when they'd put a cuff on his ankle and chained him to the wall. Even when they'd shut the door and left him in complete darkness, he'd not shed so much as a tear. The boy was not frightened. His father would come for him. He knew it without a doubt. He would make them pay. The door opened suddenly, and he raised his hands in front of his face, blinded by the brightness.

"You really are your father's son, aren't you? Not so much as a peep out of you. He must be so proud."

It was the blond man, the one his papa had called Luka. His uncle, whatever that meant.

"Please, forgive my men their rudeness. They mistook you for a prisoner."

Teo did not trust his smile. Still, he didn't shrink away. Anger and hate were stronger than fear.

"If I'm not captured, then give me my papa back." Luka's grin looked as though it had frozen to his face.

"Yes, of course. If you'll just follow me, I'll take you right to him."

He motioned for a soldier to unlock the cuff. Teo stood up, unsteady. His ankle hurt from the tightness of the shackle.

"Where is he?" he asked, suspicious. Luka put a friendly hand on the boy's shoulder.

"This way," he said, leading him out. Teo shoved him away with an ill-tempered grunt, crossing his arms defiantly in front of his chest. He failed to notice how tightly Luka's fists were clenched and how distant the escort of soldiers was staying. Had he been older, he might have guessed at the reason for the man's anger. He might have realized that Aleksei had escaped. For now, all he could think about was the fact that it would all be over as soon as he saw his father. Finally, they reached a large door. Luka opened it, shoving Teo inside so hard he fell to the floor, hitting his head. The boy shot to his feet, ready for a fight. He drew back when he saw the long knife in his uncle's hand. Fear flooded him at last.

"Where's Papa? You said he'd be here!" he shouted, hating how helpless he felt.

"I lied." Came the simple answer. "Now…you're going to do exactly what I tell you to, or I'll carve a pretty pattern on your pretty little face. Understand?"

Teo nodded reluctantly, eyeing the knife nervously.

"Good boy."

Luka handed him a microphone. "Call your father. Tell him how I hurt you. How I *will* hurt you if he and his sidekick don't surrender in the next few minutes. I'm feeling generous, so I'll give them three."

Teo swallowed back the tears that finally threatened to escape. He knew what he had to do.

"Papa. I'm okay. Don't come, all right? Go find Mama!"

He cried out in pain as Luka, furious, struck him to the ground again. The cut on his forehead now bled freely, burning his eyes. He lay there, sobbing in pain as the enemy spoke to his father.

"You hear that, little brother? It's nothing compared to what will happen if you don't turn yourself in."

Teo clamped his lips shut at those words, trying with all his small being not to make a sound. He couldn't help but scream though when Luka dragged him upright by his hair. Struggling only made the pain worse. Never before had anyone dared mistreat him.

"Papa! Papa, don't come! He'll hurt you!" he sobbed, praying his father would listen.

"Two minutes left, Aleksei, before I carve your precious son's face into an American jack-o-lantern." Luka snarled, pressing the cold blade onto his victim's face. Not enough to hurt, just scare. For now.

"One minute."

Ivan was only able to hold Aleksei back because of the beating Luka had given his friend. Under normal circumstances, it would have been impossible to keep him from getting to his son. The sound of Teo's sobs over the loudspeakers was heartbreaking.

"Let me go! I have to find him! Let go, damn you! That's my baby he's hurting!" Aleksei shouted, fighting to free himself.

"Stop it, you moron! *Pridurak!* Luka'll kill him whether you're there to watch or not. He has to keep him alive for leverage as long as you're free. Once he has you, he'll kill you both! What's going to happen to Cassy then? She'll be all alone with a new baby and no husband to protect her from Luka. Is that what you want?"

Aleksei went limp as though all strength had fled his body at the mention of Cassy. Cautiously, Ivan let him go. Both men were breathing hard.

"One minute." Luka's voice came on again. Teo whimpered in the background. In his heart, Aleksei knew his son would never forgive him for surrendering. He also knew he could not live with himself if he left his son to suffer. The choice was taken out of his hands a split second later.

CHAPTER 7

I don't know how I did it, but I managed to convince Cassy to stay put a while longer. Luka must have taught me something after all. The weather helped, I suppose. Gale force winds and snow will do that. She helped me pin our coats over the entrance so we wouldn't get too cold, but I still wish we had a fire or something. Luckily, I'd thought to bring my penknife so all we had to do was cut the fur-lined hood from my jacket and wrap the baby in it. She hasn't named him yet. It bothers me, having to call him "Baby" all the time. So I came up with one myself, one that I use only in my head or when she's asleep. And she does sleep a lot. The crying she does when she's awake tires her out, I think. It's a relief when it stops. It makes me feel guilty, and I hate it.

The baby starts fussing, and I pick him up carefully so he doesn't disturb his mother.

"Hush, little Nickolai. Your mama needs rest." I whisper, rocking. He likes it and is already nodding back off to sleep, his small fist clenched around my pinky. Before today, I'd never seen, let alone held, such a tiny baby. It's a good feeling, being so trusted by another person. True, he doesn't know right from wrong yet or that I almost took him to the most evil man on the planet, but still, I think he likes me.

"That name…it means something to you?"

I jump, startled. Cassy is awake, looking at me curiously. Slightly embarrassed that she heard, I nod.

"It means victory. It's a strong name. It'll protect him, make him brave."

"Who teach you this?"

I shrug.

"A woman I knew, back when I lived on the streets. She was all into folklore and superstition. Names were very important to her. She used to say that I was weak because *Dmitri* is a weak name. It means earth."

Cassy sits up slowly, and I give her back Nickolai. I hope I didn't offend her. Instead, she nods approvingly.

"I like Nickolai. It is good name. My son will need strength. Thank you."

I grin, feeling a little sheepish. It's the first time anyone has ever praised a decision of mine. How strange to have suddenly so much pride over such a small thing.

Outside, the storm rages on, trying to force its way into our shelter. For two days we sit there, cold and hungry. The only food we have is what I brought with me: a few crackers and some jerky. It doesn't last long. On the morning of the third day, we wake to find things quiet outside. I push aside the coats carefully and step out. The world has gone completely white, as though God grew tired of the ugliness and decided to wipe everything clean. Cassy follows, wrapping Nickolai even more tightly to protect him from the cold. She looks almost otherworldly, set against the empty background, with her flaming red hair fluttering loosely in the breeze. I wish she was my mother. I know she would never let anything hurt me ever again, never let Luka beat me, or make me feel worthless. That's when I make myself a solemn promise not to leave her side so long as I live. Why couldn't she be my mother? After all, Luka was my father. What does being blood-linked matter? Nothing! Not when I could have a mother, and one or maybe even two little brothers. Provided, of course, the other is still alive. I hope Aleksei isn't. I don't want a new father. Fathers only hit you. Mothers take care of you. Luka's wife was always trying to get me to wash and eat better and stupid things like that. She'd try to comfort me after a beating too, but I never let her. That would have been weak. I don't tell Cassy any of this yet. Maybe I will in a few years, when we're all living together in a nice house in Moscow where I'll have my own room and toys to play with, and no one will make me take cold showers or stand outside at attention in the rain. Maybe when I'm ten I'll tell her everything. It won't matter as much then because we'll be so happy she won't care. Yes. It's a good plan and even relieves some of the guilt I had from lying to her. It's not the same if I'm planning on telling her later.

"Dmitri, I can't wait longer. I have to find Teo, my other son. Will you be helping?"

I nod. Of course I'll help. I'm not about to let her go toward Luka all by herself. She smiles and ruffles my hair with her free hand.

"You are good child, Dmitri. Not weak."

I redden at the compliment. She doesn't know me yet.

We trudge through the snow a long while in silence. Cassy walks slowly, still tired and weak from labor. We pass by the crashed van, the bodies completely covered by the snow. It still impresses me how she managed to overpower the soldiers.

Something appears suddenly in the distance. A black speck on the white ground. A chill goes through me that isn't a result of the weather. I've had enough training to recognize a person even at this distance. Whether it's one of Luka's or someone else, it means trouble for me. More than likely, they'll know if Aleksei really is dead or not. Worse, I could be recognized. It's too late though. Cassy has already spotted him. She holds baby Nickolai tightly in one arm, shielding her eyes against the glare of sun on snow with a free hand.

"Ivan!" she cries as the man comes close enough to be identified.

"Cassy?" he's as surprised to see her as she is him.

"What happened? I thought Luka had taken you?" he asks as he reaches us at a sprint. I hang back, forgotten for the moment. She shakes her head.

"I get away. Made crash the van. Ivan, look. This is Nickolai. This is my new baby!" she says proudly, showing him the newborn. He grins, happy for her.

"Why Nickolai? Did you and Aleksei decide on it together?"

Her jaw tightens at the mention of her husband, but she stays strong.

"No. We didn't. This young boy, he helped me. He says it's a good name, and I trust him."

The man gives me a strange look. "What's your name, kid?"

I almost lie, catching myself just in time.

"Dmitri," I mumble, not meeting his gaze. I get the odd impression he knows who I am. Yet he remains quiet about it, turning to other matters.

"Well then, come on, both of you. Let's get you somewhere warmer. The few of us who made it through are camped not too far from here. Aleksei's mother and siblings finally made it too. I was out looking for more survivors. I'm very happy I found you. Maybe you can convince Aleksei to stop acting like a madman and stay put."

I could slap him for opening his big mouth. I hate him. He's ruining everything. Cassy stops walking, her green eyes wide with surprise and delight.

"Aleksei's alive? He's all right?"

Ivan frowns in confusion. For an instant, I imagine his gaze flicked toward me, but then he's talking again as though nothing had happened.

"Of course he is. I mean, Luka beat on him a little, but other than that, physically at least, he's fine. Who told you he was dead?"

"It doesn't matter. Just take me to him, Ivan, please!"

He nods. This time I'm sure of the glance he gave me. It's not particularly friendly. I hate him. I hate him! Why did he have to come and ruin everything? It's not fair. It was all going so well until he showed his ugly face. Luka should've killed him a long time ago. Too late now. I curse him silently. I hate him.

———

For a moment, Aleksei dared not believe his eyes. Then he saw the flash of red hair again through the crowd, and hope surged in him.

"Cassy!" he yelled, shoving his way forcefully toward her. She was here, she was safe. He wrapped his arms tightly about her, kissing her forehead, her nose, her lips, not caring that everyone was watching.

"I thought I'd lost you again! Are you hurt? Is everything all right? Did he hurt you?"

"I didn't give him time to. I'm fine, I promise. Just a little tired. Don't you want to meet your son?"

She laughed at the shock on his face. "Nickolai, this is your daddy. Isn't he cute when he's all worried and bothered?"

Aleksei's shock vanished in an instant, replaced by a look of sheer delight. He peeled back a fold of the hood, revealing the tiny face.

"*Dobro pozhalovat' v mir, malysh!* Welcome to the world, little one. Come to your papa!" he said, lifting the miniature bundle into his arms. For a precious second, he was focused entirely on Nickolai instead of what had happened to Teo. Then he caught sight of a blond, surly little boy standing awkwardly behind Cassy. The looks he was throwing him were far from friendly.

"Who is that?" he asked in English.

"A boy who found me and helped deliver the baby. I…I thought you'd been killed, so I let him help name our son. We can change it, if…"

Aleksei took her face in his gloved hand.

"I don't care, *lyubov*, as long as Luka hasn't won this round, it doesn't matter. Come on, let's get you both somewhere warmer. We need to talk."

He handed her back the baby, putting an arm about her, kissing the top of her head. She leaned against his shoulder as they walked, her exhaustion finally catching up to her.

"Where's Teo, Leksei? Ivan said your mother is here. Is he with her? I should go see him, make sure he knows I'm all right," she said sleepily. His jaw tightened and he hesitated before answering.

"That's one of the things we need to talk about. Cassy...Teo... isn't here."

She stopped, pulling away from him.

"Where is he? Aleksei, tell me. Please."

The accusation in her voice, the fear in her eyes were almost too much for him to bear.

"I lost. I lost him. Luka...he's with...Luka. Cassy, I'm sorry. I'm so sorry. I swear to you I did everything I could. Ivan—he wouldn't let me go after him."

"You let Ivan stop you, of all people?"

"I was hurt, weakened. If I'd been stronger..." He let the phrase go unfinished. "But I wasn't. I was weak. I failed, all right? I know that. Go ahead, you can say it! I failed as a leader, and worse, I failed my own son. Do you think I don't know that? Because believe me, I do. And it's killing me, Cassy. It's killing me. So don't you start!"

He strode away before she could get in an answer. The tears that streamed down her face now were no longer happy ones.

"Cassy, please. Don't blame him. If it's anyone's fault apart from Luka's, it's mine. I'm the one who held him back so he couldn't turn himself in to save Teo. There was no choice. I ended up having to knock him out with the butt of my pistol. If he'd gone, Luka would've killed them both." Ivan explained, putting a comforting hand on her shoulder. She slapped him away savagely, anger and grief playing for dominance on her face.

"Don't touch me! Ivanovich Petrov, I swear to you on all that I ever held dear, if anything has happened to my son, I will make you pay for it dearly. Do you understand?" she hissed, then turned to run after her husband. No one could have missed the triumphant smirk on the little blond boy's face.

CHAPTER 8

Luka paced nervously in his newly acquired office. He had to face facts. In another day, the boy would die of his wounds, and he would have lost his leverage. He was disappointed. He'd truly believed his brother would run to the rescue. Ivan must have stopped him somehow. Aleksei was far too attached to his son to simply stand by and let him scream like he had. Now the five-year-old was curled up in a corner of the office that had once been his father's, barely conscious despite Katya's attempts to help. Luka had spared her from a beating only so she could tend to the boy. Her efforts had been in vain though, and he'd had her locked in the cells until he could deal with her disobedience.

The dictator resisted the urge to kick at the small body. It wouldn't help his problem.

"Children shouldn't be made to fight their parents' wars. Your father abandoned you, forcing me to extremes. How you must hate him for it," he whispered, crouching next to his nephew. He'd even gone so far as to allow Katya to bandage up the boy's face a day or so ago. True, it was more for the carpet's sake than the child's, but he still considered it a great act of kindness on his part.

"Liar," Teo breathed, his voice barely audible. Luka smiled to himself. At last, a sign of life.

"Am I now? What, so your papa didn't abandon you to save his own skin? You can't say he exactly rescued you either."

A tiny tear escaped from behind the bandages, landing on the man's hand. He wiped it away in disgust. Crying was for the weak.

"Told…him…go," the boy sobbed.

"Yes, you did, didn't you. Do you regret it now?"

The answer was so soft, he had to ask him to repeat it. "No, you don't regret asking not to be rescued? You're a strange little child. I wish my adopted son had been like you. Sadly, he fled at the first sign of battle. Now I'll have to kill him if he shows his face again. It's a pity, really. He had a lot of potential."

"Don't care," Teo whimpered, sniffling. The answer took Luka by surprise.

"You're half-dead and still you have the guts to back-talk? I'm impressed. Truly. I might seriously start considering making you my new heir. God knows I can't count on Katya to provide one. You'll have to live long enough too, which might prove a challenge."

"Want…Mama. Not…you!" he wailed, his sobs getting louder. Luka got to his feet, relieved. The boy was stronger than he'd assumed. He would live, and the scars would eventually heal. They would always be there though, a constant reminder of his father's failure and his uncle's triumph. Luka had made sure to cut deep enough to make certain of that. Of course, just to be on the safe side, he would probably summon Katya again. It was important that the boy live.

Days passed. Luka began to feel more than a little disappointed by the lack of rescue attempts. Finally, he lost patience. Gathering his troops, he had his wife loaded onto one truck, and his prisoner onto an ambulance. The weak child had taken a turn for the worse again, and he would not risk him in a normal truck. Orders were issued to the troops to return to Moscow immediately. After all, their purpose for coming had been at least partially fulfilled, and there were rebel captives to interrogate back at headquarters.

The soldiers were all delighted to be headed home. They laughed and joked with each other as they boarded the army transports, morale rising visibly, especially compared to the last days of inactivity. Most were teenagers and eager to get back to their sweethearts. Luka did not allow women into combat, knowing full well that, because of the age range of his troops, having females around would only distract from the fight.

The man himself left by private jet, complete with flight attendants, soft cushions, and a mini bar. As a consequence, he arrived a full day and a half before everyone else. So by the time it was noticed that the ambulance was missing, they were at least three days too late.

At the news, Luka flew into one of his famous rages, murdering anyone in his path. No one could calm him. Normally, after an hour or so of exhausting himself with shouting and throwing things, he would calm slightly. Not this time. This time, it would take a special sort of person to achieve a temporary peace. The boy had not yet been tested in the field, but Luka had trained him up well, making him as cruel and vindictive as himself, teaching him to make others into the same twisted thing. Through his puppet, Luka would achieve the revenge he'd been striving for, for six long years. The Shadow was coming.

―――

Senka would not let Aleksei near Teo. No matter how he raged, threatened, or pleaded, she insisted that her grandson needed rest, not more aggravation. The truth was, she feared his reaction. She'd seen what lay beneath the bandages, and she knew her son too well to believe he would stay put once he saw for himself the damage. Cassy was a different matter. Teo needed his mother at his side if he was ever to recover. Besides, unlike Aleksei, her baby's health mattered more to her than vengeance. The child hadn't woken yet since his rescue. She held him in her arms, rocking gently and humming a soft tune. Cassy did not cry. Her tears had been spent. All that counted now was that Teo was safe.

"Mama?"

The little voice was so faint, she almost missed it.

"I'm here, Teo. I'm here, baby. You're going to be all right now. Mama's here." She whispered, kissing the top of his head.

"It hurts!"

"I know. It'll get better soon, I promise."

"Where's Papa?" he whimpered, reaching up to take the cloth from his eyes. She stopped him gently.

"I'll go and get him if you promise not to take the bandages off."

"But I wanna see!" he complained.

"Not yet. You're still bleeding too much. Soon. And I'll have a surprise for you then too. But only if you keep the bandages on, okay?"

Teo nodded reluctantly. Satisfied, Cassy set him down carefully on the little cot and went out. Dmitri had fallen asleep, waiting for her to exit. He insisted on following her everywhere she went, like a lost puppy. Since he hadn't been allowed inside, he'd taken it upon himself to keep watch. Stepping over him, Cassy went in search of Aleksei.

She found him sitting on a log, looking dejected. Tati, his sister, was making futile attempts to cheer him up. Ever since Ivan had forcefully brought him back, he hadn't been himself. Several people in the camp had volunteered to take turns keeping an eye on him, in case he tried anything stupid. It was a good thing they had. He'd ignored their warnings and their rescue plan, trying to sneak out in the middle of the night. In the end, Tatiana had had to threaten to exclude him from all further plans to keep him still. "Aleksei."

He turned, a slightly wild look in his eyes. Cassy smiled at him for the first time since he'd announced his failure.

"Teo's awake. He wants to see you."

"He doesn't hate me?"

"No. At least, I doubt it. He's…in a lot of pain, and he has a bit of trouble talking."

Aleksei said nothing, letting her lead him silently to the tent. They walked hand in hand, their fingers intertwined with each other's. She leaned her head once again on his shoulder, letting him wrap an arm around her waist. It was her way of telling him that everything would be all right, that he was forgiven, and that, for good or bad, she would be at his side.

"I love you, *dorogaya*," he whispered in her ear, almost smiling.

"I love you too." She grinned, standing on the tips of her toes to kiss his cheek.

"Don't stay too long. He needs his rest, and so do you."

"I won't. I promise."

Aleksei, ignoring the malevolent glances the now-awake Dmitri was casting him, went inside. Dragging a chair forward, he sat next to the cot, quiet for a long moment.

"Teo. It's your papa. Can you hear me, *detka*?" he asked, taking one of the tiny hands in his large ones. The boy nodded, his lower lip trembling.

"I knew…you'd…come," the boy whispered, tears soaking through the bandages. "I…was strong like…you. I was brave, Papa."

Aleksei swallowed the lump that rose in his throat. "I know you were. I'm very proud of you, Teo. You showed more courage than anyone I've ever met. Not even your mother or I could have been so brave. But you have to rest now, okay? You have to get better. It's a different sort of battle, but just as important as standing up to Luka. And when you're all better, I'll get you your own gun, just like you wanted, and we can practice together. Would you like that?"

He nodded again.

"Luka…Luka said you…abandoned me."

Aleksei shut his eyes tightly, waiting for the wave of anger to pass. The next time he and his brother would meet face-to-face, one of them would die. He had no doubt which of them it would be.

"And what did you tell him?"

The ghost of a proud smile flickered briefly across the boy's lips. "Called him liar."

His father laughed in surprise.

"I'll bet he didn't like that very much, did he?"

Teo giggled, grimacing at the pain the effort cost him. He gripped Aleksei's hand tightly, his own barely half the size.

"It hurts, Papa! Make it stop!" he wailed. The man stroked his son's small head, the pain the boy was feeling mirrored in his own dark eyes. They were so alike, the two of them. Little bits of the same heart and soul. It went so much deeper than simply looks. Cassy had seen it from the moment her son could walk. His first steps had taken him straight into his father's arms, not hers. It had taken longer for Aleksei to realize it.

"I can't, *detka*. Believe me, if I could take away your pain, I would do it in a heartbeat. But I can't. No one can but you. This is your fight now. Your struggle. And whatever happens, you can't give up. You're strong, remember? You beat Luka all by yourself, you can win this. I know you can!"

"I didn't beat him, Papa! I was…so scared!" he sobbed.

"You lived, didn't you? You lived, and you're here. That means you won. I was once told that courage isn't lack of fear, it's the power not to let that fear keep you from doing what needs to be done. You have that power, Teo, and no one can take it from you."

"Am I…brave, Papa?" he hiccupped, his small body trembling from pain and exhaustion.

"Of course you are, you're my son. You take after me. Now get some rest, all right? Or your mother will be angry with me." Aleksei planted a soft kiss on the little hands, getting to his feet.

"G'night," the faint voice whispered.

"Good night, Teo."

He hadn't the heart to tell him it was closer to noon.

───

The boy was tall for his six years, black hearted, and every bit Luka's equal, young as he was. His cold eyes saw the world with disdain. They were beneath him. He was superior. Luka was proud of his puppet. He'd raised the boy in darkness, training him to be as ruthless and brutal as he was. A shadow among shadows, people called him, the unseen death. One never would know he was there until he'd struck, and by then it was far too late.

"Have you found them yet, Mikhail? Or are they proving slippery again?"

The boy stiffened, blinking uncomfortably even in the low light.

"I don't like being called that. It's not my name," he answered, ignoring his master's hint at failure.

"It's the name your mother gave you. Surely you want to keep that tie to her?"

"Why? I don't owe her anything."

"True. She relinquished her rights when she sold you to me. So, then, what am I to call you? I take it you've found a name for yourself?"

He hesitated, the child he was showing for a moment in his uncertainty. Luka tapped a finger impatiently on the desk. He didn't like being reminded that it would be several more years before his weapon was old enough to be of some use.

"I like…Sergei. It means glory, sort of."

"Alright, *Sergei*, why did you want to see me? I know you don't like coming out in the daytime, so I assume it's important."

The boy took a deep breath. This was his moment to prove to his master that he wasn't too young, wasn't too inexperienced, that he was ready to be in the field and ready to kill men not strapped to chairs.

"I know how we could get rid of your brother."

"To capture him, you mean?"

"No, sir. To kill him."

Luka grinned. "Go on. I'm listening."

CHAPTER 9

Two months later.

Teo stared at his reflection in the mirror he'd taken from his mother's bedside, hypnotized. He touched the still-red scars gingerly, tracing their paths. One was from the left temple, across the nose, and to the right cheek. Another was from his forehead to the nose on the other side. The last one, the one that cut the corner of his mouth down to his chin, had been the deepest and most painful, taking nearly a month longer than the others to heal.

"They'll fade with time, you know. Not completely, of course, he made sure of that, but it'll get better."

Startled, the boy dropped the mirror as he spun round, shattering the glass. One long piece of it sliced his hand. No cry of pain passed his lips though. In fact, he barely noticed it.

Aleksei, saying nothing, crouched down, took a handkerchief from his pocket, and wrapped the wound gently.

"I know people look at you a little strangely now," he said, tying the makeshift bandage securely. "But it's no excuse to start avoiding your own family. What? You thought I hadn't noticed you sneaking off all the time to stare at yourself? You have to stop. It's not good for you."

Teo shrugged. He'd been so withdrawn and distant since they'd taken off the bandages. It made the whole camp uneasy. They'd gotten used to his laughter and pranks before the battle. He'd been the life of the rebel cause. Now, there was only silence.

"I don't like Dmitri," he confessed, lowering his gaze and pulling away. Aleksei sighed, pretending not to notice the change in subject.

"Neither do I. Ivan says he's Luka's, and I believe him, whether the kid denies it or not. It's better to keep him close where he can be watched. Nobody likes the little brat, and he only likes your mother."

"And Nicko. He likes my little brother."

His father grimaced.

"*Da.* So he does. Too much, if you ask me. He throws a fit every time I try to go near my own son. It's a pity your mama won't let me kick him."

The boy smiled for the first time in two months. It was a mere shadow of his former grin, but it brought Aleksei hope.

"I got him in the face with a snowball yesterday. Told Mama it was an accident."

"That's my boy! Did you make him cry?"

"No, but Mama yelled at him for trying to get back at me, and that was fun. He won't let me near Nicko either. I don't like him."

Aleksei gathered Teo into his arms and carried him back toward the campsite. The child nestled his head between his father's neck and shoulder with a sigh.

"Will they ever go away completely, Papa? I don't like the way people stare."

"No, Teo, they won't. But you'll get used to them, and so will others. Let them be a source of pride, *detka*, not shame, and it's how people will see them too."

Cassy met her boys as they left the forest. She did not look happy.

"Aleksei, I can't stay here. Your mother is making my life miserable, and Dmitri won't let me go to the bathroom without being three steps behind. At least back in the building, we had our own place, with privacy. I'm going to go insane if we stay much longer."

He nodded, thoughtful. "I know. I've been thinking the same thing. With Ivan gone to Moscow to rescue his family and so few people left willing to fight, there's not much reason for us to stay. Remember where we were when this whole thing started? I could build us a house. Let the boys grow a little before rejoining the resistance. Would you like that?"

She beamed, aglow with the prospect. Her delight expressed itself in a long, happy kiss. Teo made a face, turning away in disgust. He swore to himself he'd rather die than let a girl do that to him.

I listen to their conversation in mounting dread. I was right. He's going to take her away where I'll never see her again. I can't let it happen. I won't. There has to be a way to get rid of him and that brat and stop Cassy from leaving. The only solution going through my mind at the moment is not a good one. Besides, getting to Moscow and back would take too much time. They'd be long gone. If only Aleksei would let me tag along. I could be very useful to them. But he never will. He and that scar-faced twerp hate me for some reason. Maybe it's because Cassy loves me more. I bet they're jealous.

I sneak away before I can be spotted. I'll go and talk to Nickolai. Whenever I need someone to listen, I go to him. He may not be able to answer, but it doesn't matter. Sometimes, just saying things aloud helps me focus.

When I get to the tent where he's napping though, his grandmother, Aleksei's mother, is already there. She never lets me close.

As always, I'm shooed out unceremoniously. Seething, humiliated, I stalk off into the woods alone.

"Fine!" I mutter to myself, "Fine! You don't want me, I won't stay. I can make it on my own. And when I'm big and strong, you'll regret this!"

I'll make them all pay. Luka, Aleksei, his mother, his brat of a son Teo, all of them. Only Cassy and Nickolai will be left, and we'll have a big house in Moscow just like I dreamed, and I'll have a mother, and a brother, and no one will look down on me again.

I walk a long time, struggling through waist-high drifts. I wish I was taller. My legs tire fast. If only I were stronger. The day passes by faster than expected, night comes, enveloping me in frozen darkness. I'm cold and wet, and I wish I'd never left. It's too late now to turn back. Cassy'll look for me. I wonder if she'll be worried enough to go out into the darkness to find me. I hope she doesn't get hurt in the process. No, Aleksei will probably stop her anyway. Thinking about it, it's really all Ivan's fault that he hates me. He's the one who told him Luka adopted me. How he found out, I don't know. From what I overheard, he met Katya, and she's the one who talked. Well, as much as she can "talk" to anyone without her vocal chords. Luka had them cut as punishment for her trying to run away. I'm glad he did. She deserved it for being a bad wife to him, and she was always nagging me. I had to burn her supply of paper just to get some peace.

Exhausted, I plop down into a snow drift. I was stupid not to bring supplies. All I have are a couple of crackers in my pocket, and they barely make a dent in my hunger. I'll go back in the morning. For now, sleep is the best option. I drift off easily, no longer even aware of how cold it is.

———

A swift kick in my side wakes me completely. I sit bolt upright, snow in my hair and eyelashes. Blearily, I try to see who hurt me. My attacker kicks me again before I can focus.

"Stop that!" I shout, leaping angrily to my feet. He's younger than me. Everything about him is dark. Dark coat, dark sunglasses, dark hair, even his skin is a deep tan. Something about him scares me, even if he is smaller.

"What's a little worm like you doing out here all alone?" he asks, condescending. The insult sounds strange coming from such a young child, but there's something oddly familiar about the tone, like he's mimicking an adult. I shudder.

"Nothing! I'm not doing anything. And I'm not alone. My family's nearby, and they'll be very angry with you for hurting me."

He gives a snort of disgust and lands a surprisingly powerful punch to my midriff, making me double over in pain.

"I hate lying little brats like you. Now tell the truth before I shoot you!"

Anger blinds me, and I yell before thinking things through.

"You can't hurt me! Baby! If you touch me, Luka himself'll make you pay! You should run back to your mommy and have her change your diaper! Baby!"

He shrugs, then barks out a high-pitched laugh, so unlike a child's, it truly frightens me.

"And why would Luka care about you?"

"Because he's my father and I'm on a mission for him! I'm important, unlike you. You're just a baby."

I want to take back the words the instant they leave my lips, but it's far too late. The damage is done.

"Is that right? Well why didn't you say so? I'll take you to him."

Panic makes my chest tight. He'll kill me for sure. I've been missing for two months, he probably thinks I betrayed him, went over to the other side. I realize with mounting horror that that's exactly what I did. I run, tearing through the trees like a madman. I don't get far before slamming face first into someone. I fall back, breathing hard.

"Well, well, well. This *is* a surprise. Fancy finding little Dmitri all alone way out here. Strange place to run into a traitorous toad."

I'm so frightened, I can't move. The one person in the world I'd prayed never to see again is standing in my path.

"I-I-I can…explain!" I stutter, unable to look away. He smirks.

"I'm sure you could. Sadly, I'm not interested."

Luka draws his gun, cocks it, ready to shoot.

"I was doing it for you! I followed them, found their camp. I can take you there! I only stayed so long because Cassy was nice to me and I liked helping her with the baby."

Even I'm not sure of the truth anymore. Maybe, deep down, it really was the plan all along. In any case, it makes him pause.

"They're only about a day's walk from here. I'll take you to them if you promise not to hurt Cassy and Nickolai, her new baby."

He's thinking about it. I can almost see the gears turning in his mind. Finally, he shrugs.

"We've been looking for this camp for over a month. So, okay, I'll give you one last chance. You take us there, and you get to live. Betray me again, and I kill you."

"Promise Cassy and Nickolai won't get hurt."

"Of course not. I am only after Aleksei. I have no grudge against his family."

He's lying. I know he is. But what choice is there? I have to trust him. I don't wanna die. I'm only eight. I've got my whole life ahead of me. Besides, he'll do it in a painful way. I don't wanna be hurt. Not again. I nod.

"Okay. It's a deal."

He grins, pleased, and holsters the gun. I rise cautiously, carful not to make any sudden moves in case he changes his mind. This is, after all, Luka we're talking about. Not someone sane.

"Sergei," he says, looking at a point behind me, "don't shoot the little cockroach yet. He's just agreed to take us to the camp in exchange for his life. Small price, I know, but why refuse such a good deal?"

I turn and find the boy who attacked me earlier. He gives the ghost of a smile.

"Pity. I was looking forward to blasting his head off."

CHAPTER 10

Cassy turned onto her side, laying her head on Aleksei's chest. It was long past two in the morning, and in all the camp, she was the only one not asleep. Dmitri's disappearance worried her. If Ivan's suspicions had been right about the boy, did that mean he'd gone to betray them to Luka? She could not seem to be rid of a sense of foreboding, like some terrible tragedy would soon be upon them. Aleksei's hand stroking her hair did not help relax her the way it usually did.

"Can't sleep, *lyubov*? What's the matter?" he asked in a whisper, still half-asleep. She closed her eyes, not sure how to answer. No one and nothing could ever make her feel as safe and protected as when she was in his arms. Yet tonight, even that wasn't enough to chase away the feeling of impending disaster.

"I don't know," she admitted. "Bad dreams, I guess."

"Liar. Can't fool me. You're worried about that kid going back to Luka. I am too. But we'll be leaving soon, and they won't find us, not for a long, long time. Now go to sleep, while Nicko lets you."

"Ivan found us."

He yawned, wrapping his arms around her. "Only because I showed myself. If I hadn't, he'd still be wandering through Siberia looking for us."

"Maybe. Maybe not. I don't think I'll feel safe until we've left."

"We could go this instant if you wanted to."

"Really?"

"*Da,* and you could explain our sudden departure to my mother. Again. She still hasn't forgiven me for last time."

"Or for marrying me."

He grinned. "That too."

Cassy sighed, wishing he'd take it seriously. He never did while he was tired or sleepy though. It was moments like those when his sarcasm level reached its peak.

"It's not funny. You won't be laughing when Luka takes us away from you again," she muttered. But he was already snoring again. Eventually, she too followed in sleep. It wasn't restful though, and nightmares plagued her.

Morning came and with it, a relief from idleness. Nicko needed to be fed, bags packed, Teo kept out of trouble, and relatives soothed.

———

I hear the crack of a bullet first. Then all I can feel is a burning in between my shoulder blades.

"Who's the baby now?" a cold voice hisses in my ear, a hand shoving me forward, sending me tumbling down a steep hill. For a spilt second, there's intense pain, then, nothing. Just darkness. And a sense of peace such as I've never known before. It's over.

———

Aleksei's mother, as expected, did not agree with their decision to leave. They'd thought Tati wouldn't oppose their going, but as it turned out, she was even more against it than her mother.

"We'll come back. I just think the boys need to be older before we involve them in a war. Teo's already been hurt. I don't want his brother to go through the same thing," Aleksei argued as they cornered him.

"Then send them away. You can't leave! Not now! Without you, the whole rebellion falls apart."

"No! I won't leave my family to wander around in the wilderness for years. Besides, Cassy would never do it."

A shout interrupted any further argument.

"Medic! A boy's been shot!"

Teo. Aleksei's heart skipped a beat as screams of panic followed the announcement as people tried to figure out what had happened. Paying his mother and sister no further attention, he raced toward the commotion, yelling for Cassy. He found her at the front of a crowd, her face pale as the snow that had started falling gently.

"What happened? Tell me it isn't Teo!" he said, breathing hard. She was clutching Nickolai to her chest, looking scared.

"No, no, it's not him. It's…it's Dmitri. He stumbled in, a minute ago. He's dead, Leksei. Someone shot him in the back."

She stepped aside, showing him the small body. Crimson blood stained the snow where he'd fallen. Aleksei reacted quickly. He knew what it meant. Shaking Cassy out of her shock, he began issuing orders.

"Go find Teo, get the boys out of here. I'll find you when it's safe. The rest of you, send your families away with her, and arm yourselves with whatever you can find. Luka's coming."

For an instant, all was still as his words sank in. Then, chaos. Cassy clung to her husband, refusing to go.

"I've been fighting by your side for six years! Don't you dare tell me I can't stay now!"

There was no time to argue. Already, they could hear the tramp of soldiers' boots. Luka was not bothering with discretion.

"Find Teo! Keep him safe!"

He leaned down and gave her a long, slow kiss. "I love you, and I will come for you," he whispered, brushing her cheek tenderly before vanishing suddenly into the throng. She stood frozen to the spot, not wanting to believe what every sense in her body and in her soul was telling her. That they would not meet again in this world.

———

Luka observed the chaos with satisfaction. His brother was somewhere down below. This day would end the war. All that was needed to accomplish it was a single command. He basked in the glorious warmth of power coursing through his veins. Such a small obstacle left until the world belonged entirely to him.

"Troops!" he shouted, not looking away from the scene. "Attack!"

Instantly, seven hundred men charged forward, perfectly in step. He'd come in full force this time, leaving nothing to chance.

"It begins!" a gleeful voice hissed from somewhere below his eye-line.

"No, boy," he answered, grinning in pride and anticipation, "It ends. Remember, the family is yours, but no one touches a hair on my brother's head. Aleksei is mine."

———

Teo crouched behind a large crate, shaking with fear. The battle noise was bringing a flood of unwelcome memories. In the distance, he suddenly caught sight of his father fighting off an enemy soldier.

"Papa!" he wailed, not daring to move from his hiding place. Aleksei heard and turned toward his son.

"Teo! Get out of here!"

But the boy stayed where he was, too frightened to move.

"Go! Go find your mother!" came the order again.

"I can't, Papa! I can't!" he sobbed. In later years, he would always wonder what might have happened had he not shouted, not distracted Aleksei. The moment would forever be branded on his young mind. Out of the smoke and confusion of battle, Luka appeared, knife in hand.

"Behind you!" he shrieked, pointing. The warning came too late. As Aleksei turned, his brother drove the weapon between his ribs. Time slowed to an agonizing crawl as the hero of the rebellion fell to his knees, a trickle of blood running down his chin. Luka, a maniac grin on his face, jerked the knife free, kicking his victim in the chest. Aleksei collapsed, his dark hair mingling with the white snow and the red blood. Teo screamed, forgetting his terror completely.

"Papa!" he screeched, running forward, "Papa, no! Don't die, Papa!"

Before he could reach the body, someone grabbed him from behind, dragging him away.

"Let go! Let go! He needs me!" the boy wailed, struggling in vain.

"Stop it, Teo! There's nothing we can do except get killed ourselves. Your Mama is waiting in the forest with Nicko. We have to leave!" Tati yelled, hating herself for the lie. She didn't know what had happened to Cassy after baby Nickolai had been passed to his aunt. He, at least, was truthfully safe for the moment. Despite Teo's shrieks, kicks, and bites, she managed to get him away from the battlefield. There would be time to grieve later, she told herself, when it would all be over, and the dead could be counted and buried.

CHAPTER 11

Teo never saw either of his parents again, though he helped bury his father. Cassy's body was never found. Tati, taking charge of the boys, moved them to Moscow. Luka, believing them dead, did not pursue the little family further. For a while, there was relative peace as rebellion died down. Then new leaders arose, and it began again.

By the time he was seven, Teo had already made a name for himself in the city's crime circles as a master thief. His scarred face alone commanded respect even among adults. By the time he was eight, he was one of the top. He withdrew more and more into himself as the years went by, rarely speaking his thoughts aloud. Aleksei's death and his mother's disappearance were never mentioned. Or if they were, he simply changed the subject with a sad smile.

When Tatiana, in turn, was killed in a street riot, Nicko, though only a child of six years, followed his brother into the streets of the slum. The boy quickly became the only person Teo trusted.

Throughout all of this, Luka reigned supreme. With each passing day, his power grew. As his power increased, so did the madness within. There were times when even the boy Sergei feared him, and the Shadow was not innocent himself in the ways of cruelty.

Katya finally bore Luka an heir, if not a male one. He was pleased, all the same, and allowed her more freedom. She was allowed out of his sight now and even into the palace gardens. He was too busy to watch her every move, especially with the expansion of his weapon.

"The emperor's Shadows," people called the boy and his young followers. Shadows that came for you in the night, in the darkest alleys of the slums, in your very bed. Shadows that were never seen, nor heard, not even as the deed was done. You died without knowing you'd been killed. As the dictator's power grew, so did their renown. Children vanished under their parents' very noses, never to be seen again. Only a lucky few prospered and were spared living each day in fear. These were the cowards who, caring nothing for their fellow men, joined Luka's court for a share of wealth and power.

In this way, twelve years passed. And if Teo resembled his father more every day, Nickolai became more like his mother. He was the one who took care of his brother's cuts and bruises after street fights, who lied to protect him when the police came knocking, who made sure they had enough to eat when Teo came home too exhausted to do more than drop on his cot and start snoring. No matter the hardships though, there could not have been two brothers closer in all of Russia.

PART THREE

Teo's Cause

CHAPTER 1

I lean against the makeshift railing, staring out at the seemingly endless wasteland of slum houses. A few of them still have lights on inside, even though it's well past 2:00 am. I like this place at night. It's the only time it's relatively peaceful. Plus it's rather comforting to know I'm not the only one who can't sleep. At least I didn't wake up screaming, for once. I light a cigarette, trying to forget the nightmares.

"You shouldn't smoke, Teo. You promised."

I turn to face my little brother. Nicko's twelve and thinks he has to look after everybody, especially me.

"*Izvinite*, Nicko. Sorry. You know I can't help it," I apologize, ruffling his red hair as he joins me at the railing. We built it ourselves out of scrap metal we found lying around. The tiny, one-roomed house too, even though he was too young to be of much help at that time. I put it together on top of a hill, tall, so we'd have a view of something other than just mud and other slum houses. True, there's not much to look at, but it's better than nothing.

"If you were really sorry, you would have put it out. Just because people call you a delinquent doesn't mean you have to act like one," he grumbles. My brother has always been the only one who could make me laugh.

"I *am* a delinquent, *mysh'*. Don't you know that by now?"

He hates it when I call him a mouse. But hey, it's not my fault he's so tiny. To annoy him further, I take a long drag from my cigarette, grinning mischievously. He punches me in the arm, pretending to be upset.

"You're a jerk sometimes, Teo, I hope you realize it."

"Yeah, well, with you reminding me every day..." I tease, raising an eyebrow meaningfully.

"Did you have another bad dream?" he asks, changing the subject and growing serious again. I shrug. He knows the answer.

"You wanna talk about it?"

"Not any more than usual. What about you? What are you doing up so late?"

Nicko mimics my shrug.

"Heard you get up, so I followed. I figured either you couldn't sleep or you were sneaking out to see Sophiya again. You have a tendency of forgetting how much her father hates your guts."

I scoff, taking another puff.

"Like I care what Ivan thinks of me. She's old enough to decide what she wants for herself, and so am I."

"Doesn't mean he won't shoot you if he catches you kissing his daughter."

"He can try. He'll miss, just like he always does. His aim is as poor as his sense of humor. How many times do I have to tell you not to worry about it?"

"It's hardly my fault you're so reckless."

"I'm not reckless, I'm adventurous."

"Another word for it, that's all."

"Not true."

"Is so! Look it up in the dictionary. It'll be under *idiot*."

I roll my eyes.

"What about *annoying*? Where's that in your precious dictionary? Under *little brother* or under *show off*?"

He likes rubbing it in my face that he can read and I can't. I never had any patience for the school my aunt Tatiana tried to send us to. I have a vague memory of my father teaching me a little, enough to recognize my name, but I've forgotten the rest a long time ago. Nicko still goes to the tiny slum school every day, even if the teacher is younger than I am. He's a smart kid, my brother. He'll go far in life. Much further than me.

"Try looking under 'stupid older brothers who insist on smoking!'" he says dryly, answering my question.

"*Ish, surovyi!* Make it more obvious you don't approve, why don't you. *Oï.*"

He glares at me.

"You're not taking this seriously! Have you never heard of lung cancer, blood poisoning? Your stupid, smelly cigarettes are gonna kill you!"

"Calm down. I'll be fine. Someday you'll be a famous doctor and save my skin. For free, obviously, since you love me so much."

"*Ya tebya nenavizhu!* Jerk!" he mutters, shoving me hard before turning on his heel and going back inside, slamming the door behind him. I sigh. He'll be mad at me for days now. I usually try to hide my smoking from him. Not my fault he followed me. Sophiya doesn't approve either. Last time I made the mistake of doing it in front of her, she wouldn't kiss me for three weeks. Not that it would have made her father unhappy, had he known of it. Ivan has a hero complex. No one will ever be good enough for his only daughter, especially not me. Who cares what he thinks though? He doesn't control my life. Nobody does that but me.

I finish my cigarette and drop it over the side of the railing. I figure I'll try getting some sleep again. Tomorrow's going to be busy. The job I've been given is a break-in, and I still have some details to take care of beforehand. Nicko pretends to be asleep when I finally head inside. For once, I let him get away with it.

In the morning, I'm woken by a loud banging on the door.

"Come on, Teo, we know you're in there. Open up before I break it down."

I groan and bury my face in the pillow. It's too early for this. "You go, Nicko. Tell 'em come back later, when I've put some pants on."

My brother ignores me completely, instead giving a very loud, very fake snore. I shouldn't have made him mad. I'll be regretting it awhile. If there's one thing he's good at, it's holding a grudge.

"Teodore! Get your lazy thief's butt out here! *Now!*"

I grimace. There's only one person who ever calls me Teodore, and messing with her before she's had her coffee is never a good idea.

"*Da, da,*" I grunt. "I'm coming."

I shove Nicko as I pass, and he falls to the floor with a satisfying squawk of surprise. Barely awake, I pull back the lock and, yawning and blinking, open the door.

"Irena, what a pleasant surprise. And you even brought your lapdogs with you over for a visit. Charming."

As expected, she doesn't take kindly to my sarcasm. Her already tight lips get even tighter. She hates dealing with me more than anything in the world, and that's saying something.

Irena isn't very old, maybe late twenties, early thirties, but she tries hard to look younger. Her ash blond hair (very obviously dyed) hangs loose around her cosmetic-coated face.

"The boss wants you. He's waiting, so *move.*"

I roll my eyes. Why does she insist on calling him "the boss" like he's somebody important?

"Can I put on some pants first, maybe? Or is Janek so eager to see me that I have to go in my underwear?"

The bulldogs, as I call her two massive bodyguards, sensing their mistress's unhappiness, growl at me, hands on their guns. I grin.

"Good doggies. Down, boys."

I whistle and click my tongue, not caring that I'm only aggravating the situation. They won't shoot me, not without a direct order from Irena, and she won't give it without Janek's permission. I'm too valuable for him to give it, apparently.

"Easy, boys, don't let the brat get to you," Irena hisses, her eyes glowing with ill-disguised hatred. I smirk.

"Tsk, not very polite, that. Maybe I should talk to Janek about your rudeness."

I can tell she's just itching to slap me. She controls herself though, if barely.

"Get dressed quickly then," she snaps, heading back down the stairs. Her poodles follow suit reluctantly. I watch them go, then shut the door and turn to Nicko, who's gotten back under his blankets and is watching me. He doesn't like her any more than I do.

"Are you going?" he asks, not happy about it. I sigh, pulling on my jeans.

"Course I am. Got no choice. Janek is willing to put up with a lot, but refusing an invitation is crossing the line. You have school today anyway, don't you?"

He shakes his head, sitting up.

"It's Sunday. Teacher's day off. You were going to take me to the park, remember?"

"Yeah. I do. Of course I do. Don't worry, it'll be quick. I'll be back in an hour or two, and we'll go then, okay? Otherwise maybe Sophiya can take you. She was supposed to meet me there anyway."

He grimaces. Nicko loves the rich people's park. It's the only place in the whole city, apart from Luka's private gardens, where there's grass and trees. It would have been the perfect place to watch the house I'm breaking into tonight.

"I don't like it when she comes. You only pay attention to her and not me. Anyway, she won't go if you're not there. I wanted to go with you, Teo. Not her."

I sit next to him on the bed. "I promise we'll go together. But right now, I have to take care of this. We have the whole day ahead of us, so stop worrying so much. And I thought you were mad at me anyway?"

He slides out from under the blanket, swinging his skinny legs over the side, thinking.

"Only an hour or two?"

"Tops."

"Promise?"

"Yes."

"Say it. Say you promise."

I roll my eyes but comply.

"I promise I'll be back in two hours and that I'll take you to the park. Satisfied?"

He nods reluctantly.

"Good. Now hand me my sweater so I can get this over with."

Nicko obeys, scurrying quickly across the room and tossing it to me. I pull it over my head and step outside. The sun has barely risen.

"I'll have breakfast ready when you come back, okay?" he shouts after me. The prospect warms me despite the frosty air. The kid is a skilled cook. Much better than I am.

"You do that, *Mysh'*. See you later!" I call back as I race down the stairs before he can get mad at me for calling him a mouse again.

To my surprise, Janek himself is waiting in the black car across the street. He rarely shows up in person. Last time he did, I ended up unconscious in a gutter for two days. Nicko wouldn't let me out of his sight for weeks after.

"You're late. Irena went to get you ten minutes ago. What took so long?" he asks dryly as I settle myself in the leather seat next to him.

"I had to take care of something," I answer simply. It's never a good idea to advertise to these sorts of people that you have family you care about. Luckily he drops the subject.

"I have a favor to ask you. Do you know this man?"

He hands me a photograph of a gray-eyed, fierce-looking man. I take it, pretending to think hard. Finally, I shake my head.

"No. Sorry. Never seen him." The lie comes easily. I've had a lot of practice. "Why do you want to know?"

"Word around the streets is he's some sort of rebel leader. Luka's put quite a high price on his head. Rumor has it he fought with the great Aleksei himself. If you could…locate him, for me, there'd be a good chunk of reward in it for you."

I snort, faking hesitation. I may not like Ivan, but I'm not about to sell him out either.

"Since when do we work for Luka? And Aleksei's been dead a long time. I thought his army had all been wiped out?"

"Since Luka is rich and willing to pay a few of his millions to have this man caught. He's been quiet awhile, it's true. There hasn't been a rebellion in nearly six years, ever since the last one was put down. Recently, though, this man has become active again. My sources tell me he's planning something. Unfortunately, we don't know what, and we can't find him. You're the best at this. Can you do it or not?"

I sigh inwardly. Better me than someone who really will try.

"Of course. It might take some time, but it's not impossible."

"I don't care if it takes you months. The price can only go up the longer it takes. Just find him and bring him to me."

CHAPTER 2

Luka opened the door quietly, careful not to wake his daughter. She lay fast asleep in her dark-red canopy bed, clutching a giant teddy bear. Various toys and dolls littered the polished wood floor. He would have to talk to the nanny about cleaning up. Such a mess was not suitable for his angel girl. Anastasiya, or Anya for short, was every bit the apple of her father's eye. She was the only being to whom he ever showed affection, even love sometimes. It had bothered him at first that she was not a boy, but he'd gotten over it fairly quickly. Especially after her first word had been *Papa*. The second, *kill*, had pleased him just as much. She was so much like him in so many delightful ways.

"Anouchka," he whispered, stroking her blond curls, "you want to come have breakfast with Daddy?"

The seven-year-old blinked awake groggily.

"I have to leave on business today, and I'll be back very late, so I thought we could eat together before I go," he explained. She nodded, holding out her arms for him to pick her up. He gathered her to him, lifting her out of bed.

"Did you sleep well?" he asked as she let her head drop onto his shoulder. She picked at her pink nightdress absentmindedly, nodding.

"I had good dreams," she said, still half asleep.

"Oh? What were they about?"

"You and me, and we were ruling the whole world and killing all our enemies, and everyone was so afraid of me, they all bowed and worshipped me, and all the girls had to wear red to make me happy because it's my most favorite color."

Luka planted a proud kiss on top of her little head.

"That's my girl. Don't worry, your time to rule will come very soon."

They reached the dining hall, and he set her down beside him at the great oak table. Instantly, slaves appeared with steaming platters of food. Sausages, bacon, pancakes dripping with syrup, bowls of fresh fruit covered in chocolate sauce, and cups filled with milk, both warm and cold, coffee, juices of every kind, and wine for Luka, should he desire it.

"It's a simple breakfast today, love. Unfortunately, I haven't got much time," he apologized. She nodded understandingly.

A young slave appeared at a wave of the dictator's hand.

"Coffee this morning," was the order.

The boy poured the steaming liquid into a cup, careful not to spill a drop, while another served sausages and quail eggs.

"What do you want to eat, Anouchka?" he asked, using his pet name for her. She considered a moment.

"Pancakes and hot chocolate. Can I have caviar, Papa? Nanny let me try it at dinner last night, and I liked it."

"It's not really a breakfast item, but I don't see why not. You heard her!" he snapped at the slaves, sending them scurrying. They ate in silence a minute, enjoying the good food.

"Papa," she said, breaking the calm, "can I ask you something?"

"Of course, my angel, anything."

"May I have a slave my age to play with? Nanny never knows any good games, and I'm getting too big for her to handle anyway."

Luka thought about it. She was only seven, still in need of a nanny's supervision, no matter what she claimed. But a pet wouldn't hurt. Slaves were easy to come by and easy to dispose of if they displeased her.

"Yes, why not. I'll find you a suitable one when I return, all right?"

Anya grinned and jumped up to kiss his cheek and throw her arms around his neck.

"Thank you, Papa! Thank you!" she cried, delighted. Her sudden movement startled the young slave who'd been serving coffee earlier, causing him to slip as he was refilling. The cup, upset by his hand, tipped over, staining the white tablecloth, and worse, Luka's perfectly ironed suit pants. The dictator roared in pain as the hot liquid scalded him, and he leapt to his feet. A deathly silence filled the room as everyone waited in terror for his next move. Even Anya felt frightened for a split second. She'd seen her father's anger before, even if she'd never been on the receiving end herself. It was a terrible thing to behold.

"You!" he snarled, turning on the hapless slave. Terrified, the boy threw himself to the ground at his master's feet.

"Forgive me, master, I beg you! It was an accident! It won't happen again! Forgive me!" he pleaded, keeping so low he was nearly flat out on the cold marble floor.

"Have him whipped, Papa! Teach him a lesson," Anya crowed, suddenly transformed from a sweet little girl into a ruthless dictator. No one could have doubted whose daughter she was.

"Forgive me, master! Forgive me!" the boy begged, touching his forehead respectfully to the tip of Luka's shiny black shoe. Still breathing hard, Luka composed himself.

"Guards!" he shouted. "Take this vermin away to the dungeons. I'll see to his punishment on my return."

Two soldiers dragged the poor boy to his feet, removing him from the room. They could still hear his screams long after he'd vanished.

"Someone clean up this mess. I'm going to get changed," he snapped at the still frozen slaves. "I'm sorry, Anouchka, I have to go now. We'll talk more about getting you a playmate tomorrow."

"Okay, Papa," she answered, smiling and holding out her cheek to be kissed. He obliged, feeling rather proud of her reaction to the whole incident. She was truly her daddy's little girl.

———

"*Pridurak!* Watch where you're driving, moron!" I shout, making a rude gesture at the chauffeur of the limousine that nearly ran me over. He honks and sticks his hand out of the window, returning the motion.

"*Ublyudok,*" I mutter, dragging Nicko out of the road and onto the sidewalk facing the park. I'm not used to watching out for cars. There aren't many inside the slum limits. It's too narrow, and the roads aren't paved, making them dangerous in bad weather. Janek's ride is a rarity he can afford only thanks to my exploits.

"Go and play with the ducks or something for a while. I'll be right there," I tell my brother, catching sight of a familiar figure in the distance, sitting primly in the crook of a low branch. He gives me a disgusted look, guessing rightly who it is, but moves on anyway.

I creep up behind her and wrap my arms around her waist, kissing her neck. She turns, grinning.

"You made it! Finally. Do you have any idea how long I've been waiting?"

I shrug, trying to look as innocent as possible.

"I had some things I needed to take care of. Sorry. How was Prague?"

"Don't change the subject, Teo. Were you out stealing for Janek again? He'll stab you in the back one of these days, you know."

I grin.

"He can try. Who cares? I'm smarter than he is."

I encircle my arms around her middle again, pulling her in close for a kiss. She lets her hands drape over my shoulders, melting into it, relaxing, heart beating steadily against mine. Her father took her to Prague for three weeks to visit her grandmother, possibly as an excuse to get her away from me. In any case, I've missed her. We've only been dating for the past two years, but we've known each other nearly all our lives. She's got her father's clear gray eyes and her mother's nut brown hair. It's cut fairly short, which I don't like, but as Sophiya always tells me, "I'll grow it out when you stop smoking and swearing." Meaning, when pigs fly.

"Teo! Teo, run! It's Ivan! He's coming!" Nicko's shout draws me back to reality. I pull away, cursing to myself. Too late. He's seen us.

"Come by the house tomorrow. My brother'll cook up something special, all right?" I whisper quickly, giving her one last quick kiss on the cheek before turning away reluctantly. She nods, her face flushed bright red. A quick glance at Ivan spurs me on my way. He's running now, shouting something. I grab Nicko and tug him back toward our end of the town. The last thing I need is to get shot today.

———

"What'd you have to go and do all that for? It ruined everything!" Nicko complains as I force him to go faster. I can hear Ivan yelling at his only child behind us. Poor girl's going to be in a mess of trouble because of this. I should have been more careful.

"Just go before he catches up. You'll understand these things when you're older."

We make it across the street just in time. I can't catch exactly what he's shouting at me, but I can guess.

"I thought he was a good friend of our papa's?" the kid says, confused.

"He was his right-hand man."

"So why does he hate you so much?"

I hesitate before answering. It's a problem that's been bothering me for a long time.

"Because he thinks I'm a coward, and therefore unworthy of his daughter."

"What? Why?"

I sigh.

"Because I won't...because I won't join his cause against Luka. I'm not a rebel, so that makes me a coward in his eyes."

My brother gives me a strange look, like he doesn't quite believe me.

"But, Teo, you fight all the time. Just last week, you broke that kid's arm because he was shoving me around. Then his big brother knocked out your back tooth, and you—"

"Okay, okay, I get it," I say, making a face at the recollection.

"That's street fighting though. It's different. I'm not risking your life, or mine, doing it. This family has already given their share of blood against Luka. Dad's whole family and Mom's too. They're all dead. I won't have us added to the list."

I barely notice he's struggling to keep up with me. The subject is one which I'd much rather avoid. I hate remembering my parents. Unfortunately, I've been gifted with a photographic memory, meaning I don't have much of a choice. Nicko's lucky. He was just a baby when they died. It's why he can sleep at night without waking up screaming. Truth be told, I envy him that. He claims he never dreams at all, good or bad.

"Teo, slow down!"

"No. Walk faster, *mysh'*."

"Don't call me that!" he yells, almost running now, his short legs struggling to stay by my side. I decide to take pity on him and shorten my stride.

"I'll stop when you get taller."

"I can't help being short, anymore than you can help being a jerk."

I sigh inwardly, rolling my eyes, then stop suddenly. I pretend to be busy pulling out a cigarette, all the while keeping my attention on the street.

"Teo! No!" Nicko protests, indignant. He's on the verge of launching into one of his famous lectures when I cut him off harshly.

"Shut it, Nickolai. Get home, you hear me? Get out of here." I hiss. He trusts me enough to know I wouldn't talk to him that way without reason. He looks suddenly frightened.

"Don't get hurt, okay?" he says, giving me a worried look before scurrying off, sticking close to the walls just like I taught him. I hate to admit it, but I'm rather proud of the kid. He's turned out a far better person than I am, despite my efforts to corrupt him.

I light the cigarette, taking a deep breath of it to calm my nerves. There's a fight coming. I can feel it in the stillness of the air. As I watch, my suspicions are confirmed. Two groups of boys materialize out of the darkness of the trash-strewn alleys. Most are carrying clubs and other various weapons. The rest have only their bare hands. I recognize most of them. Kids I've grown up with, gone on jobs with. This is why I've always refused to join one of the many gangs. The pointless violence gets old fast.

"Teo, come fight with us! Teach these punks a lesson!" one calls out, catching sight of me. I wave back.

"Not today, Simon. I'm just waiting for the passage to clear so I can get home," I shout back. He shrugs, disappointed. A split second later, it's begun. I've seen it all before though, and it doesn't affect me the way it did the first couple times. I used to throw up easily in those days. I suppose I'll lend a hand if it gets really ugly, but for now, it's best to stay out of it. Broken bones should be the extent of the damage this time around. They don't seem serious enough to kill. More than likely, the fight was only arranged out of boredom. Then something happens that makes everything much, much worse. Sirens sound off close by, followed by the tramp of rhythmic boots. I drop my cigarette and leap into the fray.

"Simon! *Politsya! Ot syuda!* Get everyone out of here!" I shout. The cry is taken up quickly by others.

"*Politsya! Politsya!*"

Panic spreads like wildfire as each tries to flee to save his own skin. If the police catch you, they take you away and brainwash you into joining the army. You'll never see your friends or family again. Not that you'd even want to.

In the chaos, I don't see the fist until it's too late. It cracks hard against the side of my jaw, knocking me to the ground. Instantly, I'm kicked and trampled by dozens of panicked pairs of feet. It's all I can do to shield my face. Something smacks into my ankle, and I swear I can hear the bone crack. I scream in agony, trying desperately not to black out. The pain is so awful, my stomach heaves, throwing up my breakfast. Just when all seems lost, a strong hand reaches toward me, pulling me up.

"It's not over yet, kid. Come on, let's get you home."

I shake my head, grimacing in pain as he drags me out of the chaos.

"No. No, I don't…I don't want my brother…to see me like this." I groan, leaning all my weight on his shoulder.

"Not much choice. It's either him or my house. Pick one."

"Nicko."

Ivan grins, not in the least surprised.

"Figured that's what you'd say. Besides, he's probably seen worse. He'll be kinder to you than I would be."

We walk, or rather he drags me, quickly away from the scene. I must have blacked out at some point because the next time I open my eyes, we're almost there.

"Which one is yours?"

I point, not bothering to ask how he knows which street we live on.

"The house with the stairs? I might have guessed. All right, let's do this."

I bite my lip bloody trying not to scream every time my ankle hits a step.

There's no answer from inside when he knocks. I almost grin in spite of the pain. Smart kid. Better to pretend there's nobody home than open the door and get shot.

"It's okay, Nicko. Just…just…me." I breathe, panting hard. It opens a crack, then completely as he sees I'm telling the truth.

"You idiot! I told you not to get hurt!" he yells, his voice shrill and panicked.

Ivan helps me to the bed, and I collapse gratefully onto it.

"Yeah, well…since when do I listen…to you?" I grunt, reaching for my pack of slightly smashed cigarettes. Before I can light one, he snatches it out of my mouth and tosses it outside. His face is pale with fury.

"Give it back," I protest feebly, holding my hand out for the rest of the pack.

"You smoke?" Ivan asks, surprised and slightly disgusted.

"Not anymore he doesn't," Nicko answers before I can.

"*Vyrezat*, Nicko, give it. Stop being a brat."

He ignores me.

"You promised. You promised you'd stop fighting, you promised you'd stop smoking, and you promised you'd stop breaking your promises! Why are you always lying to me? I hate you!"

I lean my head back against the wall and close my eyes. I'm so tired of all this. I wish my father were here. He'd know exactly what to say to make it all better. I groan and mutter curses under my breath. I don't have his gift with words.

"Come here," I say, beckoning. His lower lip trembles, and he wipes a hand savagely across his eyes. At twelve, I guess he thinks he's too old to cry.

"Come on!" I tell him, motioning again. He drops the packet and runs over to me, burying his face against me and sobbing. I must look really awful to have scared him this badly. Even when he was little he rarely ever cried.

"I know I let you down. But you have to trust me now when I tell you everything's gonna be all right. I'm not the perfect big brother, I'm not even a very good one, but you gotta give me a chance to at least try. What would I do with my little *sovest'* by my side? I would've been in jail or dead a long time ago, that's what. So what do you say? Willing to give me one last try at it? Hmm?"

He nods, bawling too hard to speak, barely able to breathe between sobs.

"*Spasiba*, little brother. I owe you one." I whisper, planting a kiss on his red hair. I don't care that Ivan is watching all this. In fact, it seems to be bothering him a lot more than it is to me.

"Look, I came to warn you to stay away from my daughter, not to save your life. I only did it because I know Aleksei would have done the same for me. Next time I catch you anywhere near Sophiya, I'll shoot you, understand?" he says suddenly as though only just remembering why he's standing there. I nod. I understand. It doesn't mean I'll stop seeing her. Saving my life doesn't make him in charge of it.

"Good. Well...I'll go now."

Neither of us tries to stop him as he leaves.

CHAPTER 3

"Sire."A lieutenant saluted sharply as Luka passed.

"What was so urgent you had to interrupt my day?" The man handed over a series of photos.

"These were taken only an hour ago in a slum raid. We believe we've finally caught sight of the terrorist leader known as Ivan."

Luka studied the pictures with sudden interest.

"That's Ivan, no doubt about it. But what about the boy he's helping? Who is that?" he asked, frowning.

"We don't know, sir. All we've been able to find out is that he's a dweller."

"a *what*?"

"A…a slum dweller, sir. A boy who probably lives, breathes, and eats the place."

Luka handed back the photos.

"Get me clearer pictures. I want that kid's name, his family, everything. Talk to the ones that were brought in today, see if any recognize him. No need to ask gently if they don't comply right away. And send a team to pick up Ivan. He's been causing trouble lately, and I'm running low on patience."

Soldiers scurried around, looking like panic-stricken ants. He paid them no mind. So long as he got results, it didn't matter how they went about they went about getting them.

As he stepped into his office, he was met by the icy feel of the barrel of a gun to his temple. He smiled, unconcerned.

"How long have you been waiting?" he asked, not bothering to turn around.

"To kill you? Since the day I was born! It has been what I've lived for, planned for, every moment of every day. Now you will die, and the people shall be free from you!"

Luka sighed.

"I meant hiding behind the door of my office, but I suppose that works too. If you're so eager, shoot me then. There's no one to stop you. My bodyguard is gone on a mission."

He turned slightly, watching his attacker for signs of weakness. Her hand was trembling slightly, and her eyes were wild. It was hard to make out her features properly in the dim light—he always kept the shades drawn for his bodyguard's sake—but she seemed young, impressionable and, more importantly, terrified. She wouldn't pull the trigger, not if handled right.

"What's your name?" he asked, making his voice soft, almost kind.

"Don't talk to me, monster! Murderer! I am going to kill you! Tyrant!"

"Strong words. Have you ever shot anyone before? It's not as easy as it seems. It takes something I don't believe you have."

The girl's chest swelled visibly as she sucked in a nervous breath.

"And what would that be?"

His grin widened. He was enjoying this immensely. She was even more fun to manipulate than Katya.

"A killer's heart. You aren't going to shoot me."

"I am! I've been waiting for this moment...I'm just...I'm savoring having you at my mercy!"

Luka laughed, digging his hands into his pockets, fingers grasping the small knife he always kept for emergencies. Before he could turn and end her life, a shot rang out. A pained expression spread across the girl's face, mixing with surprise. She coughed weakly, blood spurting onto her chin. She collapsed at his feet. The dictator grimaced in disgust at the drops falling on his shoe. He wiped it quickly on the still body. A delighted grin lit up his features as he saw who the shooter was. He crouched down, opening his arms to her. Anya dropped the gun and ran to him, obviously relieved she hadn't done anything bad.

"She was going to hurt you, Papa. Did you see? She was going to shoot you."

Luka kissed her cheek reassuringly, turning to the soldiers come running at the sound of gunfire.

"Men, this is your future queen. You'd do well to show her the same amount of respect you do me. Understood? And someone clean up the mess."

They saluted, clicking their heels sharply.

"Yes, sir!" came the unified shout. Anya gave her father a worried look.

"I did the right thing, Papa, didn't I? I did good?"

"You did *very* good, Anouchka. You saved my life. That's the best anyone could ever do, *dorogaya.*"

He canceled his plans for the rest of the day, deciding instead that the time was better spent forming his future heiress.

Later that evening, as he was reading her a bedtime story of his own composition—"Great Tyrants and Their Magnificent Deeds"—he was interrupted by a nervous-looking guard.

"Keep reading, *lyubov*, I'll be right back," he told her. She nodded sleepily. It had been a long day for her.

"You have the pictures?" Luka asked, shutting the door behind him.

"Yes, sir. And one of the captured boys recognized him."

He handed over the enhanced photos. "He said his name is Teo. There's also a younger brother, Nickolai, that he's very protective of. No other family. Everyone knows the older one, but few even realized there was another."

Luka took a deep breath, steadying his nerves. His worst suspicions had been confirmed. Aleksei's children were alive, probably protected by Ivan, groomed to rise against him. He could not, would not, allow that to happen.

"Have your men track down their hideout and report back. What of Ivan? Any news?"

"No, sir, not since the photos. The boys may prove less of a challenge though. Apparently the older one is a famous and well-respected thief. With a bit of luck, we'll have them in a day or two. Do you wish to have them brought in?"

"Not by your men, no. I'll send my Shadows in to take them from their den."

The guard suppressed a shudder at the mention of the gang. "Something wrong?"

"No. No, sir. I'll pass on your orders straight away, sir."

———

Down long, dark passages Luka strode, ignoring the smell of dampness and death. Very few people were even allowed to know this place existed. He'd not spoken of it to his own daughter.

He pushed open a heavy wooden door, letting the faint electrical light shine into the darkness. Most of the cages were empty, their occupants long dead or vanished. But when he directed his flashlight at the fourth, something recoiled into a corner, shivering from the draft it was so unused to.

"Still alive, then? Good. I'll be bringing you company soon. After all, twelve years is a long time to be separated from those we love."

CHAPTER 4

Irena did not take kindly to my broken ankle. Now not only would she have to find someone else for the robbery, but it would probably have to be delayed several days, ruining her normally perfect schedule. She yelled things that were not particularly kind.

"At least she didn't burn the house down," Nicko says as she slams the door behind her.

"She still might if she's feeling vindictive. It was a big job."

"Would Janek let her?"

I shrug. "Nah. He'll just find someone cheaper and probably less skilled. Too bad. I could've paid groceries for six weeks with what he was gonna give us."

I hate being forced to stay bedridden. Not being able to walk is slowly driving me insane. My brother had the local so-called doctor come earlier and put a splint on my ankle. Half of the money we usually use for food had to go into that, which hardly helped my mood.

"It's fine, Teo. I'll just skip school for a month or two and go back to work at the printer's. They'll hire me in a second. There aren't that many boys who can read and write in these parts."

I groan and smack the back of my head against the wall in frustration.

"Last time you had to do that was when I got shot and couldn't move for *weeks*. It was *horrible*! Now you're telling me it's going to be *months*?"

Nicko gives me an unimpressed glance.

"Go ahead, give yourself a concussion as well. I'm sure it'll help."

"I'm just saying I'll be fine in a couple days. You don't need to skip school."

"Oh yeah, no, that's really realistic. Your *shattered* ankle is going to *magically* heal itself in time for us not to starve. Wonderful, I'm *so* happy you told me. And then what? The wealth fairy is going to pay us a visit on her unicorn and sprinkle money from the sky?"

"It's not shattered. Just…broken a little. In a couple places."

"And that's so much better, right?"

I glare at him, annoyed. "No. Since when are you this sarcastic anyway?"

"I learned from the best. Now stop being cranky and eat." He hands me a plate of green beans and something that looks suspiciously like not meat. I grimace and pick at it tentatively before giving up.

"You have it. I'm suddenly very much un-hungry."

"Teo—"

"I won't! I hate beans!"

"God, you're such a baby when you're hurt! Just eat it already. At least we have food for now. Or do I need to force-feed you?"

"I'm injured, not handicapped." I grunt, folding my arms defiantly across my chest, daring him to try anything. He rolls his eyes, heaving a groan of exasperation.

"Injured, huh? So…I guess it hurts when I do this?" He reaches down and prods my ankle through the splint. See, Nicko's a pacifist most of the time, but there are days when I can really get to him, force him into a reaction. Today, I figure we both got scared, and this is his way of getting past it. It's unpleasant for me, but it works, I guess.

"Ow! Yes, it hurts! Get off!" I cry, not faking for once. We're both so busy yelling at each other, neither of us notices Sophiya standing in the doorway until she actually steps inside. An awkward silence falls between the three of us. I let Nicko out of the headlock I'd just grabbed him into, embarrassed.

"I could come back later?" she says, obviously as uncomfortable as we are. I shake my head.

"Don't worry about it. I was just teasing, right Nicko?"

My brother gives me a look of pure disgust.

"Yeah, don't pay any attention to him, Sophiya. He's just in a bad mood 'cause I took away his cigarettes today."

"Today? You told me you quit a month ago!"

I shrug, giving her my best innocent face, while vowing silently to murder my brother for this. He grins, faking surprise, dodging nimbly as I make a grab for him.

"Really? He told you that? Huh. Weird." And without another glance back, he strides out the door, smirking, a triumphant gleam in his eyes.

"Sophi, *dorogaya*, I swear I didn't lie to you. I really, really tried this time. I did! It's hard, you know, 'cause there's a lot of pressure what with raising my little brother all by myself, and I haven't been sleeping well lately…"

As always, it works like a charm. Being injured helps too. She sits next to me on the bed and brushes my hair out of my eyes, kissing my forehead.

"At least you tried. I'm proud of you for that. So why haven't you been sleeping? Are you having nightmares again, *detka*?"

I flinch and pull away suddenly.

"Don't. Don't call me that. Please."

"Why not?"

"Just don't, okay? I don't like it. I'm not a baby, yours or anybody's."

She runs a finger down one of my scars, tracing its path. She's one of the few people who's never asked about them. I never talk about my past, and she doesn't mention hers.

"You don't have to act tough around me, Teo. I know you better than that. Remember, when we were kids, we used to play pranks on our parents? You laughed back then. Now I can barely get a smile out of you. Why is that? Have we really changed that much?"

I sigh and pull her closer to me. She leans her head on my chest, tucking her legs under her. We stay like that a long moment, neither saying anything. It's a comfortable silence, and I dread breaking it. I guess it had to happen sooner or later though, and maybe it's time. Maybe it'll do me good to get it off my chest. After all, I've never told anyone about it, not even Nicko.

"Did I ever tell you how my father died?" I ask, knowing full well I haven't. She shakes her head, sensing the importance and not interrupting.

"Close the door, please. I don't want Nicko to hear. It's better if he finds out only when he's much older. Let him stay free of it all as long as possible."

She obeys, then comes back to press herself against my side. It's not an easy story to tell; I force myself to go on.

———

Tears ran down Nicko's face for the second time that day as he put his ear to the door. He hadn't meant to eavesdrop, not really. But Teo had never kept anything from him before. At least, that's what he'd believed. Now, hearing his brother's story, how much pain and terror he'd been through, Nicko understood better why he was the way he was. Smoking, swearing, fighting, lying—these were walls he'd built to hide the past and live a fairly normal life. But why hadn't he told his own brother about it? Nicko couldn't understand. He himself had only ever kept one secret, and that was far too big to be shared. It also had nothing whatsoever to do with Teo. Their father's death concerned them both. He could not understand his brother's reluctance to fight, either. After listening to the story, all Nicko could think of was getting revenge. It wasn't right, what Luka had done to the world, to them. How could Teo not take action? He was no coward, like Ivan assumed, so it wasn't fear that stopped him. A thirst for vengeance filled the twelve-year-old's heart. Something had to be done.

It wasn't hard to sneak through the darkened streets. Most of the boys who were still out and about were dead drunk and wouldn't have noticed him if he were wearing bells and dancing a jig.

The house he wanted was on the outskirts of the slum. It was nice compared to most, but not so much as to stand out. He knocked three times, paused, then twice more. Maia opened the door. She did not seem surprised to see him.

"Come in. They're in the living room," she said, leading the boy inside.

Ivan and another man were sitting on a moth-eaten couch, talking in heated whispers. They stopped when he came in.

"Nickolai? What are you doing here so late? I haven't got anything for you to deliver. Go home before your brother notices you're missing."

"Teo just told me everything. How my father died, how he got his scars. I've…I've made a decision. I want to do more than just deliver letters and packages. I want to fight for real. I want to destroy Luka."

Ivan sat back, thoughtful. He opened his mouth to speak, but Nicko cut him off, the words pouring out.

"And don't say I'm too young. I'm not. This is my fight more than yours. You know, Teo's not a coward. He's just trying to protect me. But I don't need protection. Not anymore. Don't try to stop me. I'll fight no matter what you say."

Ivan smiled.

"I was just going to say how we could use you in this. It's useless to try and stop the members of your family from doing anything they set their minds to. I learned that a long time ago. You're all far too stubborn. So have a seat. I'll fill you in on the plan."

The boy obeyed, uncertain whether he was merely being pacified or not.

"By the way, this is Sam. He and his brother Charlie are from the American Resistance. Sam, this is Nickolai, the boy I was telling you about."

"Aleksei's kid?" he asked, his Russian nearly flawless. Ivan nodded.

"Pleasure to meet you. I was a good friend of your dad's. Welcome to the rebellion. Oh, and please, call me Sammy. Everybody does these days."

It felt strange at first to call the huge American such a childish name. Nicko quickly took a shine to the big man though, and within minutes, they were teasing each other and arguing like the oldest of friends. After an hour or so, the conversation turned more serious as Aleksei was discussed.

"I was a skinny little runt back then, only about nine years old. Your dad came as an exchange student, supposedly. I never did find out why he was really there. Couldn't stand me at first. I wouldn't stop pestering him with questions. He only stayed a few months before vanishing. At the very end, we were getting along better, and I'm proud to say I was his friend. Everyone panicked when Ivan and Aleksei disappeared. There was another one too, a girl named Cassy. I never met her though. Then things got even worse. The girl's family was murdered, a dead body was found in an airport garage, and just when things were settling down again, Luka took over. He'd been infiltrating and planting his men for years, so it was over in barely a few hours. They killed everyone in the government who wouldn't swear loyalty, including the president. They spared his family because his wife was one of them. We watched on TV as they burned down the White House and bombed the monuments. I swore to myself that day that I'd never feel so helpless ever again. My brother, Charlie, and my father, were among the first to set up a counterattack. It…failed, miserably, and—" he paused, finding it difficult to go on. Nicko patted him awkwardly on the back, and Ivan offered a shot of vodka. Sammy drained it in one gulp, the glass looking miniature in his big hands. He put it down and went on shakily.

"Charlie got away. Lost an arm in the process, but he made it home. My father didn't. He was with the six hundred who died that day. We were forced, at gunpoint, to watch on TV as they burned the bodies. My mother…never really got over that. She made us swear never to risk our lives again. The minute Charlie turned eighteen, he was off saving the world. I was ten, and my big brother was my hero in a way no one else had ever been. I couldn't let him leave without me, so I ran away from home to join him. Just in time too because that's when they started recruiting boys my age for Luka's army. Anyway, I finally caught up to Charlie a couple months later, somewhere near the Texas border. He wasn't thrilled to see me, but it wasn't like he could just send me back. I was forgiven when I managed to save his skin three times in less than an hour. After that, we started building the Network. We use old things that can't be tapped, like underground telegraph wires and Morse code. That way, we can communicate with other bases all over the States without Luka eavesdropping. About a year ago, Charlie went and settled in Canada. Even got married to a girl up there. Can't remember her name for the life of me though. Never met her, you see. She's in charge of the Canadian Resistance. Me, I got sent here. No real use in fighting if Luka isn't taken down."

Nicko was liking Sammy more and more as time passed. By the end of the night, they were fast friends. A plan began to take shape between the three of them. All agreed without a doubt that Luka had to be weakened before being taken on face-to-face.

It took two days of little sleep and intense preparation, but at last, everything was ready.

When Nicko finally stumbled home on the evening of the third day, he was filthy, hungry, and exhausted, but triumphant. Their plan had succeeded with perfection.

He pushed open the door, ready to collapse onto his bed. Instead, he was forced to confront a red-eyed, sleep-deprived Teo. His brother looked as tired and ill-tempered as he himself felt.

"Where the hell have you been, Nickolai? Do you have *any* idea how worried I've been? Do you even *care?* I couldn't even get out of the damned house to look for you!"

Teo always swore more when he was anxious or angry. Apparently, since at the moment he was in excess of both, things were not about to calm down.

"I was just…I was out with friends, that's all."

"For three days?"

"Yeah. We…we had to hide, you know, from some soldiers-"

"*Vy izhets!* You little liar! You think I don't know about the rebels blowing up all those barracks? You think I'm blind and deaf, too stupid to realize Ivan suckered you into joining them? I gave up *everything* so you wouldn't have to worry that I wouldn't be there when you came home at night, so you could go to school and have a future! I had my own dreams! You think I enjoy living like this? Like a rat forced to cower and feed off of scraps?"

Nicko opened his mouth the interrupt, but Teo wouldn't let him. He smacked his fist into the little table, leaving a dent.

"I only did it for *you!* So you wouldn't get involved in all of it! Now you repay that by stabbing me in the back? By lying to me?"

The boy took a step back, stunned. There were tears of helpless rage in Teo's eyes and a look of such disappointment and pain, that it broke his heart. He'd been yelled at before by his brother, but never like this.

Teo slumped back in his seat, all the fight suddenly going out of him. He avoided Nicko's eyes, tracing a pattern on the table absentmindedly with one finger.

"I'm not going to force you to stay. If you want to go, then go. I won't stop you. Just don't…don't treat me like an idiot and try to lie to me about what you're doing, okay? I'm not a child."

Nicko bit his lip, staring at the ground.

"Neither am I," he whispered.

Teo's glanced up, his gaze softening.

"I know that."

"So if it weren't for me, you'd be out fighting Luka?"

He shrugged.

"*Someone* had to raise you, feed you, teach you to use the bathroom correctly. Aunt Tatiana wasn't exactly able to after she died, so yeah, I had to give up a few dreams to do it. It's in the past though. Doesn't matter anymore."

A heavy silence fell between the two brothers, full of unspoken losses and heartbreaks, secrets, and lies, but hopes too, wishes lost in the torrent of time.

"Maybe…now that I'm older…we could still do something. We could fight him together. You said it yourself, we're not children anymore. It's our battle too. We have more right to kill the bastard than anyone else," Nicko suggested at last, tentatively at first, gaining strength as he went. Teo sighed and passed a hand over his weary face.

"If we did, we couldn't join Ivan. Or at least, I couldn't. He doesn't trust me."

"Because of Sophiya?"

"Partly. We had a fight, couple years back. I called him an obsessive fanatic, and he told me, among other things, that Father would be ashamed of what I'd become. We haven't exactly been on friendly terms since then."

"Who says we need Ivan? We're Aleksei's sons, remember? We can do it on our own. He did."

A renewed spark of interest flashed in Teo's eyes. He sat up straighter, intent, almost his old self again.

"What do you have in mind?"

CHAPTER 5

Luka was feeling frustrated. The rebels he'd believed dead and buried had blown up a good portion of his army, and his nephews still hadn't been located. True, the slum was a big place, filled with mazelike alleys and streets all too easy to get lost in, but he'd expected better from his Shadows. At least their loyalty to him was absolute, never wavering, unlike that of the common army, and there was a silver lining to the whole thing. One of the survivors of the bombing had not only escaped but managed to follow Ivan back to his den. It was only a matter of hours now before he was captured. The man had also reported seeing a red-haired boy fleeing the scene. There probably weren't a great many of them in the city. He'd have the boys sooner or later. Perhaps one or both—with a little luck—of the brothers could be turned. Teo was unlikely; he'd seen and heard too much of Luka's true nature. But the younger one…twelve was such an uncertain age. You were still gullible, easily manipulated. A brother for little Anya. Someone to protect and look after her when he'd gone. It was worth a try. All that had to be done was separate the boy from poisonous influences.

"You've found them?" he asked, not turning to face his visitor. He'd appeared suddenly, as though born of the room's shadows.

Any lesser man might have been frightened, or at the very least startled, but Luka was used to it.

"We have, master. All we need is your order, and they'll be brought in."

"Good. Get me the boys, first. Forget Ivan for the moment. It's sufficient that we're keeping an eye on him."

Sergei bowed low, his dark hood covering his face.

"I trust you'll be discreet. The older one is a good fighter, and I want both alive. Unharmed, if at all possible."

"Of course, sir. As always, I will make certain your orders are followed to the letter."

Luka smiled to himself. The Shadows would get the job done and done well. He'd trained the leader expertly, and the boy, in turn, had trained his companions to perfection. It helped that he'd kept Sergei at his side from infancy, taken from the outside world and trained in total darkness for most of his and the others' lives. So much so that light, electric or natural, hurt their eyes. People were always surprised to find out how young the others were. Sergei was big for his eighteen years and passed easily for an adult, but the other four were all under ten. Luka had plans to add more children to their group, not enough for a whole army— simple pawns were a necessity, but a good number. Ten, twenty, perhaps. It took a long time to train them. At first, he'd wanted Anya to be one of their number. She might as well have made herself useful after all, despite being born a girl. Sadly, the extreme photosensitivity in the younger ones had proven to be a problem. Sergei, exposed to light more often, was not quite as weak, thankfully. Still, it was all right for a group of soldiers to venture out only at night, less so for a future dictatress of the world.

———

One rooftop, then the next. Catlike they landed, continuing their course without fault or misstep. The five were in their element. To them, heights weren't a problem, and neither were they thrown off in the least by the maze of nearly identically rundown houses. The captain stopped suddenly, crouching down. The others followed suit instantly, perfectly in sync.

"What's wrong?" Number Four asked, not seeing any reason to halt. She was seven, the youngest and only girl. He motioned for her to stay silent, drawing his knife from his belt. Five daggers flew in flawless unison at the slight sign of movement. It turned out to be only a rat, and all breathed a little easier. For Number Four and Five, it was their first time out in the open, which did not help ease the tension.

"Sergei, I'm scared. I wanna go home."

He turned to her, furious.

"You're a Shadow, Elena! Act like one! You do not know fear! And what did I tell you about using names on a mission?"

She turned scarlet, cowering.

"Not to do it?"

"Exactly. So what should you have called me if you must speak at all?"

The small girl bit her lip, thinking about it a moment.

"Captain."

"And you are…?"

She went an even brighter shade of red, muttering something unintelligible. The other stifled their snickers as he glared at them.

"Louder."

"I'm fourth. The Girl. But shouldn't I be fifth since I'm youngest?"

"Pyotr is fifth."

"But he's older."

"You were recruited fourth, not fifth."

"But—"

"Enough! We'll argue it after the mission. Now move!"

They retrieved their weapons from the lifeless body and crept on without another word. Orders were not lightly disobeyed, at home or outside.

There were no lights on in the little house. After making certain everything was quiet, they moved in.

———

I can't sleep again. I don't know why. I'm exhausted from three days of worrying about Nicko, I should be able to drop right off. As usual, I can't. Worse, I can't even get up and go outside to smoke because of my stupid ankle. It's all I can do to get to the kitchen table, let alone go out.

A shadow falls across the window suddenly, blocking out the moonlight. I sit up, ready to investigate, when something wet and sweet smelling is pressed against my mouth. I struggle, but two surprisingly strong little hands push me down.

"I got him! I got him S—I mean, Captain!"

"The small one too. He's out like a light."

Nicko. The thought of my brother being in danger brings me back from the brink of unconsciousness kicking and roaring. I throw off my attacker, elbowing him sharply in the gut, finally managing to reach the pistol I always keep under my pillow. I stumble to my feet, still in such a daze that I barely notice the pain. There's five of them, each wearing dark cloaks and sunglasses. Four seem at first to be midgets, though the fifth is about my height, maybe a little taller. Who the heck sends midgets with guns?

"Easy now. We're not going to hurt you. Just put down the gun." Their leader says, aiming at me. Through the haze, I realize suddenly that they aren't midgets. They're kids. The biggest of the small ones has got to be even younger than Nicko. I can't go around shooting a bunch of undersized, wannabe ninjas even if they are under apparent adult supervision. Reluctantly, I obey. The one I hurt gets painfully to his feet, groaning.

"You all right Ash?" the leader asks, failing to lower his own weapon.

"*Da*, I'm fine. Caught me off guard, that's all."

"Good."

Before I can so much as blink, he shoots me with a tranquilizer. I crumple to the floor, barely conscious. The big one strides over to me and gives me a swift kick to the jaw before I can black out completely.

"That's for hurting my brother," he snarls. It's the last thing I hear.

The first thing that registers is how much my head hurts. The second, that I'm lying on the softest mattress ever created. My tired body sinks into it gratefully, relaxing. Sitting up, I realize that the room itself isn't so bad either. Large windows let in just the right amount of sunlight, the floors are polished wood, and paintings in golden frames line pure white walls. The bed itself is a massive four-poster, with tied-back red hangings. I swear there are more pillows than I could count. My ankle is in a real, actual plaster cast instead of the makeshift splint. I have to touch it before admitting to myself it's real. My old clothes too, dirty and sweaty from too much use and not enough washing, have been replaced, and I'm wearing soft, gray pajamas instead.

What, I wonder, is going on? I was expecting a prison, not a palace. Maybe I'm dead, and this is heaven. Can you be hungry in heaven? Because in all honesty, I'm starving.

Just when I thought things couldn't possibly get any weirder, I notice a pair of crutches leaning against the wall, perfectly placed within my reach. Without thinking twice, I grab them and hobble toward the large double doors. They're sure to be locked, but it's worth a try. To add to my surprise, they aren't.

Clinging to my newfound crutches, I emerge into the most luxurious hallway I've ever seen. Tapestries and paintings line the red walls, crystal chandeliers hang every couple of feet. The bare toes of my right foot sink into white carpet so deep I lose sight of them. Questions churn in my mind. Where am I? The only person I've ever heard of to live in such wealth is Luka, and I'm fairly certain if he knew I was alive, he wouldn't treat me so kindly. Who were those kids, and why aren't I still their prisoner? Daylight streams in through floor to ceiling windows. How long have I been out? More importantly, where's Nicko, and what have they done to him? Is he lying hurt somewhere, waiting for me to find him?

I hop forward tentatively, unsure where to go. A door is ajar at the far end of the hall, and the amazing smells coming from it wipes all thoughts other than food from my mind. Besides, maybe my brother will be there already.

"Nicko?" I shout, swinging toward it, "Nicko, where are you?"

But there's no answer, and the room turns out to be devoid of people. I can't exactly say empty because of the food, though. Piles and mountains of sausages, eggs in every shape and form of dish ever invented, and platters of stuff I can't even name are all delicately arranged on a huge wooden table. My mouth waters. My stomach growls. I let out a whimper of pure joy, wiping drool from my chin. I have never, in all my life, seen so much food. It's a teenage boy's dream come true.

For a mere instant, the temptation to dig in is so strong, I can actually taste those steaming strips of bacon. Something stops me, despite my stomach's pleas. I've learned the hard way to be suspicious, and all this seems suddenly too good to be true, too perfect. I don't trust it.

Turning away from that feast is one of the hardest things I've ever done, but I do it all the same. I do it for Nicko, wherever he is.

"I won't eat until I get my brother back!" I shout, fairly certain I'm being watched. "You hear me? I want Nicko or I'll let myself starve!"

"I'm sure you would," a soft, sickeningly familiar voice replies. My hand flies up to my face instinctively, tracing the old scars, remembering all too vividly the pain, and the cruelty with which they were inflicted.

"Ah, good, so you do know who I am then," Luka says, stepping out of the shadows. My heart pounds furiously, threatening to burst from my ribcage. I push down the fear I haven't felt in twelve long years. My jaw tightens as memories flood my mind. He's haunted my nightmares for so long, it's hard to resist the urge to run, flee to safety.

"I do. I remember how you let me bleed almost to death in a corner. I remember you murdered my parents. Now you take my brother from me? Why? What have I ever done to you for you to hate me so much?"

He shakes his head slowly, motioning for me to sit down. I stay where I am, anger starting to slowly chase away the fear.

"Teo, Teo, Teo. Murder? Hardly," he replies, ignoring my last question completely.

"You were just a child then. Are you certain you know the whole story?"

I scoff. "What's your side of it then?"

"Sit, and I'll tell you."

I comply reluctantly, lowering myself onto the cushioned chair, wishing for my gun. I would blow his brains across the fancy walls right here and now if I could, and end it.

"Your father, my brother, was not the hero everyone has made him out to be. No, hear me out. Please. Before you were born, the countries ruled themselves. Frankly, it wasn't working. The world was a mess. War, poverty, famine, crimes against the very nature of people's humanity; it was awful. Russia was…just as bad, if not worse. Our government kidnapped children, forcing them into horrible conditions in the army. I know what you're going to say. How am I any different? It's true. I too take children. But only with their parents consent, and they are well treated, unlike in the old days. Aleksei, your father, was one of the best agents the government had. I tried many times to get him to join me. But he was stubborn, like you, and refused to hear reason. He believed the government was just and fought to restore it. I only want the good of the people. He and his so-called rebels only wanted to rule them. I'm sorry, Teo, but the truth is, I'm not the villain here. Your father was. He was a tyrant bent on destruction, willing to risk even his own family's safety in his quest for glory. Those scars, he gave them to you, not me."

I sit back, absorbing it all. I'd always wondered how Luka had won the world, why people followed him. Truth be told, I'm tempted to believe him myself. He makes it sound so reasonable. Snake Charmer—I've heard him being called in the streets—Velvet Voice, Whisperer of lies, and King of manipulators. I never understood why till now. The trouble comes when the snake doesn't like your voice. Then the spell is broken, and he bites back.

"You know…" I say, choosing my words carefully, "Credit where it's due, you're really very good at this."

He smiles, certain of his victory. I lean forward, eye to eye with the devil himself and give an apologetic shrug.

"Sadly, I'm not buying it. I loved my father very much. Photographic memory, you see. It's more a curse than a gift, usually, but every once in a while, it really comes in handy. It's the first time I'm actually grateful for it. So thanks for that. Now where's my brother?"

Luka's smile doesn't waver. He was expecting me to refuse.

"You really are a lot like him, you know that? Stubborn, unable to be reasoned with. Such a pity. I could have made you great, Teo. I can't say I'm surprised though. Before I go, one question."

"Ask away."

"What would you do if I told you that unless you join me, you'll never see little Nickolai again? Or worse, that I'll kill him?"

I barely manage to keep a lid on my anger.

"My brother is *everything* to me, you bastard. He's one of only two people I have left to care about. If you take him from me, if you hurt him, I will rip out your guts one by one until you beg for mercy. I will come after you, and this time, I'll have nothing to lose. Trust me, that's not something you want to happen. Because I swear on my parent's graves, if you harm so much as a hair on his head, I will make you wish you'd never been born." My voice shakes, but not with fear. I mean every word, and he knows it. Just as he knows I'll hunt him down to my last breath if anything happens to Nicko.

He flicks his wrist suddenly, and two burly soldiers grab me from behind in the blink of an eye. I struggle, but one kicks me in the kneecap, forcing me to the ground at Luka's feet.

"I'm a little disappointed, you know. Even Aleksei would have paused to think twice before opening his big mouth."

He pours himself a cup of steaming coffee, lounging back casually in his chair. I can tell by the look on his face that I'm in serious trouble. The guard shoves my head down none too gently, growling something about my not being worthy to look the great dictator in the eyes.

"I just hope your brother shows a bit more sense. Take him away, men. He'll not see the light of day for a long, long time to come."

CHAPTER 6

I'm half dragged, half carried through passageway after passageway, until I can barely tell them apart anymore. We cross bewil-
dered-looking servants, who turn their heads away the moment
I try to meet their eyes. One of them, a woman better dressed
than the others, looks confused at the sight of me, as though she
knows who I am. She raises a hand timidly to stop the guards'
progress, but they shove her aside unceremoniously, and she falls
hard on the marble floor. I manage a glance back before I'm taken
into a dark corridor. The brutality doesn't seem to have affected
her much as she simply gets up, brushes herself off, and moves on.
I suppose she must be used to it. There were enough bruises on
her face to suggest as much.

Once through a sliding wall, everything gets more dismal as
any trace of luxury disappears. The walls are unadorned, dripping
with mold and damp, the floor is more mud than rough stone. On
any other occasion, I could easily have made a run for it; unfortunately, my crutches are back with Luka.

I'm finally tossed unceremoniously into a dark cell. My head
smacks against the ground, hitting a stone, and I taste blood from
a split lip. I don't have time to rise before a great wooden door is
slammed shut, and I'm left in complete darkness.

It's the first time in my life I feel complete hopelessness. Nicko was always there before to cheer me up, keep me going. Now even he's been taken from me.

"Hello? Is someone else there?"

A soft voice in the darkness. I sit up, pricking my ears. "*Da*. Who are you?"

There's a stifled sob from somewhere to my right. My heart sinks a little as I realize we aren't in the same cell. Still, a fellow prisoner far away is better than none at all. It takes a long time for her to stop crying long enough to talk coherently, despite my attempts to comfort her.

"Sorry. It's...it's been...such a long time...since I've had anyone to talk to. My friend Luka comes by maybe once or twice a year, but he can never stay very long. I sing, sometimes, to not lose my voice. Do you sing?"

She starts sobbing again, this time for no obvious reason. I decide to ignore the fact that she just called him her friend for the sake of calming her down. I'll get to the bottom of it eventually, though I'm not sure I want to. How anyone could think of Luka as friendly is best left a mystery.

Strangely, her voice is vaguely familiar to me. I can't place it though. The only women I interact with are Sophiya and Irena. I edge closer to the bars as she calms.

"Who are you? Why were you locked in here?"

"I don't know! I don't remember!" she wails, voice rising almost to a shriek. I suppose, after being trapped in here too long, you start to lose your sanity a little.

"No, wait. I do know...I know my name! Cassy. I'm Cassy. I'm here because...because I loved Luka's brother." The sobs start up again, even more hysterical this time.

Still I swear my heart skips a few beats, and I forget to breathe for an instant. I choke on my words, never having imagined I'd say them again.

"Mama?"

Sophiya pulled the army cap lower down over her eyes, grateful she hadn't listened to Teo whining about how short her hair was. The uniform had been easier to acquire than the rifle. Luckily, Sammy had been all too willing to lend a hand for both. The big American was a softie beneath all the muscle and had been heartbroken to hear of Nicko's capture. No one doubted it was Luka who'd taken the boys. It was the only possible explanation. Not even Teo's boss, Janek, would have been stupid enough to try and take them. He knew they were under Ivan's protection. She smiled briefly to herself. Had Teo known how much her father had done to guarantee their safety, he would have been furious.

Sophiya pushed through the crowd of listless, bored boy soldiers, praying the uniform was as shapeless as it had seemed in the mirror.

"Hey you, new kid!"

She turned reluctantly as a hand gripped her shoulder.

"I'm squadron leader here. I'm to ask you if you've been to see His Glorious Majesty yet."

She shook her head, stifling a laugh at the pompous title.

"I didn't know I was supposed to."

"New law," he said, handing her a slip of paper, "all new recruits are to submit to an interview and examination. It's to prevent spies and girls from joining. Follow me. I'll take you to his office."

She obeyed, a sick feeling of dread building in her gut. It was said that Luka could not be tricked, that he always knew when he was being lied to. What would happen to her when he found out she wasn't a boy? Or worse, if he figured out who her father was? Likely he would come up with a punishment worse than death. At the same time, Sophiya knew that her best chance of finding the brothers lay in meeting with the enemy.

The soldier led her through the palace, through hall after hall of magnificent tapestries and marble floors, until they reached two imposing golden doors. She raised an eyebrow skeptically at the sight. Luka certainly liked to show off.

"Wait here," the boy told her crisply, knocking twice before turning the handle and going in. Frowning, she bent down for a closer look at the knobs. They were blood-red and glowed in the sunlight streaming in through the windows. Ruby doorknobs in golden doors. This was more than just showing off. He was sending visitors a message. He could do what he liked, when he liked, no matter the cost, and get away with it. Clever madman. Any sane person would have been intimidated. Luckily, she was far too focused on her task to bother being afraid.

"Sophiya? What...what are you doing here?"

She turned, surprised.

"Nicko? Are you escaping? Do you need any help? Where's Teo? I was looking for the two of you, though mostly Teo now, I suppose."

Her words echoed hollowly, and she was suddenly uncertain what to think. He was clean, well dressed in a white- and gold-braided uniform. He didn't look frightened, or panicked, or in any way as though he were on the run. Nor did he seem particularly happy to see her. Nicko bit his lip and avoided her accusing gaze, focusing on his black shoes instead as he spoke.

"You shouldn't be here. Teo's gone. It's no use looking for him. Go home while you still can, Sophiya."

"Nicko...did you join with Luka? Is that what all this is about? Where's Teo? What happened?"

The boy took a deep breath. "Yes. I joined. Not at first, but eventually I saw reason. Teo didn't. He's dead now. Even if I didn't believe Luka's story, which I do, where else would I go? There's nothing for me out there without my brother. Besides, Luka is family. He's my uncle."

She stared at him in horror, unable to bring herself to believe what she was hearing.

"No! Stop this! I'm not falling for it! Teo's alive. I know he is. This isn't you. You're not this gullible. Your family gave their lives so you could be free. You would never betray that. Whatever is going on, I'm going to find out, and I'm going to get you both out of here."

Nicko's face remained impassive, his normally bright green eyes dull and cold.

"Don't bother. You'll just get caught for no reason. I saw my brother die. He was stubborn and wouldn't adapt. I would rather live."

Sophiya shook her head.

"You'd better be lying. Otherwise, I swear I'll kill you myself."

At that moment, the door opened, and the squadron leader reappeared, followed by a small blonde girl in a blindingly pink, frilly dress.

"Luka will see you now," he stated as the child swept past, a smug look on her angelic face. Nicko sighed.

"That's Anya. Luka's daughter. She can't stand her own mother or the nanny, so I'm supposed to be her new playmate. I don't like it, but it's not like there's much of a choice. Please. Give up. Don't come back."

Without waiting for her to answer, he turned and followed the child, leaving Sophiya to face Luka alone, but not before she'd seen the deep pain his gaze.

CHAPTER 7

Nickolai was miserable. He'd half lied to Sophiya when he'd explained his behavior. Teo was dead, executed while he was forced to watch from afar, but he did not believe Luka's story about his family. Pretending to be loyal was the only way he could get close enough to slip a dagger between his enemy's ribs or drop poison in his golden cup. His brother would be avenged, come what may. At least the little girl was no threat. All she did all day was play with expensive toys and order slaves around while hanging onto her father's every word. He'd met her mother briefly and did not wish to renew the experience. Katya was a broken creature. She crept from room to room, silent, ready to cower. Nicko was surprised she'd survived this long. What would happen to the little girl when Luka was brought down? Would she be just another abandoned child in the streets? At least she wouldn't be alone. Luka had torn apart a great many families with his stupid war.

Frustrated, he kicked at a pillar, stubbing his toe. The curses that erupted from his mouth would have made his big brother proud.

"You shouldn't swear in front of ladies," a pompous little voice scolded from behind him. How he hated her smug indifference, her superior glances, and worse, her passionate love of creepy dolls.

"When I see one, I'll be sure to be careful of my language."

She frowned, uncertain whether or not he was insulting her. Sarcasm, due to the servants' fear of her, still eluded her grasp.

"Come play with me," she ordered, letting the matter go before it made her think too hard.

"I just did. Leave me alone!"

Anya stamped her foot angrily. "If you don't obey, my papa will have you whipped, slave!"

"I'm not a slave, I'm your cousin. Where's your nanny? Go play with her for once. Or go torture your mother. You like *that*, don't you?"

"I hate my nanny. And Mother is in the garden again. She's never very interesting to play with anyway. Besides, Papa agrees that I'm getting too old to be forced to hang around adults all the time, especially nannies."

She tossed a blonde braid over her shoulder importantly and gripped his arm.

"Someday, I'll rule this place. A future queen doesn't need mothers or nannies, or even fathers, though mine is a particularly fine and handsome one. As your future queen, I order you to come play with me."

Nicko rolled his eyes, swearing under his breath. The brat was really getting on his nerves. "Fine. I'll play with you a few minutes if you promise to leave me alone for the rest of the day. "Deal?"

"Okay."

She led him to her room, satisfied for the moment.

For over an hour Nicko indulged her whims, until he felt ready to burst from an acute lack of patience. Then something happened that changed the way he saw the flowery, overdramatic little girl.

Anastasiya got frustrated with one of her dolls. A strange look came over her face as she grew suddenly very calm.

Without a word, she skipped over to her closet and pulled out a strange contraption.

"What is that?" he asked as she placed the doll's head in a small hole. Anya didn't answer. Instead, she tugged on a rope and stood back. Nicko jumped as the blade fell with a swish, slicing the luckless toy's head off neatly. She grinned, pacified.

"That's better. Can't have insubordinates going unpunished."

"Insubordinates? The thing wasn't even alive! What is *wrong* with you?"

Her lips pressed into a pout.

"My papa made it for me. He says it's good practice."

"Do you disagree with my methods, Nickolai?"

Nicko turned to face Luka, harsh words dying on his tongue instantly. He hung his head, faking remorse.

"No, sir. It just took me by surprise. I'm used to violence from the streets, but not from such young children."

The dictator almost allowed himself a smile.

"Children have the greatest potential for cruelty. That's why I choose my soldiers young. They don't have any of the barriers adults carry for the sake of propriety."

A shiver crept up the boy's spine. Clever madman. Get them small so they trust you no matter how badly they get hurt. Teo had been very young when he'd been given his scars. It had hardened him. But Teo was gone now. It was up to him to be strong.

"That's very smart, sir. I'll be sure to remember it." He forced himself to say it, not looking up in case the enemy saw the loathing in his eyes. Luka frowned, not fooled. Anya, running to stand next to her father, imitated his stance and manner perfectly.

"Something wrong?"

Nicko could not stop the tears from falling this time. "I just— I…I miss…my brother, sir. I w—I wish…he were here."

How he hated admitting weakness to his enemy, hated the childish hiccups that escaped him.

"Anya, give us a moment of privacy, please, *dorogaya.*"

She obeyed instantly and without question, shutting the door quietly behind her. There was a pause, then Luka tilted his nephew's chin up so they were eye to eye.

"It's all right to miss loved ones when they've gone," he said gently, placing a hand on the boy's shoulder. "But we must not allow grief to interfere with our duties. Teo, God rest him, died because he let your father's death rule his life. In a way, he was already dead to the world. It was merciful, what I did. He was suffering a great deal inside. In any case, it had to be done. Do you understand what I'm trying to say?"

Rage and hatred such as he'd never known filled Nicko's soul, cool and refreshing, clearing his mind of anything but the icy feel of anger's grip. Luka would die by his hand, and no one else's. He would make it his life's goal.

Miraculously, he kept his face blank of emotion. "I understand, Uncle. And I promise I am trying. I loved him very much, and I'm saddened he couldn't see reason."

With the words came a coldness unfamiliar to him. A killer's heart was growing within him, ruthless, vengeful. Already, Nickolai could feel himself changing, growing. No longer a mouse, but a cat.

———

Luka is good at making people suffer. I can hear my mother, I can speak to her, but I can't see or touch her. It's torture for me as much as I know it is for her. Mama's pain is probably even greater, despite the madness of her mind. For twelve years she's been trapped here, far from her family, not knowing whether we were alive or dead. I had to tell her about Papa, which wasn't easy. She cried for hours, and even after that it was hard to get much sense from her.

I thought, at first, we would see light when they brought us food. Luka made sure the system was foolproof though, and bowls of cold mush are shoved in through a contraption that allows not the slightest sliver of light to enter.

"What about Nicko? You haven't mentioned him. Why?" she asks suddenly in a moment of lucidity. I've been dreading the question.

"I don't know. I haven't seen him since we were taken. He's not very much bigger than the last time you saw him. I call him mouse. Took me awhile to grow too. He'll get there, eventually if…" I break off, not wanting to say it aloud.

"If he's still alive?" she lets out a harsh, barking laugh that makes my skin crawl.

"Don't shield me, Teo. I'm no weakling child. My entire family, including my husband, was murdered. I'm used to death."

"But I'm not," I whisper, more to myself than to her. I can barely stand the thought of losing my brother. We've been through so much together, I don't want to think that this might be our last adventure.

Eventually, I drift off. My dreams are a strange mix of memory and fiction and when I wake a little while later, it's hard to tell the difference between the two.

Night and day blend into one. I lose track of how long I've been here. My mother and I don't talk much. Every time I try to start a conversation about what's been going on in the world or about the past, she breaks into hysterics or yells at me not to treat her like a child. It's better, in a way, that she stay within her own dream world. I don't want to have to tell her about the misery of the streets, about the piles of garbage we found our food in, or the dampness of the alleys we slept in.

The door opens suddenly, flooding us with light. I shrink back, blinded after days of complete darkness. When I'm able to open my eyes, I half I wish I hadn't. Luka is standing in front of me, grinning.

"How are you enjoying your new home? Comfortable?"

I force myself to return his smile. "Very. I appreciate the company as well."

"Oh, still not dead, is she? We may have to remedy that and put the poor creature out of her deranged misery. She's lived for far too long already."

I let my gaze wander discreetly, trying to find my mother. Unfortunately, she's curled herself into a corner, as far from us as possible, so I can't see her face.

"Why didn't you? I mean, why keep her locked up? She's of no use to you without my father." The words slip out before I can stop them. Luka ponders the question a second.

"Well…I do like to have trophies to remind me of my victories. Besides, killing would be the merciful thing to do. I wasn't feeling very generous at the time. I'm still not. In any case, I'm not here to talk about her. I'm here to report a great victory."

My blood runs cold. *Please not Nicko, please, please don't be about Nicko.*

"Your little brother has shown far more common sense than you. He's rethought his loyalties and joined me. Isn't that wonderful news? You must be so proud!"

I feel sick, like I'm about to pass out or throw up, or both. A punch to the stomach would have hurt less. He's lying. He has to be. Nicko's smarter than that. He wouldn't. He couldn't. *Not my brother, oh God, don't let him have turned my brother*, I pray.

"Liar!" I croak, fighting down panic. His grin widens triumphantly, gloating.

"Am I? You've called me that before. It's not very polite."

"Let me see him. I want to talk to him! He would never join you. He's better than that. I raised him to be better!"

If I could stand up and reach through the bars to strangle my enemy, I would without hesitation. I hate my ankle for holding me back, hate not being able to move as I please.

Luka smirks, running a finger casually across the bars, obviously doing his best to infuriate me. It works too.

"And have you change his mind? No, I don't think so. At first I wasn't sure he'd really seen reason. Likely, little Nickolai wasn't certain of his loyalties either. But now… well…let's just say I trust him. You *did* raise him well. He speaks highly of you."

I don't believe it. I won't. He's a master of lies. Why would he tell me the truth now? Unless…unless he knew truth would cause more pain than lies. I have to see Nicko. I have to find some way to talk to him, make him see what he's really gotten himself into.

"Let me see my brother. Please. I want to hear it from him. I don't trust you."

Luka shakes his head, wagging a finger mockingly. I hate him like I've never hated anyone before, not even Janek when he beat me.

"I'm afraid I can't allow it, Teo. See, he's still very fragile in his faith. Perhaps I'll let him visit you in a few years, when he's stronger."

My hand grips at the dirt on the ground. If only I had a rock or something to throw. For once, my prayers are answered. I clench the stone tightly, talking all the while to distract him.

"He's probably lying to you, you know. Nicko's good at that. Even had me fooled a couple times. I know him. He'd die before he betrayed his family and friends."

"Nobody lies to me! I always know. Your brother is just a child, alone and friendless in a cold world. He needed someone to turn to, someone to be there for him, and I happened to be there, unlike you. The boy needs guidance. A father figure."

I struggle to my feet, ignoring the pain my ankle gives me. Rage is stronger. "He has me!" I hiss, hurling the rock at his face as hard as I can. My aim flies true, sailing between the bars with perfect accuracy. It smacks his nose with a sickeningly satisfying crunch, and his hands fly up to stem the sudden flow of blood.

"You…you little—"

I don't let him finish his sentence, grabbing his collar and forcing him to look me in the eyes.

"I. Want. My. Brother!" I snarl, pulling back so his forehead smashes against the bars. He recovers much faster than expected, drawing his gun and pressing it against my temple. I let go, feigning defeat. Before he can draw back, I strike his wrist as hard as I can, forcing him to drop the gun. Cursing, Luka stomps his foot hard on my broken ankle, making me howl in pain as I lose my balance and fall to the floor, grimacing. Quick as a flash, his uninjured hand snakes through the bars to take back the weapon. Breathing hard, he wipes away the blood dripping down his chin.

"You will rot here for the rest of your miserable life, I swear to it. Nickolai is mine. In another month, he'll have forgotten he ever even had a brother."

He takes a step back, as though about to leave, then changes his mind.

"Guards!" he shouts, "Give this pathetic vermin the whipping he deserves. Teach him to respect those better than he."

Luka watches as I'm dragged upright, my wrists chained to the ceiling so my feet dangle a few inches off the ground. It hurts terribly, but I manage not to give him the satisfaction of seeing it.

One of the guards tears off my shirt, leaving me shivering in the cold air. Discomfort stops mattering the instant the first stroke of the whip rips through my flesh. I have to bite my tongue bloody to keep from screaming. All the while, Luka simply watches, grinning more broadly as each lash falls, stripping the skin from my back. By the fifth blow, I'm close to passing out. By the seventh, blissful darkness envelopes me, blocking out the hated face.

I'm brought back rather brutally with a bucket of ice cold water in my face and a kick from Luka. They've let me down, but my arms still burn like hell itself.

He bends halfway to whisper in my ear.

"If you defy me again, it won't be you hanging from the ceiling, and I'll make you listen to his pitiful little shrieks while you stand, helpless, unable to comfort him."

Then he's gone, the door slamming shut behind him.

CHAPTER 8

Nicko ducked back into the shadows as Luka and his henchmen swept past. There was blood on the enemy's face and on the bottom of his pants. He looked angrier than the boy had seen him be in the two weeks he'd been spying. Cautiously, checking that the coast was clear, Nicko inched his way forward, pushing against the wall the same way he'd seen Luka doing. It slid open easily enough, and he found himself in a dimly lit corridor. He flinched as his hand accidentally brushed against the damp, mold-covered wall. Grimacing in disgust, he wiped it on his pants, walking slowly forward. The whole place creeped him out. On the bright side, he'd managed to get away from Anya for the time being. In the last few days, her father had been too busy to afford her much attention, and doll heads hadn't been the only things flying. The girl had certainly learned from Luka how to throw an impressive tantrum. He had bruises from her surprisingly strong punches.

The wooden door was heavy to push, but Nicko had been training hard in preparation for killing Luka, and he managed it better than he might have a few months previously. Beyond, there was only darkness. He'd been stupid not to bring a flashlight.

Everything had happened so fast, he hadn't had time to think before throwing caution to the winds and tailing after Luka.

Pushing the door open wider, he could make out rows of what, at first glance, seemed to be cages. Hope rose in him. Could Teo be alive after all? Had it all been a trick, born of the dictator's twisted mind? In any case, it was at least worth a look.

"Teo?" he called softly, hardly daring to hope for an answer.

"Nickolai?"

Disappointment filled his heart. It was a woman's voice.

"How do you know my name?"

"I'm…I'm your mother, Nicko. I'm your mama."

He scowled, instantly suspicious.

"No, you're not. My mother's dead. Teo told me so. Why should I trust you?"

"I need your help. Please. Teo's hurt. He won't answer when I talk to him. Luka hurt him. I couldn't do anything to help, and now he won't talk to me."

Nicko almost forgot to breathe. He'd been right. His brother was alive.

"Where is he?"

The woman was crying now, her sobs shrill and slightly hysterical.

"I just got him back! I just got my baby back, and Luka wants to take him from me! It's not fair! It's not fair!"

He was seriously starting to doubt her sanity, but a small chance was better than nothing.

"I can help. Really. But you have to tell me where he is."

She stopped crying abruptly. The boy leapt back, terrified, as a nightmarish face appeared, pressing itself against the bars and into the light. Her cheeks were sunken, hollow, her eyes abnormally wide, and completely white, blind from searching the darkness for so long. What must once have been long, beautiful red hair was gray in areas, thinned and stringy. Her clothes hung from her skeletal body in filthy rags.

"You're with him!" she hissed, baring her teeth in a snarl.

"You're with the enemy!"

Nicko back away so quickly he tripped over his own feet, falling backward.

"No! I'm not with Luka! I swear! I just wanna find my brother, if he's alive."

"He's dead! He's dead, and it's all your fault!"

The boy fled, fear and adrenaline fueling him to run faster than he ever had before. Her screams of "Traitor!" followed him a long time, long after everything had gone quiet. There was no way a monster like that was his mother.

Sleep eluded him that night. Each time he shut his eyes, he saw her face again, horrifying, more terrible than any nightmare. In the end, he gave up, swinging his legs over the side of the tall four-poster. There was only one person left in all of Russia who could help him now. He just prayed she really hadn't bought into the lie.

———

Sergei listened with rapt attention to another of Luka's speeches on the glory still to come. Even as a child, he'd loved to simply stand by and let the words wash over him. On the outside, he tried to appear patient, attentive—the way he knew Luka wanted him to be. Inside, he was boiling with impatience. There were still pockets of growing resistance all over the world. He was eighteen now and felt that his master was not making full use of his potential. But of course, Luka knew best. He always did. From the very beginning, he'd led them to victory time and again, even when Sergei was uncertain of the plan. The boy had never questioned his master. He'd taught the other children to follow in his footsteps, trusting their lives over to the Cause completely. Deep down, he was sure Luka must be proud of him, even if he couldn't show it. The master treated him more kindly than he did the other soldiers, more like his own child than a slave to be used and disposed of quickly. Lately, things had been slow though.

There'd been no activity from Ivan or the rebels, and no one to crush or intimidate. He was growing restless, like a dog too long tied to a leash.

"Are you listening to me?"

Sergei snapped to attention.

"Of course, master. Always. You know I enjoy your speeches. I've been inactive too long, that's all. I'm eager to go on a new mission, as are the others."

Luka smiled benevolently. "I understand. I was young, once, believe it or not. It's difficult to restrain one's zeal. But you must be patient. Your time will come very soon now, I promise. In a few weeks, the American rebellion will be ripe to be crushed. I have men working on it now. Then you and the young ones will accompany me to help speed their destruction. For now, rest. Train. Let the little Shadows know what is expected of them."

Sergei returned the smile, relieved. Knowing action was coming soon made the wait easier. He could spend the time planning. "Yes, master. I look forward to it."

At a wave from Luka's hand, he slipped gratefully into the blessed darkness of the hallway. Electric lights were a curse on humanity. If he could have, he would have convinced Luka to have them banned.

The soft sound of hushed whisperings made him pause. Someone was up to no good.

Creeping as silently as the shadow whose name he'd stolen, he drew closer.

There were four of them, arguing heatedly about something. A small, red-haired boy he knew to be Luka's nephew, a girl clearly trying to pass herself off as a soldier, and two men, one average-looking, the other a hulking tower of muscle. They reached a decision suddenly, and the boy moved forward, pressing his hands against the wall. It slid open soundlessly, as Sergei had known it would, and the group vanished inside.

His curiosity aroused, he followed them. Of course, each had a flashlight to guide their blind, groping way in the dark. He cursed them silently. The brightness hurt his sensitive eyes, diminishing considerably his ability to see in the dark. Worse still came when one of them flipped a light switch, flooding the tunnel with artificial light. Sergei was forced to hang back as the muscle-mountain pushed open a huge wooden door. For once, even the custom-made sunglasses, designed specially to correct his weakness, didn't help. He let out a low hiss of dissatisfaction, looking forward to the moment he'd turn them in to his master for punishment.

Then the shouts started. A woman was yelling something about traitors.

"Stop it, Cassy! It's me. It's Ivan, remember? I'm not going to hurt you. We've come to free you and Teo. Don't you want to come?" one of them shouted at her above the noise. Her screeches faded, replaced by whimpers. There were two loud bangs, like doors being torn from their hinges. Then, silence.

Sergei ducked back as the group started through the tunnel once more. The strong man carried in his arms the small boy's brother, the one the shadows had captured only weeks before. He didn't look very alive, hanging limply, like one of Elena—number Four's—rag dolls. Behind them, the nephew and the girl, both obviously distressed by the injured one's condition. Lastly, the normal man, leading a scary-looking woman. She was clinging desperately to his arm as though if she let go, she might fall.

Sergei realized suddenly that it was because she was blind. What could the master have wanted with such a woman? Why hadn't he said anything about it? As his bodyguard, it was his right to know.

They passed by without seeing the Shadow leader, too intent on getting out. He kept trailing after them, knowing he should raise the alarm, yet more curious to know what they were up to.

Besides, there was no time to call his team. He would have to follow on his own.

"It's this way," Luka's nephew whispered, leading his friends through the maze of corridors.

As they reached their exit, the kitchen back door, trouble arose. Shocked by the sudden feel of fresh air, the blind woman refused to go further.

"Don't wanna go," she moaned, dropping to the floor and curling into a fetal position, rocking back and forth.

"Cassy, come on. Don't do this. We have to get everyone to safety. It's going to be all right, but we've gotta go now."

"No, no, no, no, no, no," she whimpered, blocking her ears and shaking her head. "I want Aleksei. I want him, and I'm not leaving without him."

Despite Ivan's attempts to reason with her, she remained stubbornly uncooperative. The strong man was visibly worried. Time was ticking. The servants would be active soon.

"Ivan, we can't stay. It'll be light soon. People are going to see us."

"I know!" he snapped. "But I can't just leave her here either. I made a promise, and I intend to keep it."

Sergei heard the distress in his voice and smiled. They would still be there by the time he raised the alarm, and his master would be pleased at the capture. A slight movement caught his eye, stopping him. A woman stepped forward shyly. He recognized her instantly, and a shiver of disgust crept up his spine.

The girl, reacting quickly, drew her gun. The man called Ivan stopped her, an incredulous, slightly baffled look on his face. He seemed unable to tear his eyes away from the sight of the beaten little creature.

"It's all right. She's a friend. Come here, Katya. We're not going to hurt you, I promise."

Relieved, she gave the first real smile Sergei had ever seen on her face. Trembling slightly, she took a few steps forward, scribbling something on a small piece of paper, as was her habit when Luka allowed her to communicate. Ivan read it quickly, and then nodded.

"I would be grateful for your help. And don't worry. I won't abandon you again."

Katya crouched in front of the blind woman, brushing her stringy hair with gentle fingers and radiating such kindness; instantly, the other calmed, taking her hand hesitantly, allowing herself to be led outside. Luka's nephew's jaw dropped in surprise.

"What did she do?"

Ivan shrugged, grinning.

"I don't know, but it worked."

Sergei stared in growing loathing and astonishment as they calmly exited, no one stopping them, no one noticing them. He had to go warn Luka before it was too late. His master would have a plan to get them back. He always did.

CHAPTER 9

The first time I wake, someone is setting me down gently on a soft bed. Everything is a blur, and I barely have the strength to keep my eyes open, let alone say anything. I feel safe though, as if deep down something in me knows I'll be cared for. It makes it easier to let the darkness win me over again.

The second time, I catch fragments of whispered conversation, including a familiar voice. Nicko. *What's he doing here? Where am I?* My brain is able to ask the questions, but the rest of me is too weak to take action. After that, I lose track of how many times I come and go. All I know is that I get a little stronger as the days or weeks or years pass. An eternity goes by, in which all I can do is lay there and heal. For once, being bedridden doesn't affect me too badly. Everything hurts too much.

Surprisingly, the final waking up is the hardest. I have trouble seeing straight. All I can hear is soft snoring nearby. Smiling to myself, I ruffle my little brother's red hair weakly, rousing him. He raises his head sleepily from where he'd dropped off next to me on the mattress, taking a second to realize who woke him up.

"Hey *mysh'*," I whisper, grinning at the look on his face. He bursts into tears, wrapping his arms around my neck.

"Luka-killed-you-so-I   pretended-to-join-him-and…then-I-followed him-and…Cassy was really, really scary, and you weren't dead-and…Katya-calmed-her down-and-Sophiya-she-dressed-as…a boy-and-you…you wouldn't wake up—" he sobs, hiccupping.

"Slow down, kid. Breathe, okay?" I order weakly, my head pounding from trying to keep up with him. He nods but can't seem to obey. His eyes are so red, I figure it's not the first time he hasn't been able to calm down. So I just hold him awhile, stroking his head reassuringly, neither of us saying a word.

Little by little, as he quiets, the whole story starts to come out more clearly. I may hate Luka with all my being, but he does deserve credit for his scheme. It was genius, in a particularly twisted way, to kill off some poor sap in my place, making Nicko believe it really was me. But my brother was clever too, much more so than I was. Instead of blowing up and telling Luka what he thought of him, like I did, he went along with it, fooling even the master of lies himself. I kiss the top of his head fondly.

"You did good, kid. I'm proud of you."

He looks up in surprise, his nose runny, cheeks tear-stained. "You're…not mad?"

"Why would I be? You just did the bravest thing I've ever heard. Even better, you stayed alive."

"But I betrayed you, I cooperated with him."

"There's a difference between turning traitor and pretending to, believe it or not. Especially when you knew he had the power to kill you at any moment. In a relatively sane world, that's called bravery, not betrayal."

His eyes fill up again, and he rubs a hand savagely across his face, trying to hide it from me.

"Cassy…*she* won't believe me. She keeps calling me a traitor and a cry-baby. I hate her." He hiccups, sniffling.

"Twelve years is a long time, Nicko. It's not surprising she's lost it a little. We'll just have to be patient with her, okay? She's still our mama."

My strength, though far from fully restored, is coming back quickly.

"I guess. I mean, there are moments when she's sort of okay, but most of the time, she's either yelling at me or sitting in a corner mumbling to herself. She sings when the mood strikes. Are you sure she's our real mother?"

I shrug. "What does Ivan say about it?"

A pained grimace contorts his face. "Same as you. That we gotta be patient."

I lie back with a sigh, thinking. "How long was I out?" I ask finally, not sure I want to know the answer. Nicko shrugs, hanging his head and shuffling his feet, mumbling.

"How long?" I say again, more firmly. He doesn't look up.

"Two...about..."

"Two what? Days?"

"Weeks. Would've been three if you hadn't come around in another couple days. We were all really worried about you. Except Ivan. He's too busy trying to keep Cassy from jumping off the roof. She tried that once. It didn't end well. Sophiya pretended she wasn't scared you wouldn't wake up, but even Sammy caught her in here a couple times, crying and trying to get you to talk to her."

"Who's Sammy?"

He blinks in surprise, confused for a moment before remembering how hard I worked to stay away from anything that had to do with Ivan's rebellion.

"He's an American, a good friend of Papa's. He carried you here. Katya seems to really like him. She was Luka's wife before we rescued her. She's mute because Luka cut her vocal chords, but she writes a lot when she's got something to say."

I make a vague attempt to listen to his ramblings before interrupting. Something weighs heavily on my mind, and I'd rather get it over with.

"Nicko, would you mind asking Ivan to come? I need to talk to him."

It's clear to me now that no matter how much time passes, Luka will never give up coming after this family, not until we're all either dead or insane like my mother, kept in cages as trophies for His Majesty's entertainment. Something has to be done. I just hope I didn't realize it too late. Nicko nods, understanding. He probably had the same conversation months, even years, ago.

My brother scurries out of the room, shutting the door quietly behind him. In the brief pause that follows, I'm able to take in my surroundings. They're really not that different from every other slum house, except maybe for the size and the fact that there are other rooms beyond this one. The bed too is considerably more comfortable. The stillness of the place almost lulls me back to sleep. Before I can nod off, my mother appears suddenly, making me jump. It comes as a shock to me that she's blind and looks even more unstable than I'd imagined. No wonder Nicko got nightmares.

She sways slightly as she stands at the foot of the bed, seeming more ghost than human.

"Have you seen him?" she asks softly, her face sad.

"Seen…who?"

"He's gone. Luka told me. You told me. But I still hope. The others, they think I'm crazy. I'm not, you know. Luka didn't break me. Not like he broke your brother. It makes me so sad. Your father would be so disappointed."

She sounds almost rational for an instant. Then it's gone as she turns to leave, humming to herself, hugging the wall.

"He'll come for me, you know. He always does," she says with a little smile, before pulling the door shut behind her. A minute later, the shouting starts. The words are muffled, but it's obvious who she's crying for. It hits me then. I haven't gotten my mother back at all. The woman she was died in the battle that took almost everything from me. If not for Nicko, I would have died too. It's a depressing thought, and I do my best to shake it off. Luckily, Ivan comes in just then, distracting my attention. I try to sit up, but he motions for me to lie back down. Pulling up a chair, he sits, thoughtful for a moment before speaking.

"I take it you want revenge?"

I shake my head. "No. Justice. Not just for me, but for everyone he's wronged. On the streets, all of my friends are orphans because of him. I starved, stole, and slept in gutters with dozens of other kids because Luka massacred their families on a whim. It has to stop."

"What changed your mind?"

"It was never really personal before, even with my parents dead. I thought I could stay out of it, and he'd leave us alone. He brought me into the fight when he tried to separate me from my brother."

Ivan grins, pleased with my answer.

"I was hoping you'd say something like that. I know exactly where to put you. For now, rest. Don't die on me, all right? That's my first order to you."

I wince as he gives my shoulder an overfriendly slap. As he gets up to leave, I call after him.

"So does this mean I can date Sophiya openly now?"

He laughs. "No."

The door slams shut behind him. After awhile, I drift back to sleep, suddenly exhausted.

CHAPTER 10

Being woken by your girlfriend kissing you is decidedly more pleasant than coming out of a coma with a raging headache. I grin, not bothering to open my eyes.

"You miss me, *dorogaya?*" I whisper. She smacks me across the head playfully, jerking me awake.

"I was only worried I'd have a dead body to get rid of," she teases, kneeling next to the low bed, head on her hands. My laugh turns quickly into a cough. Despite resting, I'm still weak. Sophiya, her smile turning into a worried frown, hands me a glass of water.

"I'm fine," I tell her, after draining the cup. "Stop looking so anxious. You should be more worried about your father coming in than my health."

"Still not reconciled? I would have thought, with you suddenly wanting to fight, you'd be the new favorite."

"Doesn't mean he wants me dating you."

She giggles, happier than I've seen her in a long time. I grow serious for a moment.

"Nicko told me what you did to try and get me back. It was pretty brave. Thanks." I take her hand in mine. She shrugs, going bright red.

"You would've done the same for me. I love you, Teo. I wasn't going to let Luka have you."

"I love you too," I whisper, pulling her in for another kiss. Nicko, of course, chooses that instant to come in.

"Ew," he complains, grimacing. "Ivan's gonna kill you if he finds out."

As usual, I ignore him. "Help me up instead of standing there like an idiot. I'm sick of not being able to walk," I say, pretending not to hear their protests. To my horror, my legs won't respond. My whole body feels heavy, numb. Catching the look in Sophiya's eyes, suspicion rises in me.

"What did you do?" I ask, fighting hard not to sleep again. She grins.

"Only thinking ahead, in case you proved to be an idiot and tried to get up."

The water.

"You...you—"

I can't get my thoughts together. Everything goes fuzzy, blurred.

"You..." I try again. Sophiya plants a kiss on my cheek, ruffling my hair while I can't fight her off.

"I know, I know. I'm a terrible person. Poor baby." She says mockingly, grin widening. "But I love you," she adds in a sing-song voice.

"Nicko—"

"Came up with the idea. I guess you could say he knows you well enough by now."

My indignation is beyond words. All I can do is open and shut my mouth, lost for words. That they would stoop so low as to drug me when I've barely woken from a two-week coma is making me angrier by the minute. Unfortunately, I can't protest as it's already taking effect. I'll get them back for this, if it's the last thing I do.

———

Sophiya shut the door behind her, humming to herself. It was a rare occurrence for someone to get the upper hand on Teo. True, the sleeping draft's effect wouldn't last very long, but it was enough, hopefully, to keep him drowsy for some time. At least he was safe for now, not only from those who might do him harm, but from himself as well.

As she walked down the narrow hall, closely followed by Nicko, her gaze strayed to the window, attention caught by a flurry of movement outside. Fear flooded her veins.

"Nicko! Go back! Go back to Teo! There's a gun under the windowsill. Use it if you have to!" she hissed, shoving him toward the door. He was about to protest when he too saw the sleek black car parked outside. The sound of a gunshot from the front of the house sped them into action.

Sophiya burst into the kitchen, ready for a fight. Her mother was crying softly, holding her father's head in her arms. There was blood pooling on the floor around him. Before she could reach for a weapon, someone grabbed her from behind.

Luka ignored the girl's shriek of pain as he twisted her arm behind her back.

"I will find them, whether you cooperate or not. It's your choice, really, to keep your limbs whole or broken," he hissed in her ear, his breath hot on her neck. She didn't bother trying to pretend she didn't know what he was talking about.

"I would rather die than give them away!"

He gave a low chuckle. "That, too, can be arranged." Shoving her away, he turned to the hooded figure behind him.

"Well done, Sergei. Find the boys and I'll hold my end of the bargain."

The boy gave an eerie grin. "Gladly, sir. My crew will have them for you in a few minutes."

To her credit, Sophiya did not cry, though her arm blazed with acute pain. Instead, she kept an eye on her mother, counting each of her father's frail breaths as they got shallower, less visible. She thanked God silently that Katya and Sammy hadn't been home. They were out, supposedly shopping for food in the black market. As they went nearly every day, rarely bringing anything back, Sophiya suspected something of a different nature had grown between the two. Even so, she'd said nothing aloud.

Taking advantage of Luka's distraction, she ran to her father's side, landing a quick kiss on his forehead.

"Please don't die, Papa," she whispered. Without him, all organized resistance to the tyrant's reign would vanish. He was the last of a first generation of fighters. The last of those who'd fought side by side with the legendary Aleksei, save for her mother. She felt no fear as Luka raised his gun, aiming at her head, only anger and a will to live, stronger than anything she'd ever felt before.

"Don't fret, little girl. When I'm done with you, I'll send your boyfriend and his brother your way, so you'll have plenty of company in hell."

Sophiya got slowly to her feet, eyes alight with fury.

"Go ahead. Shoot me. But you'll never get Teo. Whether when I die I'll go up or down, I don't know. But believe me, hell would be *nothing* compared to what will happen to you if you pull that trigger. Teo is a hundred times his father's son, and he'll make you pay dearly."

Luka gave a maniacal grin. "Nice speech. Noble last words, as they say. Better than my brother's anyway. He wasted his last breath begging me not to go after his family. Then again, he never really was very smart, despite what everyone said."

Before the girl could form a reply, Sergei reappeared.

"We found them. The older one isn't conscious, and the small one thinks he's some sort of hero, waving a gun around. The others are keeping them pinned down."

His expression was difficult to read behind his dark shades, but to Sophiya, he looked almost disappointed at the ease with which his objective had been accomplished.

Lightning fast, Luka whipped out his hand, grabbing a fistful of the girl's short hair. She shrieked as he dragged her forward.

"Maybe I'll wait a moment longer then, just so you can watch me take my vengeance," he mused cheerfully, his breath hot on her face as she struggled to free herself.

"Lead the way," he ordered Sergei, at the same time keeping her neck in a firm grip with the crook of his elbow.

The whole way down the hall, she prayed silently that the Shadow was wrong or leading Luka into a trap or that some miracle would happen. But heaven stayed silent, and in another minute Teo was opening his eyes to the barrel of a gun pointed at her head. Nicko too had been made prisoner all too quickly.

It took Teo a second to realize what was happening. A look of panic flickered across his face, and he struggled to sit up, fighting to get enough breath into his lungs to say something. Luka did not give him time.

"Good evening, nephew. I trust you've had a restful few weeks? I certainly have, planning this little reunion."

"Don't—" Sophiya cried, trying to warn him. Her captor clamped a free hand over her mouth, holding her jaw shut so she couldn't bite.

"Pay the girl no mind. This is a friendly visit. In fact, we're going to play a game."

He made a vague attempt at what was obviously meant to be a cheerful smile.

Teo took a deep breath. "Let them go. I'm the one you want. They've got nothing to do with it." He tried, knowing full well it wouldn't work.

Luka shook his head, the insane grin returning. "No, no! You're not playing right. I have to tell you the rules first."

He paused for effect, waiting for his victim to answer.

"Fine. Tell me so we can get this over with."

"You're going to pick a number—one, two, three, or four. You, the little liar over there, and your girlfriend are all one of those. Pick the correct number, and I let them go, killing only you. Any of the other three, and they die with you. Choose your own, and I'll make them shoot each other. Before killing you, of course."

"So...no matter what...I die?"

"*Da.* It's no fun otherwise. Ready? You have three minutes."

He pressed a button on his watch. "Personally, I hope you pick yours. It would liven things up nicely." He gave a gleeful giggle, like a toddler discovering an unexpected present on Christmas morning.

Teo's mind was racing, trying to find a way out of the madness.

"Two minutes and forty-five seconds."

He was good at plans. Something would come to mind. It had to.

"Two minutes. Tick-tock, nephew. I'm losing patience."

He shut his eyes tightly, thinking, thinking. Why was his brain suddenly so useless?

"One minute, thirty seconds."

Nicko whimpered.

"One minute. Better hurry."

There was note of childish disappointment in Luka's voice.

"Stop. Stop it! Leave them alone!" Teo shouted suddenly, hating how helpless he felt. He struggled unsteadily to his feet, Sophiya's drug still making him dizzy. One of the Shadows, the girl, had him back on his knees in the blink of an eye.

"Twenty seconds."

There was no way out this time. No plan. No rescue. Wouldn't it be better to all die at the same time? It was all over anyway. Luka had won the final round, as he'd always known he would.

"Ten..."

"Three."

"N-what's that?"

"I played. Now let them go."

Luka laughed, long and low, a true villain's elated chuckle.

"My poor, naïve nephew. Didn't you hear the rules? To free them, you would've had to pick correctly. And you didn't. Say good-bye to your girlfriend."

Sophiya was calm as she heard the gun being cocked. He'd let her go in order to get a better aim. She dropped to her knees, pressing her forehead to Teo's.

"I'm sorry, Sophi. I tried. I'm so sorry. I tried so hard," he whispered, fighting back tears. She smiled.

"I know, *lyubov*, I know. He wouldn't have let us go anyway."

She kissed him softly, taking his face in her hands.

"I love you."

Luka snickered, doing his best to ruin the moment. At that instant, in a delayed reaction, heaven decided to answer the girl's earlier prayer in a completely unexpected way.

Luka barely had time to turn as something came barreling through the open door, knocking him flat. Shots rang from every direction. Amidst the confusion, Teo was able to reach out and pull Nicko to the floor, holding him close.

"Vuk, Elena, Pyotr, Ash, out! Get to the roofs!" Sergei shouted. As suddenly as it had started, it was over. The Shadows had vanished, leaving their former master in the hands of his enemies. Not that it would matter very much longer. As the dust cleared, Teo saw him lying on his back, a trickle of blood running slowly down his chin, eyes already glazing over.

The three teenagers stayed where they were for a moment, too stunned to move.

"H-he's…he's dead," Nicko said in astonishment, checking the tyrant's pulse.

"But…I don't understand. He had us. He was going to win. What happened?" Sophiya asked.

"I think...she did," Teo breathed, crawling carefully over to a figure curled up in the corner. Gently, he pried the kitchen knife from her stiff fingers, turning her onto her back.

"Mama? Can you hear me?" he whispered, trying to ignore the gunshot wound in her stomach. Cassy's eyes flickered open.

"Did I get him, *detka?* Did I save you?"

"*Da*, Mama, *da*. It's over. He's dead."

She gave a weak grin, taking his hand in her already cold one.

"Nobody...hurts my babies. Nobody," she grimaced in pain.

"Is she gonna be all right?" Nicko asked in a small voice, not daring to come nearer.

"Yes. In a way, I think she is. At least now..." he choked on the words, managing to compose himself with difficulty. "At least now she'll be with Papa."

Teo passed a hand over her still face, shutting her eyes gently. She'd been herself at the end. That was all that mattered.

EPILOGUE

Luka's army held together for less than a day after hearing of his death. There were mixed reactions. A few cheered, but most stumbled out into the street looking dazed and lost without their leader. Some simply sat down where they were, unmoving, eyes glazed over in shock. The rest vanished into the coming dark, never to be seen again.

As for the civilians, those who'd suffered so terribly under Luka's rule, for them it was months of celebration, of dancing and feasting and singing.

Only one really mourned him.

The night of his death, a little girl cried herself to sleep, alone in her deserted palace, no second thought given her on the servants' part. People wanted to forget the hard days. It would hurt a long time, remembering. And who wants to care for the child of a madman?

Anastasiya was relegated to the care of a kindly psychologist three days later when she finally let hunger win out and showed herself.

Teo, taking along only his brother and a medical transport, made the long journey back to his father's grave. It took them a long time to find it, but when they did, Cassy was buried at his side.

Many people had been in favor of a military funeral with full honors, but those who'd known her agreed that it was best kept quiet, leaving the lovers in peace for the rest of eternity.

Instead, the glory was given to Ivan, who was laid to rest in the big city cemetery. Strangers who'd never met him wept bitter tears that day.

As for Luka, despite public opposition, he was accorded a quiet cremation for his daughter's sake, and the girl was allowed to keep the ashes.

Nicko, out of pity, visited her often in her new, doll guillotine–free home. Though it would take a great many years, they became fast friends in the end, and his children and grandchildren never knew her as anything but a kind, slightly mad, old woman.

Sammy and Katya left Russia, settling permanently in America, where they were eventually married and had six children.

Two years after the fall of Luka's reign, in the midst of reconstruction, Teo finally found the time and courage, to propose to Sophiya. She smacked him for having waited so long and agreed.

A year later, they were naming their first child—a girl with eyes as dark as her father's and grandfather's. So Alexandra came into society, bearing the name of a legendary rebel, whose fame would know no end for hundreds of years to come.

As for the Shadows? Perhaps they still roam the dark of night, somewhere in the vast world, grieving their lost master. Who could ever know for sure?

For the moment, Teo wrapped an arm around Sophiya and held her close as the golden sun set in the distance. The future did not matter. There would be more adventures, but for now, all was still. All was perfectly, gloriously still.